DEVLIN'S BOSS IS FERGUSON, an English-man he cannot trust.

DEVLIN'S QUARRY IS FRANK BARRY, an Irish terrorist whom the world's governments cannot catch and whom his own superiors cannot control.

DEVLIN'S ALLIES ARE MARTIN BROS-NAN AND ANNE-MARIE AUDIN, an American scholar-soldier and a daring, beautiful French-woman who cannot afford to put their love before their mission of death.

DEVLIN'S JOB IS KILLING and even he cannot stop it once it begins. . . .

TOUCH THE DEVIL

"EXCRUCIATINGLY TENSE ... bloody confrontations that defy predictions on how they will end. It's safe to predict, however, that this will be Higgins's sixth bestseller."
—*Publishers Weekly*

"BREATH-BATING, SMOOTH, SMARTLY-PACED!"—*The Houston Post*

"ONE OF THE BEST ... UTTERLY MESMERIZING ... EXPLOSIVE SOLID SUSPENSE!"—*Buffalo News*

Ø

The Best in Fiction from SIGNET

TOUCH THE DEVIL

By
Jack Higgins

A SIGNET BOOK
NEW AMERICAN LIBRARY
TIMES MIRROR

PUBLISHER'S NOTE

Copyright © 1982 by Jack Higgins

For information address Stein and Day, Publishers, Scarborough House, Briarcliff Manor, New York 10510

This is an authorized reprint of a hardcover edition published by Stein and Day, Publishers

SIGNET TRADEMARK REG. U.S. PAT. OFF. AND FOREIGN COUNTRIES
REGISTERED TRADEMARK—MARCA REGISTRADA
HECHO EN CHICAGO, U.S.A.

SIGNET, SIGNET CLASSICS, MENTOR, PLUME, MERIDIAN AND NAL BOOKS are published by The New American Library, Inc., 1633 Broadway, New York, New York 10019

First Signet Printing, September, 1983

1 2 3 4 5 6 7 8 9

PRINTED IN THE UNITED STATES OF AMERICA

For Margaret Hewitt

Between two groups of men that want to make inconsistent kinds of worlds I see no remedy except force. . . . It seems to me that every society rests on the death of men.

—Oliver Wendell Holmes

PROLOGUE

VIETNAM 1968

The Medevac helicopter drifted across the delta at a thousand feet, her escort, a Huey Cobra gunship, keeping station to the left. Rain threatened, the clouds over the jungle in the far distance heavy with it, and thunder rumbled on the distant horizon.

Inside the Medevac, Anne-Marie Audin sat in a corner, eyes closed, her back supported by a case of medical supplies. She was a small, olive-skinned girl, with black hair razor-cut close to the skull, a concession to the living conditions of the Vietnam war front. She wore a camouflage jump jacket, unzipped at the front, a khaki bush shirt, and pants tucked into French paratroopers' boots. The most interesting features were the cameras, two Nikons strung around her neck by leather straps. The pouches of the jump jacket contained not ammunition but a variety of lenses and dozens of rolls of thirty-five millimeter film.

The young medic squatting beside the black crew chief gazed at her in frank admiration. The first two buttons of the khaki bush shirt were undone, giving a hint, no more, of the

9

firm breasts rising and falling gently as she slept.

"A long time since I saw anything like that," he said. "A real lady."

"And then some, boy." The crew chief passed him a cigarette. "There's nowhere that girl ain't been. Last year she jumped with the 503rd Paras at Katum. You name it, she done it. You see that *Life* magazine story on her six, seven months back? She's from Paris, would you believe that? Her folks own a piece o' the Bank of France."

The boy's eyes widened in amazement. "Then what in hell is she doing here?"

The crew chief grinned. "Don't ask me, kid. I don't even know what I'm doing here."

"Have you a cigarette? I seem to have run out," Anne-Marie said.

Her eyes were greener than anything he had ever seen, the crew chief realized as he tossed a pack across to her. "Keep them."

She shook one out and lit it with an old brass lighter fashioned from a bullet, then closed her eyes again, the cigarette lax in her fingers. The boy had been right, of course. What was she doing here, the girl who had everything? A grandfather who doted on her, one of the richest and most powerful industrialists in France. A father, an infantry colonel, five times decorated, Chevalier of the Legion of Honor, who had survived Indochina only to die in Algeria. An authentic hero and just as dead.

Her mother had never recovered from the shock, had died in a car crash near Nice two years later. The thought had often crossed Anne-Marie's mind that perhaps it had been a deliberate turn of the wheel that had taken the Porsche over the edge of that mountain road that night.

Poor little rich girl. Her mouth twisted in a derisory smile, her eyes still closed. The houses, the villas, the servants, the good English schools, and then the Sorbonne—and a year of that stifling academic atmosphere had been enough—not forgetting the affairs, of course, and the brief flirtation with drugs.

It was the camera that had saved her. From her first Kodak at the age of eight, she had had an instinctive genius for photography, which had developed over the years into what her grandfather described as Anne-Marie's little hobby.

After the Sorbonne, she had made it more than that. She had apprenticed herself to one of the finest fashion photographers in Paris for six months and had then joined *Paris-Match* as a staff photographer. Her reputation soared astonishingly within one short year, but it was not enough—not nearly enough—and when she asked to be assigned to Vietnam, they laughed at her.

So, she had resigned, turned freelance, and, in a final confrontation with her grandfather, had forced from him a promise to use all his formidable political power to obtain for her the necessary credentials from the American Department of Defense. It was a new Anne-Marie he had seen that day: a girl filled with a single-minded ruthlessness that had surprised him. And yet had also filled him with reluctant admiration. Six months, he had said. Six months only, and she had promised, knowing beyond any shadow of a doubt that she would break that promise.

Which she did, for when her time was up it was too late to turn back. She was famous, her material used by every major magazine in Europe and America. *Time, Paris-Match, Life,* all clamored for the exclusive services of this mad French girl who had jumped with the paratroopers at Katum. The girl for whom no assignment was too rough or too dangerous.

Whatever it was she was looking for, she had discovered what war was about, at least in Vietnam. No set-piece battles. No trumpets in the wind. No distant drum to stir the heart. It was savage street fighting in Saigon during the Tet offensive. It was the swamps of the Mekong delta, the jungles of the central highlands. The leg ulcers that ate their way through the bone like acid, leaving scars that would never go away.

She had spent this morning waiting in the rain at Pleikic trying to arrange transportation to Din To, until she'd managed to thumb a lift in the Medevac. God, but she was tired—more tired than she had ever been in her life, and it occurred to her, with a slight frown, that perhaps she'd reached the end of something. And then the crew chief called out sharply.

He was hanging in the open doorway, pointing to where a flame had soared into the sky a few hundred yards to the east. The Medevac swung toward it and started to go down, followed by the Huey Cobra gunship.

Anne-Marie was on her feet and standing beside the crew chief, peering out. There was the burnt-out wreck of a helicopter in a corner of a paddy field, several bodies sprawled beside it. The man who waved frantically from the dike was in American uniform.

The Medevac started down, her escort circling warily. Anne-Marie locked a lens into place on one of her Nikons and started to take pictures, one after the other, braced against the crew chief's shoulder. He turned his head to smile at her.

When they were no more than thirty feet up, she realized, with a strange kind of detachment, that the face she was focusing on below was Vietnamese, not American. A couple of heavy machine guns opened up from the jungle fifty yards away, and at that range they couldn't miss.

The crew chief, standing in the open door, didn't have a chance. Bullets hammered into him, punching him back against Anne-Marie, who was hurled against the medical supplies. She pushed him to one side and got to one knee. The young medic was huddled in the corner, clutching a bloody arm. As another solid burst of machine-gun fire raked the cockpit, she heard the pilot cry out.

She lurched forward, grabbing at a strut for support. At the same moment the aircraft lifted violently, and she was thrown out through the open door to fall into the mud and water of the paddy field. The Medevac bucked twenty or thirty feet up in the air, veered sharply to the left, and exploded in a great ball of fire, burning fuel and debris scattering like shrapnel.

Anne-Marie managed to stand, plastered with mud, and found herself facing the man on the dike in American uniform who, she could see now, was very definitely Vietnamese, and the rifle he pointed at her was a Russian AK47. Further along the dike, half a dozen Vietcong in straw hats and black pajamas climbed from the ditch and moved toward her.

The Huey Cobra swept in, its heavy machine guns kicking dirt along the dike, driving the Vietcong backward into the ditch. Anne-Marie looked up and saw the gunship hovering. Then forty or fifty North Vietnamese regular troops in khaki uniforms appeared from the jungle on the far side of the paddy field and started to fire at the gunship with everything they had. The gunship moved toward them, loosing off its rocket pods, and the Vietnamese beat a hasty retreat back into the jungle. The gunship turned and flew away to the south for perhaps a quarter of a mile and proceeded to fly around the entire area in a slow circle.

Anne-Marie crouched against the dike, trying to catch her breath, then stood up slowly. It was very quiet as she looked about her at the carnage, the burnt-out helicopter, the bodies partially covered by mud and water. There was nothing, only desolation on every side, and a great bank of reeds thirty or forty yards away. She was alone at the point of maximum danger in her life and could be saved only by the reinforcements the Huey Cobra would undoubtedly have radioed for. Until then, there was really only one thing she could do.

The Nikons around her neck were plastered with mud. She took another from one of the pouches in her jump jacket, another lens, and opened a fresh roll of film. Moving knee-deep through the water, she started taking pictures of the bodies swirling around her. She was cold, dispassionate, totally detached. And then she turned and found three Vietcong standing fifteen or twenty yards away.

There was a moment of perfect stillness, the grave, oriental faces totally without expression. The one in the center, a boy of fifteen or sixteen, raised his AK47, and took aim very carefully. Just as carefully Anne-Marie raised her Nikon. Death, she thought. The last picture of all. A beautiful boy in black pajamas. Above their heads, the sky rumbled its thunder, rain falling in a great solid downpour, and there was a cry, high through the rain, strangely familiar. The cry of a warrior, unafraid and facing fearful odds.

The Vietcong started to turn, and behind them a man erupted from the tall reeds, plunging toward them in a kind of slow motion. Khaki sweatband around his head, camouflage jump jacket festooned with grenades, the M16 rifle in his hands already firing, mouth wide in that savage cry.

She swung the camera in a reflex, kept on filming as he fired from the hip, knocking out one, then two, the M16 emptying as he reached the boy who still fired stubbornly, wide to one side. The butt of the M16 swung in a bone-crushing arc, the boy went down. Her rescuer didn't bother to reload. He simply grabbed her hand and started to plow back toward the reeds, churning water.

There were voices behind them on the dike now and more shooting. It was as if she were kicked in the left leg, no more than that, and she fell. He turned, ramming a clip into the M16, raking the dike with fire, and he was laughing. That was the terrible thing, as she tried to stand and looked up at him. When he reached down and pulled her up, she was aware of an energy, an elemental force such as she had never known. And then she was on her feet, and they were into the safety of the reeds.

*　　*　　*

He had sat her up on a small mud bank out of the water, as he sliced open her khaki pants with a knife and checked the wound.

"You're lucky," he said. "Straight through. M1 from the look of it. An AK would have fragmented the bone."

He expertly strapped a field dressing around the wound, broke open a morphine ampoule, and jabbed it into her. "You're going to need that. A gunshot wound never hurts at first. Too much shock. The pain comes later."

"Firsthand experience?"

He smiled wryly. "You could say that. I'd give you a cigarette, but I've lost my lighter."

"I've got one."

He opened a pack of cigarettes, put two in his mouth, and put the pack back in his pocket. She handed him the brass lighter. He lit the cigarettes, placed one between her lips, and examined the lighter closely.

"7.62mm Russian. Now that is interesting."

"My father's. In August '44 he saved a German paratroop colonel who was about to be shot by partisans. The colonel gave him the lighter as a memento. He was killed in Algiers," she said. "My father. After surviving this place."

"There's irony for you." He handed the lighter back to her. She shook her head and, for some reason she couldn't possibly explain, said, "No, keep it."

"As my memento?"

"Memento mori," she said. "We'll never get out of this place alive."

"Oh, I don't know. That Cobra's still on station. I'd say the cavalry should arrive within the next twenty minutes, just like Stage Six at MGM. In the nick of time. I'd better let them know they're not wasting it."

He took a flare pistol from a side pouch and fired a red flare high into the sky.

"Couldn't that be the Vietcong playing games again?"

"Not really." He fired another red flare, then a green. "Colors of the day."

Her leg was just starting to hurt. She said, "So now they know where we are. The Vietcong, I mean."

"They already did."

"And will they come?"

"I should imagine so."

He wiped the M16 clean with a rag, and she raised the Nikon and focused it. Through the viewfinder she could see the broad-shouldered six-footer close up, the dark hair held back by the sweatband giving him the look of some sixteenth-century bravo. The skin was stretched tightly over Celtic cheekbones, and a stubble of beard covered the hollow cheeks and strongly pointed chin. But it was the eyes which were the most remarkable feature, gray, like water over a stone, calm, expressionless, holding their own secrets.

"What are you?" she asked.

"Airborne Rangers. Sergeant Martin Brosnan."

"What happened here?"

"A bad foul-up is what happened. Those clever little peasants, half our size, who we were supposed to walk all over, caught us very much as they caught you. We were on our way to Din To after being picked up from a routine patrol. Fourteen of us plus the crew. Now there's only me for certain. Maybe a few out there still alive."

She took several more pictures, and he frowned. "You can't stop, can you, just like the guy wrote about you in *Life* last year. It's obsessional. Christ, you were actually going to take a picture of that kid as he was about to shoot you."

She lowered the Nikon. "You know who I am?"

He smiled. "How many women photographers have made the cover of *Time* magazine?"

He lit another cigarette and passed it to her. There was something about the voice that puzzled her.

"Brosnan," she said. "I haven't heard that name before."

"Irish," he said. "Well, County Kerry to be exact. You'll seldom find it anywhere else in Ireland."

"Frankly, I thought you sounded English."

He looked at her in mock horror. "My father would turn in his grave and my mother, God bless her, would forget she was a lady and spit in your eye. Good Irish-American, Boston variety. The Brosnans came over during the famine a long time ago, all Protestants, would you believe? My mother was born in Dublin herself. She was a good Catholic and could never forgive my father for not raising me the same."

He was talking to keep her mind off the situation, she knew that and liked him for it. "And the accent?" she said.

"Oh, that's part prep school, Andover in my case, and the right college, of course."

"Let me guess. Yale?"

"My father and grandfather went there, but I decided to give Princeton a chance. It was good enough for Scott Fitzgerald, and I'd pretentions to being a writer myself. I majored in English."

"So," she said, "what are you doing in Vietnam?"

"I often ask myself that," Brosnan said. "I was going to go straight through and do my doctorate and then I found Harry, our gardener, crying in the greenhouse one day. When I asked him what was wrong, he apologized and said he'd just heard his son Joe had been killed in Nam." Brosnan wasn't smiling now. "But the real trouble was that there'd been another son called Ely, killed in the delta the year before."

There was a heavy silence, the rain flooded down. "Then what?"

"My mother gave him a thousand dollars. And he was so damn grateful."

He shook his head and Anne-Marie said softly, "So you made the big gesture."

"He made me feel ashamed, and when I feel I act. I'm a very existentialist person."

He smiled again, and she said, "And how have you found it?"

"Nam?" He shrugged.

"But you've enjoyed it? You have an aptitude for killing, I think." He had stopped smiling, the gray eyes watchful. She carried on, "You must excuse me, my friend, but faces, you see, are my business."

"I'm not so sure about liking it," he said. "I'm damned good at it, I know that. Out here you have to be if the fellow coming at you has a gun in his hand and you want to get home for Christmas."

There was silence, a long silence, and then he added, "I know one thing, I've had enough. My time's up in January and that can't come soon enough for me. Remember what Eliot said about the passage we didn't take toward the door we never opened into the rose garden? Well, from now on, I'm going to open every door in sight."

The morphine was really working now. The pain had gone, but also her senses had lost their sharpness. "Then what?" she said drowsily. "Back to Princeton for that doctorate?"

"No," he said. "I've been giving that a lot of thought. I've changed too much for that. I'm going to go to Dublin, Trinity College. Peace, tranquility. Look up my roots. I speak a little Gaelic, something my mother drummed into me as a kid."

"And before that?" she said. "No girl waiting back home?"

"No more than eighteen or twenty, but I'd rather be sitting at one of those sidewalk cafes on the Champs Elysées sipping Pernod with you."

"And rain, my friend." Anne-Marie closed her eyes drowsily. "An absolute necessity. So that we may smell the damp chestnut trees," she explained. "An indispensable part of the Paris experience."

"If you say so," he said, and his hands tightened on the M16 as there was a stirring in the reeds close by.

"Oh, but I do, Martin Brosnan." Her voice was very sleepy now. "It would give me infinite pleasure to show you."

"That's a date then," he said softly and came up on one knee, crouching, firing into the reeds.

There was a cry of anguish, then a long burst in reply, and something punched Brosnan high in the left side of the chest, and he went over backward across the girl.

She stirred feebly, and he came up, firing one-handed at the man who charged through the reeds, that smile on his face again, and as the M16 emptied he hurled it into the face of the last man, drawing his combat knife, probing for the heart up under the ribs as they went down together.

He lay in the mud for quite some time, holding the Vietcong against him, waiting for him to die, and suddenly two Skyraiders swooped overhead and half a dozen gunships moved in out of the rain, line astern.

Brosnan got up painfully and with his good arm pulled Anne-Marie to her feet. They started to wade through the reeds toward the open paddy field.

"I told you the cavalry would arrive."

"In the nick of time? And then what?"

He grinned. "One thing's for sure. After this, it can only get better."

**PARIS
1979**

ONE

A cold wind lifted across the Seine and dashed rain against the windows of the all-night cafe by the bridge. It was a small, sad place, half a dozen tables and chairs, no more, usually much frequented by prostitutes. But not on a night like this.

The barman leaned on the zinc-topped counter reading a newspaper. Jack Corder sat at a table by the window, the only customer, a tall dark-haired man in his early thirties. His jeans, worn leather jacket, and cloth cap gave him the look of a night porter at the fishmarket up the street, which he very definitely was not.

Barry had said eleven-thirty, so Corder had arrived at eleven, just to be on the safe side. Now, it was half-past midnight. Not that he was worried. Where Frank Barry was concerned, you never knew where you were, but then, that was all part of the technique.

Corder lit a cigarette and called, "Black coffee and another cognac."

The barman nodded, pushed the newspaper to one side. At that moment, the telephone behind the bar started to ring. He answered it at once, then turned inquiringly.

"Your name is Corder?"

"That's right."

"It would seem there is a taxi waiting for you on the corner." He replaced the receiver. "You still wish the coffee and the cognac, monsieur?"

"The cognac only, I think."

Corder shivered for no accountable reason and took the cognac down in one quick swallow. "It's cold even for November."

The barman shrugged. "On a night like this, even the *poules* stay home."

"Sensible girls."

Corder pushed some francs across the table and went out. The wind dashed rain in his face, and he turned up the collar of his jacket, ran to the old Renault taxi waiting on the corner, wrenched open the rear door, and got in. It moved away instantly, and he sank back against the seat. They turned across the bridge, and the lights in their heavy glass globes made him think of Oxford with a strange sense of *déjà vu*.

Twelve years of my life, he thought. What would I have been now? Fellow of All Souls? Possibly even a professor at some rather less interesting university. Instead ... But that kind of thinking did no good—no good at all.

The driver was an old man, badly in need of a shave, and Corder was aware of the eyes watching him in the rearview mirror. Not a word was said as they drove through darkness and rain, moving through a maze of back streets, finally turning into a wharf in the dock area and braking to a halt outside a warehouse. A small light illuminated a sign that read *Renoir & Sons—Importers*. The taxi driver sat there without a word. Corder got out, closing the door behind him, and the Renault drove away.

It was very quiet. There was only the lapping of the water in the basin where dozens of barges were moored. Rain hammered down, silver in the light of the sign. There was a small judas gate in the main entrance. When Corder tried the handle, it opened instantly, and he stepped inside.

The warehouse was crammed with bales and packing cases of every description. It was very dark, but there was a light at the far end and he moved toward it. A man sat at a trestle table beneath a naked bulb. There was a map spread across the table in front of him, a briefcase beside it, and he was making notes in a small, leather-bound diary.

"Hello, Frank," Corder said.

Frank Barry looked up. "Ah, there you are, Jack. Sorry to truck you about."

The voice was good public-school English, with just a hint of an Ulster inflection here and there. He leaned back in the chair. His blond hair curled crisply, making him look considerably younger than his forty-eight years, and the black Burberry trenchcoat gave him a curiously elegant appearance. A handsome, lean-faced man with one side of his mouth hooked into a slight perpetual half-smile, as if permanently amused by the world and its inhabitants.

"Something big?" Corder asked.

"You could say that. Did you know the British Foreign Secretary was visiting the President at the moment?"

"Lord Carrington?" Corder frowned. "No, I didn't know that."

"Neither does anyone else. All very hush-hush. The new Tory government's trying to cement the *entente cordiale,* which has been more than bruised of late years. Not that it will do any good. Giscard d'Estaing will always put France at the top of his list, no matter what the situation. Their final meeting in the morning is taking place at a villa at Rigny." He stabbed at the map on the table with his finger. "Here, about forty miles from Paris."

"So?" Corder said.

"He leaves at noon by car for Vezelay. There's an airforce emergency field there from where the RAF will be waiting to whisk him back to England, to all intents and purposes as if he's never been away."

"So where's all this leading?"

"Here." Barry tapped the map again. "St. Etienne, fifteen miles from Rigny, consists of a gas station and a roadside cafe, at present closed. A perfect spot."

"For what?"

"To hit the bugger as he passes through. One car, four CRS escorts on motorbikes. No problem that I can see."

Corder was conscious of the cold now eating deep into his bones. "You're joking. We'd never get away with it. I mean, a thing like this needs preparation, split-second timing."

"All taken care of," Barry said cheerfully. "You should know me by now, Jack. I always prefer people who are working for wages. Thoroughgoing fanatics like yourself, honest Marxists who believe in the cause—you take it all too seriously and that tends to cloud your thinking. You can't beat the professional touch."

The Ulster accent was more in evidence now, all part of the deliberate exercise in charm.

"Who have you got?" Corder asked.

"Three hoods from Marseilles on the run from the *Union Corse* after the wrong kind of underworld killing. One of them has his girl with him. They'll do anything in return for the right price, four false passports, and tickets to the Argentine."

Corder stared down at the map. "So how does it happen?"

"Simple. As I said, the cafe is closed. That only leaves the proprietor and his wife in the garage. They'll be taken care of and my men in position, dressed as mechanics, from twelve-fifteen on, working on a car on the forecourt."

Corder shook his head. "From what I can

see, the convoy will be passing at a fairly high speed at that point. Remember what happened at Petit-Clamart when Bastien-Thiry and his boys tried to ambush General de Gaulle? Even with machine guns at point-blank range they didn't do any good because the old man's car just kept on going. A second is all you get and away."

"So what we have to do is stop the car," Barry said.

"Impossible. These days those VIP drivers are trained for just this kind of situation. From what I can see on the map, it's a straight road giving a good view long before he gets there. Block it with a vehicle or anything else, and they'll simply turn around and get the hell out of there." He shook his head. "He won't stop, Frank, that driver, and there's no way you can make him."

"Oh, yes there is," Barry said, "which is where the girl I mentioned comes into the picture. At the appropriate moment, she tries to cross the road from the garage pushing a pram. She stumbles, the pram runs away from her into the road."

"You're crazy," Corder said.

"Am I? It worked for the Red Army Faction a couple of years back when they snatched Schleyer, the head of the German Industries Federation, in Cologne." Barry smiled. "You see, Jack, human nature being what it is, I think that I can positively guarantee that when that driver sees a runaway pram in his path he'll do only one thing. Swerve to avoid it and come to a dead halt."

Which was true. Had to be. Corder nodded. "Put that way, I suppose you're right."

"I always am, old son." He opened the briefcase and took out a hand transceiver. "This is for you. There's a side road on a hill covered by an apple orchard that overlooks the chateau at Rigny nicely. I want you there by eleven o'clock in the morning. You'll find a Peugeot in the yard outside, keys in the lock. Use that."

"Then what?"

"The moment you see Carrington making preparations to leave, you call in on the transceiver, channel 42. You say: 'This is Red calling. The package is about to be delivered.' I'll say: 'Green here. The package will be collected.' Then you get the hell out of there. I want you at St. Etienne before Carrington arrives."

"Will you be there?"

Barry looked surprised. "And where else would I be?" He smiled. "I was a National Service second lieutenant with the Ulster Rifles in Korea in 1950, Jack. You didn't know that, did you? But I'll tell you one thing. When my lads went over the top, I was always in front."

"With a swagger stick in one hand?"

"And now you're thinking of the Somme." Barry laughed gently. "I killed an awful lot of Maoists out there, Jack, which is ironic, considering my present circumstances." He clapped him on the shoulder. "Anyway, you'd best be off. A decent night's sleep and no booze. You'll need a clear head for what you must do tomorrow." He glanced at his watch and laughed. "Correction—today."

Corder weighed the transceiver in his hand, then slipped it into his pocket. "I'll say goodnight, then."

His footsteps echoed in the lofty warehouse as he walked to the entrance, opened the judas, and stepped out. It was still raining as he moved into the yard at the side of the building. The Peugeot was parked by the main entrance, the key in the lock as Barry had indicated. Corder drove away, his palms sweating, slipping on the wheel, stomach churning.

Kill Carrington, one of the great men of his time. My God, what would the bastard come up with next? But no, that didn't apply, because now he was very definitely finished. This was it. What Corder had been waiting for for more than a year.

He found what he was looking for a moment later, a small all-night cafe on the corner of one of the main boulevards into the city. There was a public telephone in a small glass booth inside. He ordered coffee, then obtained the necessary coins from the barman and went into the booth, closing the door. His fingers were shaking as he carefully dialed the London code number and then the number following.

The security service in Great Britain, more correctly known as Directorate General of the Security Service, D15, does not officially exist as far as the law is concerned, although it does, in fact, occupy a large white-and-red brick building near the Hilton Hotel. It was that establishment that Jack Corder was calling now—and more specifically, an office known as Group Four which was manned twenty-four hours a day.

The phone was picked up and an anonymous voice said, "Say who you are."

"Lysander. I must speak with Brigadier Ferguson at once. Priority One. No denial possible."

"Your present number?" he dictated it carefully. The voice said, "If security clearance confirmed, you will be called."

The phone went dead. Corder pushed open the booth door and went to the bar. There was a man in a blue suit asleep on a chair in the corner, mouth gaping. Otherwise the place was empty.

The barman pushed the coffee across. "You want something to eat? An omelet perhaps?"

"Why not?" Corder said. "I'm waiting for a call."

The barman turned to the stove and Corder spooned sugar into his coffee. All calls to D15 were automatically recorded. At this present moment, the computer would be matching his voice print on file against the tape of his call. Ferguson would probably be at home in bed.

They would ring him, give him the number. Ten minutes in all.

But he was wrong, for it took no more than five, and as he took his first forkful of omelet the phone rang. He squeezed into the booth, closed the door, and picked up the receiver.

"Lysander here."

"Ferguson." The voice was plummy, a little overdone, rather like the aging actor in a second-rate touring company who wants to make sure they can hear him at the back of the theater. "It's been a long time, Jack. Priority One, I understand."

"Frank Barry, sir, out in the open at last."

Ferguson's voice sharpened. "Now that *is* interesting."

"Lord Carrington, sir. He's visiting President Giscard d'Estaing at the moment?"

There was a slight pause. Ferguson said, "No one's supposed to know that officially."

"Frank Barry does."

"Not good, Jack, not good at all. I think you'd better explain."

Which Corder did, speaking in low, urgent tones. Five minutes later, he emerged from the booth and went to the counter.

"Your omelet, Monsieur—it has gone cold. You want another?"

"What an excellent idea," Corder said. "And I'll have a cognac while I'm waiting."

He lit a cigarette and sat back on the bar stool, smiling for the first time that night.

* * *

In his flat in Cavendish Square, Brigadier Charles Ferguson stood beside the bed, pulling on his dressing gown as he listened to the tape recording he had just made of his conversation with Corder. He was a large, kindly looking man, distinctly overweight with rumpled gray hair and a double chin. There was nothing military about him at all, and the half-moon spectacles he put on to consult a small address book gave him the air of a minor professor. He was, in fact, as ruthless as Cesare Borgia in action and totally without scruples when it came to his country's interest.

There was a tap at the door, and his man-servant, an ex-Gurkha *naik* peered in, tying the belt of a bathrobe about his waist.

"Sorry, Kim, work to be done," Ferguson said. "Lots of tea, bacon and eggs to follow. I won't be going back to bed."

The little Gurkha withdrew, and Ferguson went into the sitting room, stirred the fire in the Adam fireplace, poured himself a large brandy, sat down by the telephone, and dialed a number in Paris.

The French security service, the *Service de Documentation Extérieure et de Contre Espionage,* the SDECE, is divided into five sections and many departments. The most interesting one is certainly Section Five, most commonly known as the Action Service, the department that more than any other had been responsible for the smashing of the OAS. It was the number of Service Five that Ferguson dialed now.

He said, "Ferguson here, D15. Colonel Guyon, if you please." He frowned impatiently. "Well, of course he's at home in bed. So was I. I've only rung you to establish credentials. Tell him to call me back on this number." He dictated it quickly. "Most urgent. Priority One."

He put down the phone, and Kim entered with bacon and eggs, bread, butter, and marmalade on a silver tray. "Delicious," Ferguson said as the Gurkha placed a small table before him. "Breakfast at two-thirty in the morning. What a capital idea. We should do this more often."

As he tucked a napkin around his neck the phone rang. He picked it up instantly. "Ah, Pierre," he said in rapid and excellent French, "I've got something for you. Very nasty indeed. You won't be pleased, so listen carefully."

It was quiet in the warehouse after Jack Corder left. Barry walked to the entrance and locked the judas gate. He paused to light a cigarette and as he turned, a man emerged from the shadows and perched himself on the edge of the table.

Nikolai Belov was fifty years of age and for ten of them had been a cultural attaché at the Soviet embassy in Paris. His dark suit was Saville Row as was the blue overcoat, which fitted him to perfection. He was handsome enough in a slightly decadent way, with a face like Oscar Wilde or Nero himself and a mane of silver hair that made him look more like a rather distinguished actor than what he was, a colonel in the KGB.

"I'm not too sure about that one, Frank," he said in excellent English.

"I'm not too sure about anyone," Barry said, "including you, old son, but for what it's worth, Jack Corder's a dedicated Marxist."

"Oh dear," Belov said. "That's what I was afraid of."

"He tried to join the British Communist party when he was an undergraduate at Oxford years ago. It was suggested that someone like him could do more good by keeping his mouth shut and joining the Labour party, which he did. Trade union organizer for six years, then he blotted his copybook by losing his cool during a miners' strike three or four years ago and assaulting a policeman while on the picket line with a pickax handle. Put him in hospital for six weeks."

"And Corder?"

"Two years in jail. The union wouldn't touch him with a barge pole after that. Deep down inside, those lads are as conservative as Margaret Thatcher when it comes to being British. Jack came over here last year and involved himself with an anarchist group well to the left of the French Communist party, which is where I picked him up. Anyway, why should

you worry, or has the disinformation department of the KGB changed its aims?"

"No," Belov said. "Chaos is still our business,
Frank, and the need to create as much as possible in the western world. Chaos, disorder, fear
and uncertainty—that's why we employ people like you."

"You haven't left much out, have you?" Barry
said cheerfully.

Belov looked down at the map. "Is this going
to work?"

"Come on, now, Nikolai," Barry said. "You
don't really want Carrington shot dead on a
French country road do you? Very counter-
productive, just like the IRA shooting the
Queen. Too much to lose, so it isn't worth it."

Belov looked bewildered. "What game are
you playing now?"

"You'll find out," Barry said, and added
briskly, "I'll still take the cash, by the way.
Chaos, disorder, fear, and uncertainty. You'll
get your money's worth, I promise you."

Belov hesitated, then took a large manila
envelope from his pocket and pushed it across.
Barry dropped it into the briefcase along with
the map.

"Shall we?"

He led the way to the entrance and unlocked
the judas gate. A flurry of wind tossed rain
into their faces. Belov shivered and turned up
his collar.

"When I was fourteen years of age in nineteen

forty-three, I joined a partisan group in the Ukraine. I was with them two years. It was simpler then. We were fighting Nazis. We knew where we were. But now."

"A different world," Barry said.

"And one in which you, my friend, don't even believe in your own country."

"Ulster?" Barry laughed harshly. "I gave up on that mess a long time ago. As someone once said, there's nothing worse than a collection of ignorant people with legitimate grievances. Now let's get the hell out of here."

The apples in the orchard on the hill above Rigny should have been picked weeks before. The air was heavy with their overripe smell, warm in the unexpected noon-day sun.

Jack Corder lay in the long grass, a pair of Zeiss binoculars beside him, and watched the villa below. It was a pleasant house, built in the eighteenth century from the look of it, with a broad flight of steps leading up to the portico over the main entrance.

There were four cars in the courtyard, at least a dozen CRS police waiting beside their motorcycles, and uniformed gendarmes at the gate. Nothing too ostentatious. The President was known to imitate General de Gaulle in that respect. He hated fuss.

For a while, Corder was a boy again lying in long grass by the River Wharfe, the bridge below him, good Yorkshire sheep scattered across the meadow on the other side. Sixteen years of age with a girl beside him whose name he couldn't even remember, and life had seemed to have an infinite possibility to it. There was an aching longing to be back, for everything in between to be just a dream, and then the President of France, Valery Giscard d'Estaing, stepped out of the house below, followed by the British Foreign Secretary.

The two men stood in the portico, flanked by their aides, as Corder focused his binoculars.

"Jesus," he whispered. "One man with a decent rifle is all it would take to knock out both of them."

The President shook the Foreign Secretary's hand. No formal embrace. That was not his style. Lord Carrington went down the steps and was ushered into the black Citroën.

Corder's throat was dry. He took the transceiver from his pocket, pressed the channel button and said urgently, "This is Red calling. This is Red calling. The package is about to be delivered."

A second later he heard Barry's reply, cool, detached. "Green here. The package will be collected."

Carrington's car was moving toward the entrance followed by four CRS motorcyclists, just as Barry had promised, and Corder jumped to his feet and ran through the orchard to where he had left the Peugeot.

*   *   *

He had plenty of time to reach the main road before the convoy, and the moment he turned on to it he put his foot down, pushing the Peugeot up to seventy-five.

His palms were sweating again, his throat dry, and he lit a cigarette one-handed. He didn't know what was going to happen at St. Etienne, that was the trouble. Probably CRS riot cops descending in droves, shooting everything that moved, which could include him. On the other hand, he had to turn up; he had no other choice, for if he didn't, Barry, being Barry, would smell an instant rat, call the thing off, and disappear into the blue as he had done so many times before.

He was close to St. Etienne now, no more than two or three miles to go, when it happened. As he passed a side turning, a CRS motorcyclist emerged and came after him, a sinister figure in crash helmet and goggles and dark, caped coat. He pulled alongside and waved him down, and Corder pulled in to the edge of the road. Was this Ferguson's way of keeping him out of it?

The CRS man pulled in front, got off his heavy BMW machine, and pushed it on its stand. He walked toward the Peugeot, a gloved finger hooked into the trigger guard of the MAT49 machine carbine slung across his chest. He stood looking down at Corder, anonymous in the dark goggles, then pushed them up.

"A slight change of plan, old son." Frank Barry grinned. "I lead, you follow."

"You've called it off?" Corder demanded in astonishment.

Barry looked mildly surprised. "Jesus, no, why should I do a thing like that?"

He got back on the BMW and drove away. Corder followed him, totally lost now, not knowing what to do for the best. For a moment Corder fingered the butt of the Walther PPK he carried, not that there was much joy there. He'd never shot anyone in his life. It was unlikely that he could start now.

About a mile outside St. Etienne, Barry turned into a narrow country lane, and Corder followed, climbing up between high hedgerows past a small farm. There was a grove of trees on the brow of a green hill. Barry waved him down and turned into them. He pushed the BMW up on its stand, and Corder joined him.

"Look, what's going on, Frank?"

"Did I ever tell you about my grandmother on my mother's side, Jack? Whenever she got a terrible headache there'd be a thunder storm within the hour. Now with me, it's different. I only get a headache when I smell stinking fish, and I've got a real blinder at the moment."

Corder went cold. "I don't understand."

"Nice view from up here." Barry walked through the trees and indicated St. Etienne spread neatly below like a child's model. The garage and pumps on one side of the road, the cafe and parking lot on the other.

He took some binoculars from the pocket of his raincoat and passed them across. "Have a look. I have a feeling it may be a bit more interesting to sit this one out."

Corder focused the binoculars on the garage. Two men, wearing yellow coveralls, worked on the engine of a car. A third waited in the glass booth beside the pumps, talking to the girl, who stood by the door with the pram, wearing a scarlet head scarf, woolen pullover, and neat skirt.

"Any sign of the car?" Barry demanded.

Corder swung the binoculars to examine the road. "No, but there's a truck coming."

"Is there, now? That's interesting."

The truck was of the trailer type, an eight-wheeler with high green canvas sides. As it entered the village, it slowed and turned into the parking lot. The driver, a tall man in khaki overalls, jumped down from the cab and strolled to the cafe door.

Barry took the binoculars from Corder and focused them on the truck. "Bouvier Brothers, Long Distance Transport, Paris and Marseilles."

"He'll move on when he finds the cafe is closed," Corder said.

"Pigs might fly, old son," Frank Barry said, "but I doubt it."

There was a sudden firestorm from inside the truck at that moment, machine-gun fire raking the entire pavement, shattering the glass of the booth, driving the girl back over the pram, cutting down the two gunmen working on the car, riddling its fuel tank, gasoline spilling on to the concrete. It was the work of an instant, no more. There was a flicker of flame as the gasoline ignited, and then the tank exploded in a ball of fire, pieces of the wreckage cascading high in the air. The devastation was complete, and at least twenty CRS riot police in uniform leapt from the rear of the truck and ran across the road.

"Efficient," Barry said calmly. "You've got to give the buggers that."

Corder licked dry lips nervously, and his left hand went into the pocket of his leather jacket, groping for the butt of the Walther.

"What could have gone wrong?"

"One of those bastards from Marseilles must have had a big mouth," Barry said. "And if word got back to the *Union Corse....*" He shrugged. "Thieving's one thing, politics is another. They'd inform without a second's hesitation." He clapped Corder on the shoulder. "But we'd better get out of this. Just follow my tail, like you did before. Nobody is likely to stop us when they see me escorting you."

He pushed the BMW off its stand and rode away. Corder followed. The whole thing was like a bad dream and he could still see, vivid as any image on the movie screen, the body of the girl bouncing back across the pram in a hail of machine-gun fire. And Barry had expected it. Expected it, and yet he had still let those poor sods go through with it.

He followed the BMW closely, through narrow country lanes, twisting and turning. They met no one, and then, a good ten miles on the other side of St. Etienne, came to a small garage and cafe at the side of the road. Barry turned in beside the cafe and braked to a halt. As Corder joined him, he was taking a canvas grip from one of the side panniers.

"I know this place," he said. "There's a washroom at the back. I'm going to change. We'll leave the BMW here and carry on in the Peugeot."

He went around to the rear before Corder could reply, and the young woman in the booth beside the gas pumps emerged and approached him. She was perhaps twenty-five, with a flat, peasant face, and wore a man's tweed jacket that was too large for her.

"Gas, Monsieur?"

"Is there a telephone?" Corder asked.

"In the cafe, Monsieur, but it's not open for business. I'm the only one here today."

"I must use it. It's very urgent." He pushed a hundred-franc note at her. "Just give me a handful of coins. You keep the rest."

She shrugged, went into her office, and opened the register. She came back with the coins. "I'll show you," she said.

The cafe wasn't much. A few tables and

chairs, a counter with bottles of beer and mineral water and rows of glasses ranged behind, and a door that obviously led to the kitchen. The telephone was on the wall, a directory hanging beside it.

The girl said, "Look, seeing I'm here I'll make some coffee. Okay?"

"Fine," Corder told her.

She disappeared into the kitchen and he quickly checked in the directory to find the district number to link him with the international line. His fingers were shaking as he dialed the area code for London, followed by the D15 number.

He didn't even have time to pray. The receiver was lifted at the other end, and a woman's voice this time, the day operator, said, "Say who you are."

"Lysander," Corder said urgently. "Clear line, please. I must speak to Brigadier Ferguson at once. Total Priority."

And Ferguson's voice cut in instantly, almost as if he'd been listening in. "Jack, what is it?"

"Total cock-up, sir. Barry smelt a rat, so he and I stayed out of things. The rest of the team were knocked out by CRS police."

"You've got clean away, presumably."

"Yes."

"And does he suspect you?"

"No—he thinks it's down to one of those Marseilles hoods speaking out of turn."

In the kitchen, Frank Barry, listening on the

extension, smiled, faceless in dark goggles. The girl lay on the floor at his feet, blood oozing from an ugly cut in her temple where he had clubbed her with his pistol. He took a Carswell silencer from his pocket and screwed it on to the barrel of his pistol as he walked into the cafe.

Corder was still talking in a low, urgent voice. "No, I don't know how much more I can take, that's the trouble."

Barry said softly, "Jack!"

Corder swung around, and Barry shot him twice through the heart, slamming him back. He bounced off the wall and fell to the floor on his face.

The receiver dangled on the end of its cord. Barry picked it up and said, "That you, Ferguson, old son? Frank Barry here. If you want Corder back, you'd better send a box for him to Cafe Rosco, St. Julien."

"You bastard," Charles Ferguson said.

"It's been said before."

Barry replaced the receiver and went out, whistling softly as he unscrewed the silencer. He slipped the pistol back into its holster, pushed the BMW off its stand, and rode away.

TWO

It was raining on the following morning when Ferguson's car dropped him outside Number 10 Downing Street, ten minutes early for his eleven o'clock appointment with the Prime Minister. His driver moved away instantly, and Ferguson crossed the pavement to the entrance. In spite of the rain, there was the usual small crowd of sightseers on the other side of the road, mainly tourists, kept in place by a couple of police constables. Another stood in his usual place by the door, not much protection for the best-known address in England, the seat of political power as well as the Prime Minister's private residence, but that didn't mean a thing as Ferguson well knew. There were others, more inconspicuously attired, situated at certain strategic points in the area, ready to swarm in at the first hint of trouble.

The policeman saluted. The door was opened, even before Ferguson reached it, and he passed inside.

The young man who greeted him said, "Brigadier Ferguson? This way, sir."

There was the hum of activity from the press

room on the right as he crossed the entrance hall and entered the corridor leading to the rear of the house and the Cabinet room.

The main staircase to the first floor was lined with portraits of previous Prime Ministers. Peel, Wellington, Disraeli, Gladstone. Ferguson always felt an acute sense of history as he mounted those stairs, although this was the first time he had done so to meet the present Prime Minister—the first time to explain himself to a woman, and a damn clever woman if it came to that. It was very definitely a new experience. But did anything change? How many attempts had there been to assassinate Queen Victoria? And Disraeli and Gladstone had both had their hands full of Fenians, dynamiters, and anarchists with their bombs, at one time or another.

On the top corridor, the young man knocked on a door, opened it, and ushered Ferguson inside. "Brigadier Ferguson, Prime Minister," he said and left, closing the door behind him.

The study was more elegant now than Ferguson remembered it, with pale green walls and gold curtains and comfortable furniture in perfect taste. But nothing was more elegant in the entire room than the woman behind the desk with the green leather top. The blue suit with the froth of white lace at the throat perfectly offset the blonde hair. An elegant, handsome woman of the world, and yet the eyes, when she glanced up at Ferguson from the paper she was reading, were hard and intelligent.

"I've had a personal assurance from the French President this morning that this whole wretched business will be hushed up. It never happened. You understand me?"

"Perfectly, ma'am."

She looked at the paper before her. "This agent of yours, Corder. If it hadn't been for him. . . ." She gestured to a chair. "Sit down, Brigadier. Tell me about him."

"We recruited Jack Corder some twelve years ago when he was still an undergraduate at All Souls. The route he chose was to immerse himself totally in left-wing politics. We often hear of moles within our intelligence service working for the Russians, ma'am. Jack was the other side of the coin. He endured prison sentences twice for his apparent militancy. Afterward, I transferred him to the European terrorist scene. Frank Barry was his most important assignment."

She nodded. "I've already spoken to the Director General of D15, and he tells me that as long ago as nineteen seventy-two one of my predecessors authorized the setting up within D15 of a section known as Group Four, which has powers held directly from the Prime Minister, to coordinate the handling of all cases of terrorism, subversion, and the like."

"That is correct, Prime Minister."

"With you in charge, Brigadier?"

"Yes, ma'am." There was a longish pause while she stared down at the paper thoughtfully. Ferguson cleared his throat. "Naturally, if you would prefer to initiate some change, I will offer my resignation without hesitation."

"If I want it, I'll ask for it, Brigadier," she said sharply. "But you can't expect me to have much faith in the activities of your section when one of the chief ministers of the Crown comes within an inch of assassination. Now tell me about this man Barry. Why is he so important and, more to the point, how does he remain so elusive?"

"A brilliant madman, ma'am. A genius in his own way. As important to the international terrorist scene as Carlos, but not so familiar to the public."

"And why is that?"

"A question of his personal psychology. Many terrorists, take some of those involved with the Baader-Meinhof gang, for example, have a craving for public display. They want people to know not only who they are but that they can make fools of the police and intelligence departments they confront any time they wish. Barry doesn't seem to have a need for that kind of publicity and, as it suits our purposes best to give him none, he has remained an unknown quantity as far as the public is concerned."

"What about his personal background?"

"I'm afraid it couldn't be worse from the

point of view of media sensationalism. He is an Ulsterman by birth. Held a commission as a National Service second lieutenant with the Ulster Rifles. Served in Korea. Excellent record in the field, I might add. He's a Protestant. His uncle is an Irish peer, Lord Stramore. Much involved in Orange politics for most of his life, but now in ailing health. Barry is his heir."

"Good God," the Prime Minister said.

"During the early years of the Irish Troubles, Barry professed to be a Republican. As usual, he did his own thing. Organized a group called the Sons of Erin, which gave us tremendous problems in the Province. Repudiated totally by the Provisional IRA. In nineteen seventy-two, when Group Four was first set up, I managed to penetrate Barry's organization with an agent of mine, a Major Vaughan. The upshot of that little affair was that Barry was very badly wounded indeed. That he lived at all was only due to the skill of the surgeons of the military wing of the Musgrave Park Hospital in Belfast."

"You had him?"

"He escaped, ma'am. Not even capable of walking, according to his doctors, but walk he did, right out of the hospital, dressed as a porter. Turned up in Dublin within twenty-four hours. We couldn't touch him there, of course. He was in and out of hospitals there and in Switzerland for more than a year."

"And afterward?"

"Since then, ma'am, he has, in some cases to our certain knowledge and in others to the best of our belief, been responsible for at least fifteen assassinations and a number of bombing incidents. His touch is distinctive and unmistakable, and political commitment seems to be the least of his considerations. A resume of his activities during the past few years will explain what I mean. In nineteen seventy-three he assassinated the general in command of Spanish military intelligence in the Basque country. Responsibility was claimed by the Basque nationalist movement, the ETA."

"Go on."

"On the other hand, he was also responsible for the murder of General Hans Grosch during a visit to Munich in nineteen seventy-five. A source of considerable embarrassment to the West German government. Grosch held a post roughly equivalent to my own in the East German ministry for state security. So, as you can see, ma'am, on the one hand Barry kills a Fascist—on the other, a Communist."

"You're saying he has no politics?"

"None at all." Ferguson took a sheet from his briefcase and passed it across. "A list of the jobs we think he's been concerned with. As you can see, his victims have been from every part of the political scene you can think of."

The Prime Minister read the list slowly and frowned. "Are you saying, then, that he works for whoever will pay him?"

"No, ma'am, I think it's more subtle than that. Everything he does falls into a pattern that causes maximum damage wherever it happens. For instance, he kills a Spanish diplomat visiting Paris in nineteen seventy-seven—a Fascist. The French government had to react appropriately and within twenty-four hours, every left-wing agitator in Paris was in police hands. Not only Communists, but Socialists. The Socialist party didn't like that, which meant the unions also didn't like it. Result, unrest among the workers, strikes, disruption."

She paused suddenly, lower down his list, and glanced up, her face bleak. "You mention here a possible involvement in the Mountbatten assassination?"

"We've the best of reasons for believing his advice was sought."

She shook her head. "It doesn't make sense."

"It does if one considers his known links with the KGB. I believe that most of the incidents he has been responsible for were commissioned by the KGB, even the assassination of those supposed to be their friends, with the sole purpose of causing the maximum amount of disruption possible in the West."

"But Barry is no Marxist?"

"Frank Barry, ma'am, isn't anything. Oh, he'll take their money, I'm sure of that, but he'll do what he does for the hell of it. I suppose the psychiatrists would have fancy terms to describe his mental condition. Psychopath would only be the start. I'm not really interested. I just want to see him dead."

The Prime Minister passed the list back to him. "Then get on with it, Brigadier."

Ferguson took the list from her automatically as she pressed a buzzer on her desk. "Ma'am?"

"Department Four has the power—total authority from this office, so it would seem. Use it, man. I'm not going to tell you how to do your own job, you're too good at it. I've read your record. The only thing I will say is that it seems obvious to me you must put everything aside and concentrate all your activities on Barry."

Ferguson got to his feet and slipped the paper back in his briefcase. "Very well, Prime Minister."

The door opened behind him, and the young secretary appeared. The Prime Minister picked up her pen. Ferguson walked to the door and was ushered out.

Ferguson usually preferred to work when possible from his Cavendish Square flat. He was sitting by the fire, drinking tea and toasting crumpets on a long brass fork, when Kim opened the door and ushered Harry Fox in.

"Ah, there you are, Harry. Got what I wanted?"

"Yes, sir, every last piece of paper in the file on Frank Barry."

Fox was thirty, a slim, elegant young man who wore a Guards tie, not surprising in someone who until two years previously had been an acting captain in the Blues. The neat leather glove that he wore permanently on his left hand concealed the fact that he had lost the original in a bomb explosion during his third tour of duty in Belfast. He had been Ferguson's assistant for just over a year.

"What exactly are we looking for, sir?"

"I'm not sure, Harry. Jack Corder was the third man I've put up against Frank Barry, and they've all ended up in a box. We've got to come up with something different, that's all I know for certain."

"You're right, sir. Takes a thief to catch a thief, I suppose."

Ferguson paused in the act of spearing another crumpet on his fork. "What did you say?"

"Jack Grand of Special Branch was telling me the other day they put one of their men into Parkhurst Prison, posing as a convict. He was attacked within two days and badly injured. I suppose the truth is most crooks can spot a copper a mile away. Frank Barry will be the same, if you think about it. He'd smell a rat in almost anyone you tried to infiltrate into his kind of action."

"You could be right," Ferguson said. "Start reading through those files. Aloud, if you please."

They were at it for six hours, only Kim dis-

turbing them from time to time to replenish
the tea. It was dark when Ferguson got up and
stretched and waved to the window.

"I'd like to know where the bastard is now."

Fox said, "The photos on him are a bit sparse,
sir. Nothing since nineteen seventy-two. The
earliest seems to be this one from a *Paris-Match*
article done by some woman journalist in nineteen seventy-one. Who are the other two with
him? Devlin, is it? Liam Devlin and Martin
Brosnan."

Ferguson crossed the room with surprising
speed for a man of his bulk and took the news
clipping from him. "My God, Liam Devlin—
and Brosnan. I'd forgotten they'd had dealings
with Barry, it's so long ago."

"But who are they, sir?"

"Oh, a couple of anachronisms from the early
days of the Irish Troubles. Before the worst of
the bombings and the butchery. The kind of
men who thought it was still nineteen twenty-
one with Michael Collins carrying the flag for
Ireland. Gallant guerrillas up against the might
of the British Empire, flying columns, action
by night."

"I think I saw the movie once, sir," Fox said.

"There was a man called Sean McEoin, a
flying column leader who later became a general in the Free State army. In nineteen twenty-
one, he was surrounded by Black and Tans in
a cottage near his own village. There were
women and children inside, so McEoin ran out

in the open with a gun in each hand and shot his way through the police cordon. Devlin and Brosnan are the same kind of idiots."

"I can't say I came up against anyone like that during my time in Ulster," Fox said, feelingly.

"No. Well, it's as well to remember that the IRA, like the British army or any other institution, consists of a very wide range of human beings. Still, you cut along now. I want to give this some think time."

Fox left. Ferguson poured himself a brandy and stood at the window, looking down into the square, thinking, with regret, of Jack Corder and the others he had sent against Barry.

"Somewhere," he said softly, "that bastard is still laughing at me."

Barry, at that precise moment, was doing roughly what Ferguson was. Standing at a window with a large cognac in his hand, only the apartment was in Paris and the view was of the Seine. There was a discreet tap at the door and when he opened it on the chain, Belov was outside.

"Well?" Barry demanded as the Russian entered.

"Considerable Service Five activity, Frank. They know you were behind the whole affair, so they're leaving no stone unturned to find you—with full assistance from British intelligence on this one, I might add. Your Brigadier

Ferguson and Pierre Guyon of Service Five are old friends."

"Well, that makes a change. I didn't think D15 and the French intelligence service were on speaking terms. How can you be sure that Ferguson and Guyon are such good pals, or have you an informer in Guyon's department?"

"Anything is possible," Belov said.

Barry showed his surprise. "I thought British intelligence had cleaned out all its moles by now. What about Corder? I had to find out about him for myself."

"To be honest, Frank, at the moment we're getting only peripheral information, but we expect that to improve."

"You'd think," Barry said, "D15 would check its employees' credentials right back to the womb."

"Perhaps they do, Frank. But in this case it wouldn't do them any good."

"At least there's no one left who can finger me at the moment, except you, of course, old son."

Belov's smile was forced. "On the whole, I think it would be sensible if you dropped out of sight for a while."

"And where would you suggest?"

"England."

Barry laughed. "Well, it's a novel enough idea. The last place they'd expect. Would you have somewhere specific in mind?"

"The Lake District."

"The colors can be glorious at this time of year." Barry poured himself another cognac. "All right, Nikolai, let's have it."

The Russian opened his briefcase and took out a selection of maps. "It's painfully simple. The balance of power as regards ground forces in Europe is hugely in our favor, mainly because we can put at least four thousand more tanks in the field than the NATO forces."

"So?"

"The West Germans have come up with a rather brilliant new weapon, light enough to be carried by any infantry section. When fired, its pod releases twelve rockets simultaneously. Imagine them as missiles in miniature—heat-seeking, of course, spreading out in a field of fire that could stop a whole group of massed tanks. What a machine gun is to a rifle this new weapon is to the bazooka. It enables one foot soldier to fire the heat-seeking equivalent of a dozen bazooka shells at once, each capable of knocking out the biggest Soviet tank. A tank thrust into Europe could be stopped dead by NATO infantry."

"Jesus," Barry said. "You'd wonder how they lost the war. What'll they come up with next?"

"We must study the weapon and develop a suitable electronic defense. We've tried every way possible to get hold of one, but so far, we've failed. We must have one, Frank."

"So, where do I come into it?"

Belov started to unfold the maps. "I've had

a report today of a rather interesting development. The Germans intend to demonstrate this weapon to the British and others at the British army rocket proving ground near Wastwater in the Lake District next Thursday. There's a team of Germans taking one over on Wednesday—an officer and six men. There's an unused RAF base at Brisingham, only twenty miles from the proving ground. They'll land there to be taken the rest of the way by truck."

"Interesting." Barry opened the maps right across the table.

"Frank, pull this off for me, and it would be worth half a million."

Barry didn't seem to hear him. "I'd need ground support. Someone I could rely on in the general area of things. A thoroughgoing crook, preferably. Could your people in London arrange that?"

"Anything, Frank."

"And more maps. English ordnance survey maps. I want to know that area like the back of my hand."

"I'll have them around to you in the morning."

"Tonight," Barry said. "I'll also need fake passports. One British, one French, and one American, just to vary things. Details like who I am I'll leave up to your experts."

"All right," Belov said.

"And keep the SDECE off my back. Tell

them I've been seen in Turkey or gone to the Argentine."

Since the *Sapphire* scandal, the intelligence networks of most Western countries had had a rather poor opinion of the French intelligence service, believing it to be penetrated by the KGB, which it was—certainly enough for Belov to be able to agree to Barry's request.

"And one more thing," Barry added, as Belov opened the door. "A banking account in my English identity for fifty thousand pounds' working capital." He smiled softly. "And it'll cost you a million, Nikolai. This one will cost you a million."

Belov shrugged. "Frank, just get it for us and you'll see how satisfactory your reward can be."

He went out, and Barry locked and chained the door, then returned to the table, sat down at the maps, and started to give the whole thing some thought.

Harry Fox was just about to step into the shower when his phone rang. He cursed, pulled a towel around himself, and went to answer it.

"Harry, Ferguson here. You know what you said earlier about setting a thief to catch a thief. You've given me a very interesting idea. Go to the office, bring me Martin Brosnan's file, and you might as well bring Devlin's while you're at it."

Fox glanced at his watch. "You mean in the morning, sir?"

"I mean now, damn you!"

Ferguson slammed down his phone, and Fox replaced his receiver and checked his watch. It was just after two A.M. He sighed, returned to the bathroom, and started to dress.

THREE

"Martin Aodh Brosnan," Ferguson said. "The Aodh is Gaelic for Hugh, if you're interested, after his maternal grandfather, a well-known Dubliner in his day."

The fire was burning well, it was four o'clock in the morning, and Harry Fox felt unaccountably alive—except for the hand, of course, which ached a little as if it were still there. That always happened under stress.

"According to the file, he was born in Boston in nineteen forty-five, sir, of Irish-American parentage. His great, great grandfather emigrated from Kerry during the famine. Made the family fortune out of shipping during the second half of the nineteenth century, since when they've never looked back. Oil, construction, chemical plants—you name it." Fox frowned and looked up. "A Protestant. That's astonishing."

"Why?" Ferguson said. "A lot of prejudice against the Catholics in America in the old days. Probably one of his ancestors changed sides, and he's hardly the first Protestant to want a United Ireland. What about Wolfe Tone? He started it all. And the man who came closest to getting it from the British government of his day, Charles Stuart Parnell, was another."

"According to this, Brosnan's mother is a Catholic."

"Unremittingly so. Mass four times a week. Born in Dublin. Met her husband when she was a student at Boston University. He's been dead for some years. She rules the family empire with a rod of iron. I believe the only human being she has never been able to bend to her will is her son."

"He did all the right things, it seems. Very Ivy League stuff. Top prep school. Took a degree in English Literature at Princeton."

"Majored," Ferguson corrected him.

"I beg your pardon, sir?"

"Majored in English, that's what our American friends say."

Fox shrugged and returned to the file. "Then in nineteen sixty-six he volunteered for Vietnam—Airborne Rangers and Special Services. And an enlisted man, sir, that's the puzzling thing."

"A very important point, that, Harry."

Ferguson poured himself more tea. "Vietnam was never exactly a popular issue in America. If you were at university it was possible to avoid the draft, which was exactly what most young men with Brosnan's background did. He could have continued to avoid service by staying on at university and taking a doctorate. He didn't. What's the word that's so popular these days, Harry? *Macho*? Maybe that had something to do with it. Perhaps he felt less of a man because he'd avoided it for so long. In the end, the important thing is that he went."

"And to some purpose, sir." Fox whistled. "Distinguished Service Cross, Silver Star with Oak Leaves, Vietnamese Cross of Valor." He frowned. "And the Legion of Honor. How in the hell did the French get involved?"

Ferguson stood up and walked to the window. "An interesting one, that. His last flamboyant gesture. He saved the neck of a famous French war photographer, a woman, would you believe, name of Anne-Marie Audin. Some ambush or other. She pops up in the story again. The photo from the *Paris-Match* article, remember, with Brosnan, Liam Devlin, and Frank Barry? The good Mademoiselle Audin took that, among others. She wrote the same story for *Life* magazine. A behind-the-scenes look at the Irish struggle. It went down very well in Boston."

Fox reached for the next file. "But how the hell did he move on from Vietnam to the IRA?"

"Wildly illogical, but beautifully simple." Ferguson turned and walked back to the fire. "I'll shorthand it for you and save you some time. On leaving the army, Brosnan went to Trinity College in Dublin to work for that doctorate we mentioned. In August, nineteen sixty-nine, he was visiting an old Catholic uncle on his mother's side, the priest in charge of a church on the Falls Road in Belfast. When did you first visit that fair city, Harry?"

"Nineteen seventy-six, sir."

Ferguson nodded. "So much has happened, so much water under the bridge, that the first wild years of the Troubles must seem like ancient history to people like you. So many names, faces." He sighed and sat down. "During Brosnan's visit, Orange mobs led by 'B' Specials, an organization now happily defunct, went on the rampage. They burned down Brosnan's uncle's church. In fact, the old man was so badly beaten he lost an eye."

"I see," Fox said soberly.

"No you don't, Harry. I once had an agent called Vaughan—Major Simon Vaughan. Won't work for me now, but that's another story. He really did see, because, like Brosnan, he had an Irish mother. Oh, the IRA has its fair share of thugs and mad bombers and too many men like Frank Barry, perhaps, but it also has its Liam Devlins and its Martin Brosnans—genuine idealists in the Pearse and Connolly and Michael Collins tradition. Whether you agree with them or not, they are men who believe passionately that they're engaged in a struggle for which the stake is nothing less than the freedom of their country."

Fox raised his gloved hand. "Sorry, sir, but I've seen women and kids run screaming from a bombing too many times to believe that one anymore."

"Exactly," Ferguson said. "Men like Devlin and Brosnan want to be able to fight with clean hands and a little honor. Their tragedy is that in this kind of war that just is not possible."

He got up again and paced the room restlessly. "You see, I can't blame Brosnan for what happened in Belfast that night in August, sixty-nine. A handful of Republicans, no more than six in all—led by Liam Devlin—took to the streets. They had three rifles, two revolvers, and a rather antiquated Thompson submachine gun. Brosnan found himself caught up in the thick of it during the defense of the church, and when one of them was shot dead at Devlin's side he picked up the man's rifle instinctively. He was far and away the most experienced fighting man there, remember. From then on he was caught up in the PIRA cause. Devlin's righthand man during the period Devlin was chief of staff in Ulster."

"Then what?"

"During the first couple of years or so, it was fine. Men like Devlin and Brosnan were able to take on the army, fight the good old-fashioned guerrilla kind of war that would have delighted Michael Collins's heart. No bombs— they left that to men like Frank Barry. Taking on the army was the way Devlin saw it. He believed that was the way to gain world sympathy for his cause. By the way, how would you feel if you were the officer commanding Northern Ireland and you went into the private office of your headquarters at Lisburn one fine morning and found a rose on your desk?"

"Good God."

"Yes, Brosnan loved that sort of nonsensical and foolhardy gesture. The rose was a play on his own name, of course. Not only did he do it to the top general, he also left one for the Ulster Prime Minister and for the Secretary of State for Northern Ireland. The implication was clear enough."

"He could have killed and didn't."

"That's right. Brosnan's rose." Ferguson laughed. "We had to make it classified to keep it out of the papers, not that they'd have believed it. Who would?"

"What happened later?"

"All changed, didn't it? An escalation of the worst kind of bloodshed, and the bombers gained the ascendancy in the movement. Devlin became chief intelligence officer in Dublin, and Brosnan worked with him as a kind of roving aide."

Reading on through the file, Fox said, "It says here he's got Irish nationality. How's that, sir?"

"Well, the American government was not exactly delighted with his activities, and then in nineteen seventy-four, Devlin sent him to New York to execute an informer who'd been helped to seek refuge in America by the Ulster Constabulary, after selling them information that had led to the arrest of nearly every member of the North Belfast Brigade. Brosnan accomplished his task with his usual ruthless efficiency and got out of New York by the skin of his teeth. When the American State Department tried to extradite him, he claimed Irish nationality, which he was entitled to do under Irish law because his mother was born there. If you're interested, Harry, I could do the same. My grandmother was born in Cork."

Fox quickly glanced through the rest of the file. "And then the French business."

"That's right. Devlin sent him to France in nineteen seventy-five to negotiate an arms consignment. The middleman turned out to be a police informer. When Brosnan arrived at a fishing village on the Brittany coast to take delivery, a rather large consignment of riot police was waiting for him. In the ensuing fracas, he wounded two and shot one dead, for which he was sentenced to life imprisonment on Belle Isle."

"Belle Isle, sir?"

"The French don't have Devil's Island anymore, Harry. They just have Belle Isle. In the Mediterranean, of course, which sounds pleasanter, but it isn't."

Fox closed the files. "All right, sir, but where is all this getting us?"

"Set a thief to catch a thief, Harry. You said it."

Fox gazed at him in astonishment. "But he's in prison, sir. You said so yourself."

"For the past four years," Ferguson said. "But what if we could do something about that?"

The internal phone rang, and Ferguson picked it up. "Fine," he said. "Tell him we'll be straight down." He turned to Fox. "Right, Harry, grab your coat and let's get moving. We haven't got much time."

He moved to the door and Fox followed him. "With respect, sir, where to?"

"Bradbury Lines Barracks at Hereford, Harry. Headquarters of Twenty-second Special Air Service, to be precise. I'll explain it on the way," and he hustled on through the door like a strong wind.

It was cold in the street outside, rain reflecting on the black asphalt, and as the big black Bentley pulled away Harry Fox leaned back against the seat and buttoned his old cavalry overcoat one-handed. So many things circling in his mind, so much had happened. Thoughts of Brosnan simply wouldn't go away—this man he had never met, and yet he felt he knew him as intimately as a brother. He closed his eyes and wondered what Brosnan was doing now.

Belle Isle is a rock situated forty miles to the east of Marseilles and some ten miles from the coast. The fortress, an eighteenth-century anachronism, seems to grow out of the very

cliffs themselves, one of the grimmest sights
in the whole Mediterranean. There is the
fortress, there is the granite quarry, and there
are some six hundred prisoners, political of-
fenders or criminals of the most dangerous
kind. Most of them are serving life sentences
and, the French authorities taking the term
seriously, most of them will die there. One
thing is certain. No one has ever escaped from
Belle Isle.

The reasons are simple. No vessel may approach closer than four miles, and the desig-
nated clear area around the island is closely
monitored by an excellent approach-radar
system. And Belle Isle has another highly efficient protection system provided by nature
itself, a phenomenon known to local fisher-
men as the Mill Race, a ferocious ten-knot
current that churns the water into white foam
even on a calm day. It is hell on earth in a
storm.

Martin Brosnan lay on his bed in a cell on
the upper tier, reading, head pillowed on his
hands. He was stripped to the waist, strong
and muscular, his body toughened by hard la-
bor in the granite quarry. There were the ugly
puckered scars of two old bullet wounds in his
left breast. His dark hair was too long, almost
shoulder-length. In such matters, the authorities were surprisingly civilized, as the books
on the wooden shelf above the bed indicated.

The man on the opposite bed tossed a pack

of Gitanes across. "Have a smoke, Martin," he said in French.

He looked about sixty-five, with very white hair and eyes a vivid blue in a wrinkled humorous face. His name was Jacques Savary, a *Union Corse* godfather and one of the most famous gangsters in Marseilles in his day. He had been a prisoner in Belle Isle since 1965, would remain there until he died, an unusual circumstance for one of his background. Usually the *Union Corse*, the largest organized crime syndicate in France, was able to use its formidable influence with the judiciary to pull strings on behalf of members of Jacques Savary's standing who found themselves in trouble.

But Savary was different. He had chosen to ally himself to the cause of the OAS. It has been said that Charles de Gaulle survived at least thirty attempts on his life, but he had never been closer to death than during the attack masterminded by Jacques Savary in March 1965. The *Union* had at least saved him from execution, settling instead for a life sentence on Belle Isle, mistakenly assuming that his release could be arranged at some future date.

Rain lashed the window, the wind howled. Savary said, "What are you reading?"

"Eliot," Brosnan told him. " 'What we call the beginning is often the end and to make an end is to make a beginning. The end is where we start from.' "

"*The Four Quartets.* Little Gidding," Savary said.

"Good man," Brosnan told him. "See, all the benefits of an expensive education, Jacques, and you're getting it for free."

"And you also, my friend, have learned many things. Can you still open the door the way I showed you?"

Brosnan shrugged, swung his legs to the floor, picked up a spoon from his bedside locker, and went to the door. The lock was covered by a steel plate, and he quickly forced the handle of the spoon between the edge of the plate and the jamb. He worked it across for a few seconds, there was a click, and he opened the door a few inches.

"The same locks since eighteen fifty-two or something like that," Savary said.

"So what? It doesn't get me anywhere, only to the landing," Brosnan said. "I never told you this before, but I once worked out a way to get out. A little climbing, a certain amount of wading through the central sewer system, and I could be outside. Found that out three years ago."

Savary sat up, his face pale. "Then why have you never done anything about it?"

"Because it gets you nothing. You're still on the rock, and there's nowhere to go."

There was the sound of footsteps ascending the steel steps at the far end of the tier, and Brosnan quickly closed the door and worked the spoon around again. There was a slight click, and he hurried across to the bed and lay down.

The footsteps halted outside, a key turned in the lock, the door opened. The uniformed guard who looked in was an amiable looking, walrus-mustached man named Lebel. He wore an oilskin.

"Stir it you two, I need your services."

"And what have we done to deserve the honor, Pierre?" Savary demanded.

"When I suffer, you suffer. You know I like you," Lebel said as they walked past him onto the landing. "The bastards have just given me the burial detail for the next month, and you know the regulations. When they take their last swim, it must be at night."

They paused for Lebel to unlock the door in the great steel-mesh barrier at the end of the landing, and Brosnan peered through it to the central hall below.

"Who's dead?" Savary asked.

Lebel looked at the paper in his hand. "67824—Bouvier. Served thirty-two years. Cancer of the bowel."

It was a sobering enough thought to kill any further conversation as they descended to the hall, crossed to the outer door where the judas gate was unlocked for them by another officer. They crossed the courtyard outside and went up the steps to the mortuary.

It was a simple enough room, with whitewashed walls and lit by a single naked light. There were several well-scrubbed wooden benches in a neat row. The corpse waited on one of them, strapped in a canvas body bag. An old convict in overalls that were too large for him, shoulders bent with age, scrubbed carbolic across the floor. He paused, leaning on his broom.

"All ready for you, sir."

Brosnan knew the form. He had performed the task many times before. Against one wall there was a simple wooden cart, which he trundled across, and he and Savary got the body onto it.

"Right," Lebel said. "Let's go."

"What about the chaplain?" Savary demanded as they maneuvered the cart down the steps.

"Said he didn't want one. An atheist."

Savary was shocked. "Hell, everybody should be entitled to a priest when he goes." He glanced sideways at Brosnan. "You make sure they do things right for me."

"You won't die, you old bastard," Brosnan said. "You'll live forever."

The guard on duty at the gatehouse emerged to open the gates, and they went outside and followed the road, not down toward the harbor but curving up to the left. It was hard work, pushing uphill. Finally, they came out onto a small plateau on the edge of the cliffs.

There was no moon, and the rock dropped sheer, a good forty feet into the water. There was an impression of waves out there, broken water, white foam, and Brosnan could feel salt on his lips like the taste of freedom.

Behind them, Lebel switched on a light above a wooden door and unlocked it. "All right, let's get the weights on him."

The small room had a wooden bench in the center on which Brosnan and Savary placed the body. One of the walls was hung with a selection of oilskins and orange life jackets. The most interesting feature was the piles of heavy steel chain coiled neatly on the floor, each one in a different weight category, according to a painted sign on the wall behind it.

"Right." Lebel consulted his document. "He weighed a hundred and five pounds at death. Christ, we can't have that. He'll float like a cork on that current." He consulted a chart on the wall. "Ninety pounds of chain according to this. Get it on him."

Brosnan took a chain from the correct pile, and they proceeded to pass it through the loops specially provided for that purpose on the body bag.

"Why all this fuss over the weights, Pierre?" Savary asked. "The way you change it, according to the body weight?"

Lebel produced a pack of Gauloises and offered them each one. "Simple. The Mill Race isn't one current, as most people imagine. It's two. Stay on the surface, you'd end on the rocks at St. Denis ten miles up the coast, and bodies drifting in as regularly as that would scare old ladies walking their dogs. But drop the body down to thirty fathoms, the current takes it out to sea. So, the weight factor is critical. Anyway, let's get this over with."

Brosnan and Savary carried the body between them to the edge of the cliff. They stood there for a moment, and Savary said, "I still say he should have a priest. This isn't right."

Lebel, his essential decency coming to the surface, removed his cap and said, "All right. Lord, into thy hands we commend the spirit of 67824—Jean Bouvier. He didn't get much out of this life. Maybe you can do more for him in the next." He replaced his cap. "Okay, over with him."

Brosnan and Savary swung a couple of times then let go. The body turned over once, plunged into white foam below, and disappeared. They stood staring down at the water.

Savary whispered, "The only way I'm ever going to get off this rock. I'm going to die here, Martin."

There was total desolation in his voice, total despair, and Brosnan put a hand on his shoulder. "Maybe—on the other hand, maybe not."

Savary stared at him, frowning, while Lebel closed and locked the door and switched off the light. "Okay, let's go."

They followed him back down the track, heads bowed against the rain.

*   *   *

At six A.M. Ferguson and Harry Fox were having breakfast in a truck drivers cafe on the A40 just outside Cheltenham. The bacon and eggs were the best Fox could remember enjoying since the officers' mess at Combermere barracks in Windsor. Ferguson was obviously just as impressed.

"What about Devlin, sir?"

"Remarkable man. He must be sixty-one now. An Ulsterman, County Down, I believe. His father was executed during the Anglo-Irish war in nineteen twenty-one for serving in a flying column. He was educated by Jesuits and took a first class honors degree in English Literature at Trinity College. He is a scholar, writer, poet, and was a highly dangerous gunman for the IRA during the thirties. He went to Spain in nineteen thirty-six and fought against Franco. He was captured by Italian troops and imprisoned in Spain until nineteen forty when the Abwehr had him freed and brought to Berlin to see if he could be of any use to German intelligence."

"And was he, sir?"

"The trouble was, from their point of view, he was a bad risk. Very antifascist, you see. The Abwehr's Irish section did use him once. They'd sent an agent to Ireland, a Captain Goertz. When he got stuck, they parachuted Devlin in to get him out for them. Unfortunately Goertz was caught, and Devlin spent several months on the run before he managed to make it back to Berlin via Portugal. From then on, Ireland was a dead end as far as the Abwehr was concerned, and Devlin took a job lecturing at the University of Berlin. Until the autumn of nineteen forty-three." Ferguson reached for the marmalade. "This really is very good. I think I'll ask him for a jar."

"The autumn of nineteen forty-three," Fox said patiently.

"How much do you know about the German attempt on Churchill's life in November of that year, Harry?"

Fox laughed out loud. "Come on, sir, an old wives' tale, that one." And then, continuing to watch Ferguson's face, he stopped laughing. "Isn't it, sir?"

"Well, let's assume it's just a good story, Harry. The scenario would run something like this. Devlin, bored to tears at the University of Berlin, is offered a job by the Abwehr. He's to parachute into Ireland, then make his way to Norfolk to act as middleman between the most successful woman agent the Abwehr had in the entire war and a crack force of German paratroopers, led by a Colonel Kurt Steiner, the object of the exercise being to apprehend Churchill, who was staying at a country house outside the village of Studley Constable."

"Go on, sir."

"All for nothing, of course. It wasn't even Churchill, just a stand-in while the great man was going to Tehran. They died anyway, Steiner and his men. Well, all except one, and Devlin, with his usual Irish deviousness, got away."

Harry Fox said in amazement, "You mean it's all true, sir?"

"It's a few years yet before those classified files are opened, Harry. You'll have to wait and see."

"And Devlin worked for the Nazis? I don't get it. I thought you said he was antifascist?"

"Rather more complicated than that. I think if someone on our side had suggested that he should attempt to kidnap Adolf Hitler, he'd have thrown himself into the task with even greater enthusiasm. Very frequently in life we're not playing the game, Harry. It's playing us. You'll learn that as you get older."

"And wiser, sir?"

"That's it, Harry, learn to laugh at yourself. It's a priceless asset. During the postwar period, Devlin was a professor at a midwestern college in America. He returned to Ulster briefly during the border war of the late fifties and went back again during the civil rights disturbances of nineteen sixty-nine. He was one of the original architects of the provisional IRA. As I said earlier, he never approved of the bombing campaign.

"In nineteen seventy-five, increasingly disillusioned, he officially retired from the movement. He's a living legend, whatever that trite phrase means. Since nineteen seventy-six, against considerable opposition from some quarters, he's held a post as visiting professor on the English faculty at his old university, Trinity College."

Ferguson pushed back his chair and they got up to go. "And he and Brosnan were friends?" Fox asked.

"I think you could say that. I also think what happened to Brosnan in France was a sort of final straw for Devlin. Still." He stood in the entrance looking across the dingy carpark and waved to his driver. "All right, Harry, let's press on to Hereford."

Barry was working at the maps in his apartment soon after breakfast, when there was a discreet knock at the door. He opened it to admit Belov.

"How about the passports?" Barry asked.

"No problem. If you would go to the usual place at ten o'clock for the photos, they'll be ready this afternoon. Is there anything else you need?"

"Yes, documentation for the Jersey route—that's the way I'll go. French tourist on holiday."

"No problem," Belov said.

Once in Jersey, he would be on British soil and able to take an internal flight to a selection of airports on the British mainland where customs and immigration procedures were considerably less strict than they would have been landing at London Heathrow.

"If I collect the package Wednesday afternoon,

you must be prepared to take delivery that night," Barry said. "Preferably a trawler, say fifteen miles off the coast."

"And how will you rendezvous?"

"We'll get whoever your people in London find to work for me to arrange a boat. A good forty-foot deep-sea launch will do to operate somewhere out of this area." He tapped the map. "Somewhere on the coast opposite the Isle of Man. South of Ravenglass."

"Good."

"I'll leave for St. Malo tonight and cross to Jersey tomorrow, using the French passport. There's a British Airways flight to Manchester from Jersey at midday. I'll meet your London contact man the following day on the pier at Morecambe at noon. That's a seaside resort on the coast below the Lake District. He'll recognize me from the photograph you keep on file at the KGB office at your London embassy, I'm sure."

Belov looked down at the map. "Frank, if this comes off, it will be the biggest coup of my career. Are you sure? Are you really sure?"

"That you'll be a Hero of the Soviet Union decorated by old Leonid Ilyich Brezhnev himself?" Barry clapped him on the shoulder. "Don't worry, Nikolai, old son. A piece of cake."

FOUR

The 22nd Regiment Special Air Service is what the military refer to as an elite unit. Someone once remarked that they were the nearest thing the British army has to the SS. This is a sour tribute to the unit's astonishing success in counterinsurgency operations and urban guerrilla warfare, areas in which the SAS are undoubtedly world experts, with thirty years experience behind them gained in the jungles of Malaya and Borneo, the deserts of southern Arabia and the Oman, the green countryside of south Armagh, the back streets of Belfast. The SAS accepts only volunteers, soldiers already serving with other units. Its selection procedure is so demanding, both physically and mentally, that only five percent of those applying are accepted.

The office of the commanding officer of 22nd SAS at Bradbury Lines barracks in Hereford was neat and functional, if rather Spartan. Most surprising was the CO himself. Young for a half-colonel, he had a keen intelligent face, bronzed from much exposure to desert sun.

The medal ribbons above his pocket included the Military Cross. He sat there, leaning back in his seat, listening intently.

When Ferguson had finished speaking the colonel said, "Very interesting."

"But can it be done?" Ferguson asked.

The colonel smiled slightly. "Oh, yes, Brigadier, no trouble at all as far as I can see. The sort of thing my chaps are doing in south Armagh all the time. Tony Villiers is the man for this one, I think." He flicked his intercom. "Captain Villiers, quick as you like, and we'll have tea for three while we're waiting."

The tea was excellent, the conversation mainly army gossip. It was perhaps fifteen minutes before there was a knock at the door, and a young man of twenty-six or seven entered. At some time or other his nose had been broken, probably in the boxing ring from the look of him. He wore a black track suit. His most surprising feature was his hair, which was black and tangled and almost shoulder length.

"Sorry about the delay, sir. I was on the track."

"That's okay, Tony. I'd like you to meet Brigadier Ferguson and Captain Fox."

"Gentlemen." Villiers nodded.

"Brigadier Ferguson is from D15, Tony. He has a job of the kind to which we are particularly suited. Absolute top priority. Seemed to me it could be your department."

"Ireland, sir?"

Ferguson said, "That's right. I want you to kidnap someone for me. My information is that he'll be spending the weekend at his cottage in County Mayo on the coast near Killala Bay. I need him within thirty-six hours, delivered to me Sunday morning in London. Do you think you can manage that?"

"I don't see why not, sir." Villiers strolled to the map of Ireland on the wall. "Only sixty or seventy miles from the Ulster border."

"Excellent," Ferguson said.

"Presumably IRA, sir? Anyone important?"

"A university professor called Devlin. You'll be thoroughly briefed."

Villiers showed surprise. "Liam Devlin, sir? I thought he'd retired?"

"That's what he thinks, too," Ferguson said. He hesitated. "Are you certain you can mount this thing right off the cuff, just like that?"

Villiers grinned and ran a hand over his hair. "That's why I never have a haircut, sir. Special dispensation. I mean, in Crossmaglen you've got to look the part." His shoulders hunched and his voice changed, the hard, distinctive Ulster accent taking over. "Personal camouflage is very important, sir. Other people use language labs to learn how to speak French or whatever. In the SAS, we can teach you how to speak with the accent of any Irish county you care to name within a fortnight."

"Soldiering," Ferguson said, "has certainly changed since my day."

The colonel stood up. "Right, gentlemen, I think we'll go over to operations now. Get this thing thoroughly sorted out. You lead the way, Tony."

Villiers flicked Fox's Guards brigade tie as they went through the door. "Which regiment?"

Fox, who knew a guardsman when he saw one, long hair or not, said, "Blues and Royals. And you?"

"Grenadiers," Villiers said. "You lost the hand over there?"

"That's right," Fox said. "Picked up the wrong briefcase."

"That's the way it goes."

It was a misty morning as they crossed the parade ground, and the clock tower loomed above them. Villiers paused. "If you're interested, the name of every member of the regiment killed since nineteen fifty is recorded up there."

Fox paused and peered at the names of men who had died in every possible theater of war. He frowned. "Good God, there's a chap listed as having died in Ethiopia in nineteen sixty-eight. What on earth was he doing there?"

"Search me," Villiers said. "Ours not to reason why, and all that sort of good old British rubbish. You might as well ask ten years from now what I was doing in Mayo tomorrow night."

Later, as the Bentley turned out through the main gates and they started back to London,

Fox said, "You really think they'll put it off, sir?"

"By the beginning of nineteen seventy-six, Harry, forty-nine British soldiers had been killed in south Armagh and not a single member of the IRA, so the SAS were moved in to operate undercover. In the year following, only two part-time members of the Ulster Defense Regiment were killed in the entire area. That result speaks for itself."

"All right, sir, but one thing worries me. So Tony Villiers and his boys are good. The two men he's taking with him were very impressive, I admit that. But Devlin's good, too. I know he's a bit long in the tooth, but what if he decides to shoot first himself . . .?"

"Just what the bastard would do," Ferguson said. "But you heard my orders to Villiers. I want him untouched by human hand. He's no use to me if he's dragging his left leg or something." He yawned. "I'm going to get a little shut-eye, Harry. Wake me at Cheltenham, and we'll have something to eat at that superb cafe."

He closed his eyes, folded his hands across his stomach, leaned back in the corner and was instantly asleep.

At that moment, Frank Barry was disembarking from the hydrofoil in St. Helier harbor on the island of Jersey, having just completed the run from St. Malo. According to the forged

French passport supplied by the KGB, he was a commercial traveler from Paris named Pierre Dubois. His hair had been soaked in brilliantine and carefully parted at one side, and he wore a large pair of black horn-rimmed glasses. His appearance fitted the photo they'd taken exactly. Amazing how different he looked, but then, as he had discovered so often in the past, a little was all that it took.

Fifteen minutes later, a taxi deposited him at the entrance to the airport. He went straight to the British Airways desk and booked a seat on the Manchester flight.

An hour to kill. He stopped at the duty free shop to buy a carton of cigarettes and a bottle of cognac, and the girl behind the counter put them in a plastic bag and smiled.

"I hope you enjoyed your visit."

"Certainly did," Barry said. "Wonderful place. Come back any time." And he walked away to the departure lounge.

The old farmhouse that nestled among beech trees on the hillside above Killala Bay enjoyed one of the best views of the entire west coast of Ireland. Devlin never tired of it. From the terrace he'd built in his spare time the year before, he could see out beyond the cliffs all the way to Newfoundland, the sun slipping into the sea like a blood orange, and to his right, Sligo Bay and across to the mountains of

Donegal. He reluctantly went back into the house.

Liam Devlin was a small man, no more than five foot five or six, and at sixty-one his dark, wavy hair showed no visible signs of gray. There was a faded scar on the right side of his forehead—an old bullet wound. His face was pale, the eyes a vivid blue, and a slight, ironic smile seemed permanently to lift the corners of his mouth. He had the look of a man who'd found life a bad joke and had decided that the only thing to do was laugh about it.

He went into the kitchen, rolled up the sleeves of his black woolen shirt, and began to prepare a stew, peeling potatoes and vegetables methodically, whistling to himself. He was still unmarried, circumstances of his life having dictated the situation more than anything else, but now it suited him. It was good to get away from the petty academic rivalries of the university. And he liked to be alone—to find his own space—although there were women enough still, even a student or two, who would have been happy to spend their weekends in Mayo with him.

He put the stew on the stove, went into the sitting room, and replenished the fire. It was dark outside now. He pulled the curtains at the French windows and poured himself an Irish whisky, Bushmills, his favorite, and settled down by the fire. He ran a hand along the shelf at the side of the fireplace, selected a copy of *The Midnight Court* in Irish, and started to read.

A breath of cold air touched his cheek, the fire stirred. As he glanced up, instantly alert, the door from the hall swung open, and Tony Villiers stepped in. He wore a dark reefer jacket and jeans, and badly needed a shave. The combination made him look a thoroughly dangerous man. The Browning automatic pistol in his right hand confirmed it.

"Would you look at that now," Devlin said softly and stood up, leaning agaist the mantelpiece of the great stone fireplace, one foot on the hearth. "And which club are you from, son? Red Hand of Ulster, UVF, or what?"

"Easy now, professor," Tony Villiers said in impeccable public school English.

"Christ Jesus," Devlin said amiably, "not you bloody lot again."

His right hand went up inside the fireplace and grasped the butt of a Walther pistol that hung on a nail there in case of just such an emergency. His hand swung, and he fired in one smooth motion, hitting Villiers in the left shoulder, knocking him back against the wall, the Browning falling to the floor.

Villiers struggled to one knee, blood oozing between his fingers where he clutched his shoulder. "Good," he said, "really very good."

"Flattery will get you nowhere, son," Devlin said, and there was a crash behind him as the kitchen door was flung open and Villiers' two companions erupted into the room, machine pistols at the ready.

"Alive," Tony Villiers cried. "Don't harm a hair on his bloody head, that's an order." He smiled savagely. "I'm expecting rather a lot, professor; they're only trained to kill. I'd advise you to drop it."

"SAS, is it?" Devlin said.

"I'm afraid so."

"Mother Mary, why didn't they send the Devil instead. Now with him, I'm on good terms." He turned to the other two. "Do you think one of you could do something about his shoulder? It's the carpet I'm thinking of— Persian, a gift from a friend."

Tony Villiers shook his head. "Later, professor. For now, you will please pack a suitcase with whatever you feel you need for an extended trip."

"And just exactly where might we be going?"

"Well, if things go according to plan, we should cross into Ulster about three hours from now. Onward transportation, courtesy of the Army Air Corps, tomorrow morning. You should be in London by noon. I'd take a raincoat, if I were you." Villiers had produced a field service dressing pack from one pocket and was opening it with his teeth. "The weather over there's been terrible lately."

Devlin shook his head. "Where did you go to school, son?"

"Eton College."

"Jesus, and I might have known. What would the Empire have been with you?"

"Not very much, I suspect," Tony Villiers said crisply. "But time is limited, professor. Please do as I say without any further delay."

"And so I will." Devlin walked to the door followed by one of the troopers. "But only because I'm fascinated. Can't wait to find out what all this is about. Help yourself to the Bushmills."

He smiled and walked out into the hall.

Morecambe is a seaside resort on the Lancashire coast, south of the English Lake District, a quiet town that even during the holiday season caters mainly to older people. Not a great deal goes on there. Someone once unkindly said that when people die in Morecambe they don't bury them, they simply sit them up in the town bus shelters to make the place look busy.

Frank Barry found it pleasant enough. Not many people on the waterfront, which was only to be expected in November, but then he'd always found seaside resorts out of season stimulating places—the cafes and shops closed for the winter, the empty boardwalks. He walked out along the pier, feeling unaccountably cheerful, and stood at the rail, breathing in the good salt air. The dark waters of Morecambe Bay were being whipped into whitecaps by the wind, and to the north, through the mist, he could see the mountains of the Lake District, a blur on the horizon.

He lit a cigarette and waited. After a while, he heard footsteps booming hollowly on the boardwalk behind him. The man who leaned on the rail on his right wore a dark raincoat and hat. He was perhaps thirty and had a young, intelligent face. His steel-rimmed glasses were giving him trouble in the rain.

Barry, who had discarded his horn-rimmed spectacles and washed the brilliantine from his hair at the motel where he had stayed the night before, smiled at him. "A hell of a problem those things in weather like this."

The young man put the briefcase he was carrying down and wiped his glasses with a handkerchief. "True, Mr. Barry. I tried contact lenses a few years ago but unfortunately had an allergy to them." His English was excellent with just a trace of an accent.

"You have something for me?"

The young man touched the briefcase with his foot. "Everything you need."

"Well, that makes a change," Barry said. "I mean, it's not often you get everything in this life."

"I have also included a contact in London by which you may reach me in the event of an emergency, Mr. Barry. Please memorize and destroy."

Barry picked up the briefcase and grinned.

"Son, I was doing this sort of thing when you were still hanging on your mother's left breast."

He walked away along the pier, his feet echoing on the boards. The young man stayed where he was. Only when the sound of the echoes had faded did he turn from the rail.

Barry picked up a rental car at Manchester airport, a Ford Cortina, and was driving it through Lancaster, turning on to the M6 motorway and heading north from the Lake District within twenty minutes of leaving his KGB contact on Morecambe pier. He drove for some ten or twelve miles, then turned into a convenient rest stop, cut the engine, and opened the briefcase.

There was, as the young man had said, everything he needed. His contact at a place called Marsh End, south of Ravenglass on the Cumbrian coast, all very convenient for the Wastwater proving ground. Details of the rendezvous for Thursday night—they'd provided a deepsea trawler for that from the Russian northern fishing fleet. And, of course, the young man's number in London. Even more interesting was the pistol with the silencer screwed on the end, a Czech Ceska 7.5mm. There were also several additional clips of ammunition and fifty thousand pounds in twenty-pound notes, neatly packeted.

"Well, would you look at that, now?" Barry said softly, hefting the Ceska in one hand.

He slipped it into his raincoat pocket. He closed the briefcase, placing it on the passenger seat beside him with the typed list on top and drove away. Occasionally, he glanced at the list memorizing the details it contained, line by line. An hour later, he left the M6 at Levens Bridge and pulled into a roadside cafe. He went into the men's room, locked himself in a stall, lit a cigarette, and touched the lighter flame to the list. Only when it was reduced to dark ashes did he drop it into the toilet bowl to flush away. Then he went outside, got back into the car and took the road to Broughton-in-Furness and the Cumbrian coast, whistling softly through his teeth.

Kim opened the door of Ferguson's sitting room and ushered Tony Villiers and Liam Devlin inside. Ferguson was at his desk, Harry Fox standing beside him. Ferguson glanced up, peering at the two men over his half-moon spectacles, then he removed them slowly.

Tony Villiers' dark reefer hung from his shoulders, loosely buttoned. Underneath, he was swathed in bandages, his left arm in a sling. His face was white and drawn, lines of pain deeply etched there in spite of the injection they'd given him at the military wing of Musgrave Park Hospital in Belfast.

"Professor Devlin, sir, as ordered," he said.

"Now then, you old bastard," Devlin said

amiably. "You've got a good lad here and you not deserving it."

Ferguson got to his feet. "You should be in the hospital, Captain, now, and that's an order. See to it, Harry. Get my car."

Villiers swayed, and Devlin moved in fast and got an arm around him. "Easy boy, you've done enough and more."

Villiers managed to smile. "Damn it, professor, but I like you. I really do, and that's a hell of a thing to say considering the situation."

"You're not so bad yourself," Devlin told him. "It's only the uniform I'm not too happy about, not the man wearing it."

Harry Fox had Villiers by the elbow. "All right, let's go."

As he opened the door Villiers said, "One thing, professor. You could have killed me and you didn't. Why?"

"The terrible waste that would have been," Devlin said, and suddenly the blue eyes were bleak. "And hasn't there been waste enough?" Villiers stared at him, frowning, and Devlin laughed. "Go on, boy, out of it, before I totally corrupt you."

The door closed behind them, and Devlin turned to face Ferguson, unbuckling the belt of his dark trenchcoat. "So, here we are."

"Here we are indeed."

"Would there be any chance of a cup of tea, would you think? It's been a hell of a journey."

Ferguson smiled and flicked the intercom.

"Tea, Kim. My usual and another pot, extra strong, Irish variety." He turned back to Devlin. "Satisfactory?"

"As long as I can stand up a spoon in it."

He helped himself to a cigarette from a box on Ferguson's desk, lit it, and sprawled in one of the chairs by the fire. "They do you well, D15, I must say."

The door opened, and Kim, followed by Harry Fox, came in with the tea on a silver tray. "I've packed him straight off in the Bentley to the special wing at Melbury House, sir," Fox said. "I've rung through and notified Colonel Jackson that he's on his way."

"Good," Ferguson said. "And let's make sure he gets only the best."

Kim withdrew, and Devlin helped himself to the tea. "And whom have we here?"

"Captain Fox is my personal aide," Ferguson said.

Devlin's eyes took in the gloved hand. "And not much time for people like me, I should imagine."

"Not really," Fox said.

"That's fine, boy. Just so we know where we stand."

There was silence. Ferguson got up and peered out of the window into the square. "You're in a bad hole, Devlin, you realize that, don't you? There are outstanding crimes listed against you which would draw you twenty years at least, if not life. How does the Central Criminal Court at the Old Bailey appeal to you?"

Devlin laughed out loud. "Go teach your grandmother to suck eggs, Brigadier. I'm not standing in the dock at the Bailey or anywhere else. You know it, I know it, and so does the boy here, if he has an ounce of sense. I was taken against my will, from one sovereign state to another, kidnapped by British troops, carried over the border from the Republic of Ireland into Ulster. Now, I know things haven't been going too well between our two wonderful countries, but if you think the British Cabinet is going to want the stink that this would cause, all the way up to the United Nations, you've lost your marbles."

He was right. He knew it, and so did they. It was Harry Fox who put it into words. "He's got a point, sir. There's no way we can make this work against his will. If he won't play, we'll have to send him back."

"Don't be a fool, Harry. I've known that all along," Ferguson said.

"So," Devlin said. "Let's be having it."

Ferguson said calmly, "When did you last see Brosnan?"

Devlin's eyes were wary. "Martin? Four years ago."

"That's right, February, nineteen seventy-five, when you sent him to France. Since when he's taken up permanent residence in a very unpleasant establishment called Belle Isle off the French Mediterranean coast, which you may have heard of."

"A small corner in hell, so they tell me," Devlin said.

"Aptly put, and he's there for life. An establishment like Alcatraz, which proudly boasts that no one has ever escaped from it."

"So?"

"What if I could get him out?"

Devlin frowned. "And how would you do that?"

"Some sort of deal with the French authorities."

"But why would you? Why should you go to the trouble?"

"Frank Barry."

There was total amazement on Devlin's face. "Frank Barry?" he said. "And what in the name of Christ has he to do with it?"

"Well, if you can keep that Irish tongue of yours still for fifteen minutes, I'll tell you."

Devlin walked up and down the room, the cigarette hanging from the corner of his mouth, smoke curling. "All right?" he said. "A fine mad bastard, Frank Barry is. I'll not deny that or my personal dislike of the man, but it's your flesh he's the thorn in and nailing him to the cross is your affair—not Martin Brosnan's and certainly not mine."

"Frank Barry is at war with the world, Mr. Devlin," Harry Fox said.

Devlin laughed. "Oh, but you have a way with the words, Captain. Is there just a touch of Irish in your blood somewhere?"

"Be reasonable, Devlin," Ferguson said. "Barry's activities never exactly helped your cause. You've got to admit that. He's done as much as anyone to blacken your image in his time, and that was before the suggestion that his advice was used on the Mountbatten affair. One of the worst things that ever happened to the IRA as far as world opinion was concerned."

"I'm with you there," Devlin said. "But you're wrong in one respect. It isn't my cause any longer."

Fox was thunderstruck. "You mean that?"

Devlin nodded. "Oh, I'm still one hundred percent for a united Ireland, but ten years is enough as far as I'm concerned. Too many dead, Captain. A bloody charnel house, and what have we got to show for it? Frankly, I think you'll find Martin Brosnan to be of the same opinion."

"Put it to him," Ferguson said. "Go and see him, that's all I ask."

"And how could that be arranged?"

Ferguson nodded to Harry Fox, who opened a file and took out a British passport which he pushed across the desk. Devlin picked it up. It was in the name of Charles Gorman and when he opened it his own picture stared out at him.

"And who would Charles Gorman be?"

"A highly respectable lawyer with offices in

Lincoln's Inn, visiting Brosnan to discuss legal matters in connection with the family business and also the possibility of an appeal for clemency."

Devlin shook his head in amazement. "Are you trying to tell me I'm expected or something?"

"Certainly. Tuesday morning, day after tomorrow. You catch the prison supply boat from a place called St. Denis, along the coast from Marseilles."

Devlin tapped the passport with a finger, frowning. "To set up a thing like this must have taken some pull over there in France, even for you."

"Not really," Ferguson said. "The right SDECE contact. Colonel Guyon, who heads Service Five now, has a vested interest in running Frank Barry to earth himself, particularly after the attempt to assassinate Lord Carrington on French soil. It's through his influence that your appointment to see Brosnan was arranged so expeditiously."

"Service Five?" Devlin grimaced. "They could have given Himmler and his bunch a run for their money. The way I hear it, they enjoy playing with electricity."

"Yes, well, we don't exactly have much choice, do we?"

"And Guyon can arrange Martin's release, is that what you're saying?"

"Not at all." Ferguson shook his head. "That

would take some delicate negotiations at a rather higher level. No, for the moment all I want you to do is see Brosnan and find out if he'll agree in principle."

"To what? Freedom, if he agrees to hunt down Frank Barry and act as a kind of public executioner for you!"

"Why not? A simple enough quid pro quo, or do you really think he'd rather spend the rest of his life in a cell on Belle Isle."

Devlin shook his head. "I don't know about this. To start with, you're making a mistake to think Frank Barry would welcome him with open arms. They always disliked each other. Martin thought him a butcher from the beginning and told him so. On the other hand, he's a very complex man, our Martin. The killer's hand is the instinctual part of him that he hasn't been able to control since Vietnam, but up here," he tapped his forehead, "is a scholar, philosopher, and poet of no mean distinction. You could never tell which way he'd jump."

"You mean he needs to be angry?" Ferguson said. "I think I can arrange that, too." Fox took a photo from the file and passed it across.

The girl in it sat on a sand dune with tall grass around her, hugging her knees, face pushed forward, laughing. She was no more than seventeen, with shoulder-length black hair and a face of extraordinary beauty. Devlin's own face was very pale as he picked the photo up.

"You recognize her?" Ferguson asked.

"Yes," Devlin said softly. "Norah Cassidy, Martin's cousin once removed, a nice Belfast girl."

"And what happened to her?"

"She died a year back, so I believe. In France." Devlin passed a hand over his face, then froze. "France?" he whispered. "And just what are you getting at now, Ferguson?"

"She went to the Sorbonne to study French in nineteen seventy-six," Ferguson said. "As you might expect from a girl with her political views, she soon made contact with various extremist political organizations at the university, and then Frank Barry appeared on the scene."

"Barry?" Devlin said. "Barry and Norah? I don't believe it."

"She was his mistress for over a year, but Belfast had left its mark. Like many young women from that city, she'd been on tranquilizers for years. In Barry's company, she progressed to harder drugs. Finally, she was mainlining on heroin. She became more and more dependent on the drug, which suited Barry because it made her more and more dependent on him. The police almost caught him on a farm in Normandy just over a year ago. He escaped by the skin of his teeth but dumped her."

"The bastard," Devlin said.

"What you're going to see now isn't nice, but

I think it necessary." Ferguson nodded to Fox. "Now, Harry."

There was a television set in the corner, a video machine underneath it. Fox switched it on, and Ferguson said, "I got this through Guyon from French intelligence. As I said, not nice, but there it is."

The video rolled for a moment then focused. Norah Cassidy's face filled the screen, ravaged, wasted, only a hint of that smiling girl in the photo. She was crying helplessly, and the camera pulled back to show her being held by two nurses. One of them pushed up the wide sleeve of the hospital robe and the camera moved in to show the dozens of tracks on her arm from the heroin fixes, running sores most of them.

The scene changed. She was in bed now, a narrow hospital cot in a white room, straps across the bed to control her as she thrashed wildly. The scene cut sharply to be replaced by another close-up of the face, in total repose, relaxed, at peace, only she wasn't sleeping— she was dead, and the camera pulled back to reveal her lying naked on a mortuary slab, her head cradled on a wooden block. The pathologist leaned over her with a scalpel.

Ferguson said, "That'll do, Harry, no need to prolong the agony."

Fox hurriedly switched off the video. Devlin turned to the window, tears in his eyes. He stayed there, shoulders hunched. He said quietly, "I'm going to be sick. Where's the bathroom?"

"Straight through that door," Ferguson told him, and Fox hurried to hold it open for him.

Devlin went out, and Fox removed the video from the machine, crossed slowly to Ferguson's desk, and laid it down carefully.

"You know something, sir?" His voice was shaky. "On the whole, I think I'd really prefer to be back in Belfast."

"I know, Harry, I know. A dirty, dirty business—you'll find that out the longer you're in it, but someone has to do it."

The door opened and Devlin came back in. He went to the sideboard and helped himself to a large Scotch and stood there, savoring it.

"Martin loved that girl like a sister, you know that? In August sixty-nine in the Falls Road, she carried ammunition to us under fire. She was all of twelve years old then."

Ferguson said, "You'll go?"

"Oh, yes," Devlin said in a low voice. "I think you could say that."

"Good. You can phone whoever you have to at Trinity College from here. Tell them you're taking extended leave or something—anything you like. You can stay at Harry's flat tonight and fly on to Marseilles tomorrow. Papers, money, everything you need you'll be provided with. You've got two days, then I want you back here."

"Fine by me," Devlin said.

"We think Barry's Russian contact in Paris is a man called Nikolai Belov. Supposed to be a cultural attaché at the Soviet embassy. Actually a colonel in the KGB. There's the address of his apartment in St. Germain in Paris and a photo."

He passed them across, and Devlin examined the photo, frowning. "Surely French intelligence knows about this man?"

"Of course."

"Then why don't they do something about him?"

"Officially he's a diplomat, so they'd have to catch him at it. And we have reason to believe that the KGB is still well entrenched within French intelligence. I think he's got friends there. One more thing that may help." Ferguson held up the old *Paris-Match* photo of Devlin, Brosnan, and Frank Barry. "Remember the girl who took this?"

"Anne-Marie Audin." Devlin took the photo from him. "Nineteen seventy-one. Belfast was crawling with journalists in those days, all of them wanting stories—secret interviews with the gallant lads of the IRA. She scooped them all, that girl."

"But then she would, wouldn't she?" Ferguson said. "After all, she'd known him in Vietnam. All she had to do was put the word out in Belfast that she was there. She must have known he'd contact her."

"Exactly," Devlin said. "She stayed with us

for a week, and a hell of a time of it she had, but what a story."

"She visited him twice in Dublin," Ferguson said. "They met again in Paris at least once. Rather more than journalistic interest, I'd say."

"That's her business," Devlin said flatly.

"Well, she *is* thirty-three and still unmarried. She's also in London this weekend on an assignment for the French edition of *Vogue*. Do you think it's worth seeing her? After all, she's hardly likely to call copper on you."

"No, she wouldn't do that." Devlin remembered those heady days in 1971, hustling through the Armagh countryside by night, crashing an army roadblock, bullets shattering the windows of their car, and flinging himself on Anne-Marie, holding her safe against the floor.

"Good," Ferguson said. "Arrange it then, Harry." He pushed the phone across to Devlin. "Only one more thing to do then. Ring the university and make your excuses."

Devlin picked up the receiver and held it for a moment. "You know, there's an old Irish saying. Touch the Devil and you can't let go."

"Interesting," Ferguson said. "And what exactly does it mean?"

"Oh, I think you know well enough. You and me, the boy here, Martin in his cell. Frank Barry. None of us can stop, can we? There's no going back. Bloody undertakers the lot of us, always carrying some poor bugger out in a coffin." He started to dial. "The trouble is, you see, that we're not playing the game anymore. The game's playing us."

FIVE

The Grenadier Guard, in black busby and scarlet tunic, stood at his post outside St. James's Palace, rigidly at attention, rifle at the slope, and stared into infinity, trying to ignore the young model in the white silk pantsuit and gold high-heeled sandals, who positioned herself against him.

It was ludicrous really, rain falling, and in spite of that her perfume filled his nostrils so that he had to breathe deeply to steady himself.

There was a lighting man, a second cameraman, wardrobe mistress with two assistants, three other models—just now changing in the large van—and a curious crowd of onlookers, pausing to watch Anne-Marie Audin at work.

She wore knee-high brown boots and a khaki jumpsuit of the kind that could be purchased at any military surplus shop. Her hair was long, shoulder length, at present held back in a ponytail. The face was very brown, and the only make-up she wore was a pale lipstick.

Fox parked the car at the curb and followed the Irishman toward the crowd. They moved around to the other side of the van.

"Has she changed much?"

Devlin shook his head. "Big for the cause of women but a darling girl, though she'd belt me for saying it."

"She and Brosnan were lovers then?" Fox asked gently.

"Oh yes." Devlin continued to watch her as she took one photo after another. "I wasn't going to tell that old bugger that, though. Tell me, Captain, when were you born? End of March, beginning of April, I'd say."

Fox was astonished. "How did you know that? It's actually the seventh of April."

"I was right though. Aries the Ram. That's the doctor's sign. Surprising to find you a soldier and you a healer by nature. Now take Ferguson. He's a Scorpio for sure. According to my favorite book of astrology, published in the eighteenth century, I might add, if his stars are badly aspected, which I'm certain they are, he's a lover of murder and thieving, a promoter of sedition, perjured, obscene, rash, and inhumane. Recognize any of his more lovable traits there?" He put a hand up. "No, don't bother to answer."

Anne-Marie turned to her assistant. "All right," she said in French. "Now we move into the park. Buckingham Palace last."

Her eyes passed over Devlin. She paused and looked back slowly. "Good day to you, *a colleen*," he said cheerfully. "God save the good work."

Anne-Marie Audin turned very pale under her tan. He took her hands and kissed them gently.

Devlin and Anne-Marie sat on a bench in the rain in St. James's Park. Below, the crew was setting up for more pictures by the lake.

The content of Devlin's French was excellent, rapid and fluent. The accent was terrible. He said, "You're wearing well, girl."

"And you, Liam. Still up to your ears in that cause of yours? I would have thought London dangerous territory for you."

"Ancient history," Devlin told her. "No more causes. I'm getting old, my love."

"That will be the day." She ruffled his hair without thinking.

He offered her a cigarette from his battered old silver case. She shook her head, and he took one himself. "Fashion photography?" He nodded at the crew by the lake. "Isn't that a bit of a comedown for France's favorite war photographer?"

"And there's the professor talking," she said. "Don't be a snob, Liam. It's the best fashion magazine in the world, and I never give less than my best. I'd have thought you'd have known that. There's always far more to any highly popular art form than the critics are willing to admit. Anyway, it's not the only reason I'm here. Later tonight I'm doing a docu-

mentary for French television on down-and-
outs in London."

"I might have known." He grinned crookedly.
"And still big for the cause of women and still
not married and all of thirty-five."

"Thirty-three," she said, and punched him
in the shoulder.

"But still not married for all that, and we
both know why." She glanced at him, face
blank, then looked out across the lake. Devlin
said softly, "Have you seen him lately?"

"The last time I tried was three years ago. I
received permission through the Judiciary Department and went to Belle Isle. He refused to
see me. Sent me a letter later, his last one, in
which he said I was to look upon him as dead."

"And?"

She smiled wanly. "I got some good pictures,
Liam. A terrible place."

"I can imagine. I'm seeing him Tuesday,
myself. It should be an enlivening encounter."

She turned instantly, eyes dark. "You are
seeing Martin? You? But how can this be?"
She frowned, glancing across at Fox sheltering
from the rain under a tree. "Who is that man,
Liam? What game are you playing now?"

So he told her, rapidly and concisely, leaving nothing out. When he was finished, she sat
there staring at him in astonishment.

"But this is incredible, insane."

"It might get him out, or would you rather
he spent the rest of his life on that rock?"

"No, of course not. I would do anything— anything to see him free," she said savagely. "Not for my own sake, Liam, not for love, but for him." Her fingers hooked painfully into his arm.

"I know, girl, I know," he soothed her.

There was a call from the lake below, her assistant waving. She said, "I'll have to go. Look, I must see you again."

"I'm leaving for Marseilles in the morning."

"Tonight at nine o'clock. I'm doing the feature I mentioned to you. Filming the work of one of the welfare canteens serving the homeless. The south side of Lincoln's Inn Fields. Please be there, Liam."

Her voice was low, urgent. He took her hand as they got up. "You always were hard to refuse."

She kissed him on the cheek and started down the slope to the lake.

It was early evening when Barry reached Marsh End, not that Marsh End itself was anything much—a scattering of cottages beside the road, most of them derelict. The place he was looking for was a mile on the other side. Iron gates stood open, a gravel drive passing through the beech trees and rhododendrons to a gray stone house beyond. The board at the gate carried the legend in gold lettering *Henry Salter— Undertaker. House of Rest and Crematorium.*

Barry drove up the drive and parked the

Cortina at the bottom of the steps leading to the entrance. As he got out, a girl emerged from the stable yard to the right and paused, looking at him. She wore rubber boots, an old raincoat, and head scarf, and carried a bucket in each hand. Her face was calm, touched by an impossible beauty in the evening light.

"Mr. Salter about?" Barry asked.

She spoke with the strong and distinctive Cumbrian accent and yet there was a dead quality to her voice.

"I'll see, sir. No one else here, with it being Sunday. Who shall I say?"

"Sinclair's the name," Barry told her cheerfully. "Maurice Sinclair. I think you'll find he's expecting me."

"I'll see then, shall I?" She went up the steps, and Barry followed her.

It was very quiet in the embalming room, and Henry Salter worked alone, his rubber apron smeared with blood. The body upon which he was working was that of a young woman, and he was in the process of removing her viscera. The door opened behind him, and the girl entered. She had taken off the scarf, revealing tangled dark hair, and the old cotton dress she wore was a size too small, the seams splitting in several places.

Salter said, "I've told you never to disturb me while I'm working, Jenny."

"There's a gentleman to see you, sir, a Mr. Sinclair. He's waiting downstairs."

Salter paused and glanced at her sharply. "Ah, yes, Mr. Sinclair. He'll be staying the night, Jenny, so make sure the spare bedroom is ready. Then you can get him something to eat."

"Yes, sir," she said in that curiously dead voice and looked down at the body. "She was really beautiful."

"I know, Jenny, but this is what we all come to in the end. Now be a good girl and run along."

She went out, and Salter picked up the body and lowered it into a stone sink filled with formaldehyde. It slid under the surface and hung suspended an inch or two from the bottom, the hair fanning out. He removed his rubber apron and gloves, went into the small washroom at the other end of the embalming room and started to clean himself up.

Afterward, he slipped on a dark alpaca jacket and straightened his black tie. The iron gray hair, the gaunt face, the rimless glasses, gave him exactly the appearance that he felt the public had a right to expect from an undertaker. Death was a serious business, and nobody believed that more sincerely than Salter himself. Certainly there was little to link the grave and respectable face that confronted him in the mirror with the second-rate thief who had served three prison sentences as a young man before coming to terms with the real facts of life.

As he went along the corridor, he wondered about this man Sinclair. The offer of the work had been something he'd found impossible to refuse. The ten thousand pounds mentioned would come in very handy indeed. Only the previous week he'd had the new incinerator installed in the crematorium. It could consume a human body in fifteen minutes, not like the older one, which was so inefficient that it was necessary to pulverize the skull and the pelvic bones later.

Another reason he'd not been able to refuse the work, even if he'd wanted to, was the source of the request—people of consequence in the London underworld whom he'd dealt with on a number of occasions.

The coast around Marsh End was a lonely, somber world of creeks and marshes, ideal for a fast boat by night, in and out, and Salter had acted as middleman for many a drug consignment on its way to London. When you'd done that sort of thing once, the truth was you could never say no again.

He went down the staircase and found Frank Barry standing by the reception desk. "Mr. Sinclair?" he said and held out a hand. "Henry Salter. Let's go into my private sitting room. It's far more comfortable."

Barry followed him along a narrow corridor, and Salter opened a door and led the way into a room that was crowded with Victorian furniture. The walls were dark green damask, the curtain a dull red velvet. Salter stirred the fire with a brass poker.

"A drink, Mr. Sinclair?"

"Not yet," Barry said. "Business first."

He took the Ceska from his pocket and placed it on the table, and Salter licked his lips nervously. Barry put the briefcase down and opened it. He took out several packets of twenty-pound notes and tossed them across.

"Five thousand there. You get the other half on completion. Satisfactory?"

"Perfectly, Mr. Sinclair." Salter scooped the money up instantly and put it in a drawer.

"Now, my requirements. You have everything?"

"You can see the boat in the morning. It's moored in a creek not far away. I thought you might like to stay the night here."

"What else do you have to offer?"

"A small farmhouse at the head of the valley, four miles from here. The two men I was asked to recruit arrived this afternoon. They're there now."

"What are their backgrounds?"

"Liverpool underworld. They have both done time for robbery with violence and the like. Rather rough, I'm afraid."

"Exactly what I need," Barry told him. "Soon enough to see them tomorrow. And the equipment?"

"Two suitcases were delivered this morning very early."

"Who by?"

"I haven't the slightest idea. A young man in a dark coat and hat. I've never seen him before." Barry smiled, and Salter said, "Your people seem remarkably efficient, Mr. Sinclair."

"And why wouldn't they be? Let's have a look at those suitcases."

Salter opened a cupboard at the side of the fireplace. The cases were well made in real leather, their catches held in place by tumbler locks, the combinations of which Barry had memorized from the list in his briefcase.

He quickly lined up the right sequence of numbers and opened the first case. It contained two Sterling submachine guns, two British army-issue Smith and Wesson revolvers, a Browning automatic, and several gas canisters. Salter's eyes opened wide. Barry closed the case, locked it, and opened the other, disclosing army camouflage uniforms, several dark blue berets, and webbing belts.

"Can I ask what all this is about, Mr. Sinclair?" Salter said nervously. "It all looks pretty heavy to me."

"That's what you're getting paid for," Barry told him. He locked the second case. "Now let's have that drink."

At that moment, there was a knock at the door, it opened and Jenny came in with a tray.

"I told you not to disturb me," Salter said angrily.

"I thought you might like some tea, Mr. Salter, you and the gentleman."

She glanced at Barry, and in the light of the room and without the head scarf he saw now that she was at best plain, with high cheekbones, olive skin, and overfull lips.

"All right, girl, run along and get a meal ready for Mr. Sinclair."

She went out, and Frank Barry, ignoring the tea, went to the sideboard, and helped himself to the Scotch. "Is she all there?"

Salter poured himself a cup of tea. "Oh, yes, just a little slow, that's all. She used to live at the farm I mentioned, up the valley, with her father, a fine old drunk. He ran his car into a wall one night and killed himself. She would have been destitute if I hadn't taken her in and bought the place."

"A philanthropist," Barry said. "I could tell right away."

"But she never seems to come to life," Salter said. "Her flesh has—has a deadness to it. She never responds." It was as if he were talking to himself for a moment, and then he looked up. "You understand me?"

"Oh, yes," Barry said in disgust. "I think so."

Salter swallowed the rest of his tea hurriedly. "Well, if you'll excuse me, I've got a job to finish. A burial tomorrow afternoon, so it won't wait. Jenny will look after you."

He went out. Barry drank the rest of his Scotch. The room was very quiet except for the grandfather clock in the corner. There was an indefinable musty smell to everything, like an old room opened for the first time in many years. It went well with the overstuffed furniture and the nature of the establishment.

When he opened the door, he could smell cooking. He followed the smell along the passage to the old stone-flagged kitchen. The girl stood at the stove stirring something in a pan with a wooden spoon. She glanced over her shoulder.

"It's almost ready," she said in that dead voice as she put down the spoon and wiped her hands over her thighs. "I'm just going out to the shed for more wood for the stove."

She took a large red flashlight from under the sink and moved to the door. Barry was there before her and opened it. "I'll come with you. You could probably do with some help."

She looked up at him, uncertain, then handed him the light. "All right, it's across the yard."

It was treacherous underfoot and Barry picked his way carefully, cursing when he stepped into a puddle. When the girl opened the door of the barn, he saw several vehicles parked inside. A black hearse, a large black limousine, a van, and a Land Rover.

The woodpile was to one side under a loft

stuffed with hay. She said, "Over here, Mr. Sinclair," and for a moment, in the light's beam, she looked as beautiful as she had at their first meeting.

She leaned over the woodpile, one knee forward so that the old cotton dress tightened across her thighs. Barry reached out, cupping a hand around her thigh, and she glanced back over her shoulder, and it was there, whatever Salter had thought, in her eyes.

Barry handed her the flashlight and smiled. "You take that, I'll carry the wood."

She stood waiting for him, her face above the light in shadow. He piled half a dozen logs in the crook of one arm and led the way out.

Like any other great city in the world, London has its share of derelicts, down-and-outs who can no longer help themselves, who sleep rough because they have to.

When Devlin and Harry Fox arrived at Lincoln's Inn Fields just before nine o'clock, a Salvation Army mobile canteen was in position, the French camera crew already setting up their equipment. Fox parked the car, and he and Devlin started walking to where Anne-Marie, wrapped in a bulky sheepskin jacket, stood talking to a cheerful-looking woman who wore the uniform of a Salvation Army major. She caught sight of Devlin and Fox approaching and came to greet them.

"Time you two met," Devlin said. "Harry Fox."

"A pleasure, Miss Audin," Fox said gallantly.

"And what would you be doing here then?" Devlin asked. "Aren't those film cameras?"

"Video," she said. "A documentary I'm doing for French television on the underside of London life." She pointed to the figures shambling out from underneath the plane trees. "Men without hope," she said. "Sometimes women. Unemployed, alcoholic, socially inadequate, or just out of prison. When the hostels are full, those who can't get in sleep out-of-doors. The soup and sandwiches they get here are probably the only food they've had today."

They watched for a while as the canteen workers served as derelict a crowd of human beings as Harry Fox had ever seen in his life before.

"This is terrible," he said. "I never realized."

"Some of them sleep over the grills in the pavement of the hotel around the corner, warmed by the steam from the boiler room," she said. "The rest wrap themselves in old newspapers and crowd together in the pavilion in the garden over there. At least it's dry."

"All right," Devlin said. "What are you trying to prove? That you care? I know that. What did you want to see me about?"

"I want to come with you," she said, "in the morning. To Marseilles. You could ask Martin to see me. He might listen to you."

"What about this?" Devlin looked around him.

"Oh, I'll get all the footage I need of this business tonight. I'd intended to return to Paris Tuesday, anyway."

Devlin turned to Fox and nodded. "She could be very useful."

Fox said, "All right, Miss Audin. We'll see you at Heathrow in the morning. No later than ten o'clock, if you don't mind. I'll see to your ticket for you. We'll meet at the entrance to the International Lounge."

"Good," she said and kissed Devlin gravely on each cheek. "Thank you, Liam. And now, I must work, I think."

She walked toward the cameras. At the head of the line at the canteen someone was being violently sick.

"Jesus Mary," Devlin said. "The one thing in this life that turns my stomach. Let's get out of it," and they hurried back to the car.

Salter led the way up a flight of narrow wooden stairs covered in cheap linoleum. The landing was long and narrow, and he opened a door at the end and switched on the light. Barry went in after him, humping the two suitcases, then put them down. There was a double bed with a brass frame, a wardrobe, a dressing table in Victorian mahogany, and a marble washstand.

"You'll be nicely out of the way here," Salter said. "The back stairs are very handy. I'm at the front of the house myself. Just you and Jenny back here." He smiled weakly. "I'll see you in the morning. We'll look at the boat first thing, then I'll take you up to the farm to meet the others."

He backed out, closing the door, and Barry took off his jacket and draped it over a chair. He stood frowning at himself in the cracked mirror above the washstand. There was something wrong. It spoke aloud in the girl's silence, in Salter's sly eyes.

"An unreliable sod if ever I've seen one," Barry said to himself and went to the door and turned the key.

He undressed, got into bed with only the lamp switched on, and sat propped against the pillows smoking and considering the job in hand. It was really very simple. Stop the truck, put the Germans and their escort out of action, drive down to Marsh End with the rocket pod, load it onto the boat Salter had arranged, and put to sea for the rendezvous with the Russian trawler later that night. Absurdly simple. So much so that something was bound to go wrong.

He lit another cigarette, and at the same moment watched the door knob turn slowly. He reached for the Ceska and was across the room in an instant, turning the key. He wrenched open the door to see Jenny walking back along the passage. She was barefoot and wore a white cotton nightdress, a shawl about her shoulders.

She turned and stared at him dumbly, her eyes taking in the gun in his hand. Yet she showed no reaction—no reaction at all. He stood to one side, and she crept past him into the room. She lay on the bed without a word, staring up at the ceiling, hands folded across the shawl. Barry locked the door, put the Ceska where he could reach it, and got on the bed beside her.

He was surprised at the strength of his own desire. When he kissed her, he was shaking like a boy, and yet there was no response, not even when his hands roamed freely over her body, pushing the nightgown up above her thighs.

She lay there passively, allowing him to do anything he would with her, still not responding, staring up at the ceiling, eyes wide. By then, he was past caring, needing her in a way he hadn't needed a woman in years.

Afterward, he rolled to one side, exhausted, and reached for a cigarette. She lay there for a moment longer, then stood up without a word, unlocked the door, and went out.

Barry lay there, smoking, looking up at the ceiling. It was crazy. It didn't make sense. It had been a long time since he'd needed anyone like that, a hell of a long time. He closed his eyes and thought of Norah Cassidy.

SIX

The tide was drifting in, gurgling in crab holes, covering the mud flats with an expanse of shining water moving among the sea asters. Somewhere a curlew cried, lonely in a somber world.

Barry and the girl crossed a narrow stone causeway and followed a path through rough marsh grass and head-high reeds. Beyond, they stretched in an unbroken line toward the distant sea on either side of the estuary, swaying, the wind passing through them with an uneasy whispering sound.

Barry said soberly, "You'd swear there were eyes watching you from every thicket."

"Spirits of the dead," she said. "My father used to tell me the Romans were here two thousand years ago. Ravenglass up the coast was a port even then." She stood there for a moment, a strange, archaic figure in the head scarf and old raincoat. She shivered visibly. "I don't like this place. It frightens me. No one comes here, no local people, unless they can't help it."

She intoned the words in that dead voice of hers like the chorus from some Greek play.

Barry said, "Fine. That's exactly how I want it."

She moved on along the causeway, and he followed. A few moments later they emerged beside a narrow creek. There was a decaying wooden jetty stretching out into the water on rotting pilings. To Barry's surprise there were two boats moored there, not one.

The first was real class, with a sharp raking prow and trim lines. It was painted white with a black line along the water mark and was obviously lovingly cared for. The name *Kathleen* was neatly painted across the bow in gold.

"Mr. Salter's own boat," she said. "He brought the other down from a boatyard outside Ravenglass yesterday."

It was a different proposition altogether, a forty-foot motor cruiser painted black, the name *Jason-Fowey* so faded that Barry had difficulty reading it. He climbed over the rail and went into the wheelhouse, and the girl followed.

"It doesn't look much, but it's a good boat at sea."

"You've been out in her?"

She nodded. "Mr. Salter uses her from time to time."

"What for?"

She shrugged. "Fishing, when he's in the mood. He won't go out in the *Kathleen* unless the weather's perfect."

"Spends his spare time polishing the binnacle and so on?"

She looked at him in surprise. "How did you know?"

"Oh, it figures." He lit a cigarette and offered her one. She shook her head, and he said, "The men at the farm, have you seen them yet?"

"I took milk up this morning."

"Old friends of Mr. Salter's?"

"I wouldn't know that. I've never seen them before."

"But you didn't like them?" They were standing close, shoulders touching, and he was filled with that irrational excitement again. She turned almost unwillingly, eyes down, and he gently stroked her face with the back of one hand. She leaned close. Outside, footsteps boomed on the jetty.

Barry went on deck as Salter stepped over the rail. "Ah, there you are, Mr. Sinclair," Salter said. "Will she do?"

"The other looks a better proposition to me," Barry said.

Salter was dismayed and showed it. "My own boat, Mr. Sinclair, a beautiful boat as you can see. You could sail to the Mediterranean in that boat. But the *Jason* here—there's more to her than meets the eye, I can assure you. She may not look much, but if you check the engine room, you'll find a Penta petrol engine. She'll do twenty-two knots. Depth sounder, automatic steering."

"All right," Barry said. "I'll take your word for it."

Salter looked relieved. "Good, and now, if you don't mind, I'll take you to the farm and introduce you to Preston and Varley. As I told you, I have a funeral today, and I really am rather pressed for time."

Hedley Preston awoke and stared up at the ceiling. For a moment, he couldn't think where he was, and then he remembered. His mouth tasted bad, his throat dry, and he got up and reached for the whisky bottle on the locker. It was empty, and he tossed it into a corner. He pulled on a pair of jeans and sweater. He was a lean, sardonic-looking man with tangled dark hair and a face that was just beginning to show the first signs of dissipation.

He lit a cigarette, coughing as the smoke caught at the back of his throat, and peered out of the window at the sodden hillside. "Jesus," he said, "the joys of the countryside." And he opened the door.

Jenny Crowther, her mouth open in fear, stumbled into him. Sam Varley was just behind her. Varley was an ox of a man, in soiled sweatshirt and corduroy trousers, and the eyes were wild in the fleshy face. Preston held the girl in the crook of his arm and fended Varley off.

"Okay, what's the problem?"

"I had a two-hundred pack of fags in my

room last night. Now they're gone. That bitch must have taken them."

His breath was sour, and not only with the stench of last night's drinking, for there was a sharp, fresh edge to it that indicated he had already been at the bottle.

"You lost the whole pack to me at poker last night," Preston said patiently. "Too bloody drunk to remember, that's your trouble."

"To hell with that," Varley said. "You're just trying to protect her."

The girl pulled herself free from Preston's encircling arm and ran. Varley shoved him to one side and went after her. She got the door open, was already on her way out when his hand fastened on her shoulder. And then he seemed to stumble, went down hard on the cobbles of the yard.

As he tried to get up, his feet were kicked from under him expertly. Flat on his back, a foot across his throat, he struggled, glaring up into Frank Barry's implacable face. Barry increased the pressure until Varley started to choke. Then the pressure was relieved. Barry took the Ceska from his pocket and touched the muzzle to Varley's forehead.

The girl cried out, a hand to her mouth, and Henry Salter said desperately, "For God's sake, Mr. Sinclair."

Barry said softly, "Touch her again, I'll put you on sticks."

And Varley knew fear then, the kind of fear

that almost turned his bowels to water, as well as rage. Barry removed his foot and stepped back. As the big man got up, Preston, lounging in the doorway, laughed.

"A touching scene." He came forward as Barry picked up his briefcase. "I'm Hedley Preston, Mr. Sinclair. This throwback to a more primitive age is Sam Varley. You must forgive him, but he's only just learned how to walk erect."

"I'll close that mouth of yours for good one of these days," Varley said and went into the house.

Preston stood to one side with a slight, mocking grin, and Barry walked past, followed by the girl and Salter. When they went into the sitting room, Varley was in a chair by the fire, clutching a bottle.

Barry put the briefcase on the table and said to the girl, "You cut along to the kitchen and make us a nice cup of tea or something." She hesitated, and he nodded reassuringly. "Go on, it'll be all right."

She went out. Salter closed the door and leaned against it. Barry nodded to Varley and said to Preston, "He starts early."

"Just his little weakness. Like they say in show business, Mr. Sinclair, he'll be all right on the night."

"Is that a fact?" Barry put the Ceska on the table beside the briefcase and unbuttoned his coat.

"So what's the job?" Preston asked.

"Simple enough. We stop a truck on a country road twenty miles from here on Wednesday morning, off-load what it contains, and bring it back here."

"And what does it contain?" Preston asked.

"That's none of your business." Barry opened the case. "This is." He tossed several packets of twenty-pound notes across. "Five thousand quid each there. You get the other half on completion."

Varley got up and moved to the table, reaching. Preston slapped his hand away. "And that's all you're telling us?"

"It's a simple job," Barry said. "Very simple. You get told what to do on Wednesday morning. Three hours work at the most and you'll be on your way. Of course, if you're not interested. . . ."

Preston said, "Oh, but we are." He quickly pushed the packets together into a neat pile. "Anything you say, Mr. Sinclair. Like the guy out of the brass lamp said, to hear is to obey."

"See that you do." Barry snapped the briefcase shut and turned to Salter. "I'll go back with you now. I want that Land Rover of yours. Somewhere I have to go this afternoon."

Preston said, "You'll be back?"

"Oh, yes," Barry told him. "You can count on it."

He and Salter went out into the passageway

as Jenny appeared from the kitchen with a tray. "You're going?" she said.

"I'll be back this evening." Barry smiled. "Don't worry. Just get on with the cleaning up. The apeman won't touch you again. The clever bugger will see to that."

He winked in a conspiratorial fashion, went out, got into Salter's limousine, and they drove away.

Watching through the sitting room window, Varley said viciously, "When I've finished with that little bastard. . . ."

"Don't be stupid, Samuel," Preston said. "Unless I'm very much mistaken, he could take you apart any time he wanted." He tapped the packets of money in front of him. "Ten grand here, Samuel, another ten to come, which means whatever is in that truck he mentioned must be very interesting indeed."

Varley smiled slowly. "Here, are you meaning what I think you are?"

"I used to study Latin at school, Samuel. *Festine lente*. Hasten slowly. That way you get it all in the end."

"Including him?"

"I don't see why not."

Varley laughed delightedly and reached for the bottle. "I'll drink to that."

Barry and Salter stood beside the Land Rover in the barn. Salter said, "I didn't try to dress them up. You must admit that. I was told hard

men were required, men who would do anything, and they certainly fit the bill."

"What's Preston's background?"

"Middle-class respectable. His father was an
accountant in Bradford, and Preston went to
grammar school there, so he's decently educated. I understand he was training to be an
accountant himself and went to prison for some
fraud or other. Since then, he's never looked
back. Was released from prison six months ago
after serving three years of a five-year sentence for armed robbery of a supermarket.
Varley, of course, is just an animal."

"A drunken animal," Barry corrected. "Still,
never mind. At least I know what I'm dealing
with. I'll see you later."

He drove the Land Rover out of the barn
and across the yard. Salter turned to the hearse,
which had a coffin inside now. He took out a
handkerchief and very carefully inspected the
whole vehicle, occasionally pausing to give the
chrome a quick polish.

The Air France jet touched down exactly on
time at Marignane Airport, fifteen miles outside Marseilles. As it was only a quarter full,
the passengers passed through customs and,
where necessary, immigration, with no delay.
Within forty-five minutes of landing, Devlin
and Anne-Marie were driving toward the coast
road in a rented Peugeot.

Devlin said, "We'll find a hotel in St. Denis

for tonight. That's where the prison supply boat leaves from." She nodded, not saying anything, concentrating on her driving and Devlin added, "You realize you can't come with me tomorrow? I mean, I'll have to see how the land lies."

"I know that, Liam." She glanced sideways and smiled. "Just as I know that he may still not wish to see me. I learned a long time ago to expect nothing from Martin."

"You really mean that?"

"Once, in Vietnam, when it looked as if we both would very probably die, we spoke of a rendezvous in Paris. A sidewalk cafe in the rain, the smell of damp chestnut trees."

"Absolutely essential," Devlin said.

She smiled without looking at him. "Dear Liam, why could it not have been you I loved? I was to wear a Paris gown, very chic."

"Just like the plugs on television. Dreams for the masses."

"Only ours came true, Liam. He took a rest from Ulster, met me in Paris. We found our sidewalk cafe, the chestnut trees behaved perfectly. Two weeks and then he went back." She shrugged. "You see, he had a mistress waiting for him, darker than me and infinitely more demanding."

They drove on in silence, for there was really nothing left to say.

*   *   *

The bar at the village pub at Brisingham was a large, comfortable room with a low-beamed ceiling, several high-backed benches, and a couple of wooden tables. There was a fire on the open hearth.

Barry was the only customer, and he stood at the end of the bar devouring the last of the beef sandwiches the landlady, a large matronly blonde, had provided for him.

"Great," Barry said, "couldn't be better." He reached for his beer. "Where's all the customers then?"

"Don't get many tourists through in the winter. Mainly evening trade. Locals."

"But I thought there was an RAF airfield here. This is Brisingham, isn't it?"

"Closed down years ago. They have a dozen men up there at the most. Oh, planes still land, but not very often." She sighed. "I remember a time twelve years or so ago when you couldn't get near the bar on a night what with the boys in RAF blue."

"That's life," Barry said. "Everything changes. Thanks for the sandwiches."

Ten minutes later, he slowed the Land Rover as he came to the perimeter fence of the airfield. He coasted along past the main gate, which was padlocked, and then picked up speed and drove on. Five miles further on, a signpost indicated Wastwater to the right, a narrow country road climbing up into the mountains.

He found what he was looking for without

too much trouble. A small wood, a plateau of grass beside the road. When he stopped the engine, there wasn't a sound except for a curlew calling. He could have been the only man left alive on the face of the earth.

He got out of the Land Rover and stood there looking around him, smiling. "Frank, me old son," he said softly. "I think this will do very nicely indeed."

The granite from Belle Isle was famous throughout France, was still so much in demand that the authorities had constructed a new deepwater jetty so that larger container ships could be used. The quarry itself was hewn out of the northern cliffs, and they were blasting as Lebel approached, the red flag fluttering in the wind.

The explosion, when it came, echoed from the cliffs like thunder as a great shoulder of rock cracked in a thousand pieces and cascaded down. A whistle blew, and convicts and their armed guards emerged from the shelter and went back to work.

Brosnan and Savary toiled together, Savary loading into a skip standing on the crude rail track beside them, Brosnan splitting larger pieces with a sledgehammer and wedge. He was stripped to the waist, his hair held back by a sweatband. The muscles in his back rippled as the hammer came down, and his prison number was clear to see, tattooed on his right forearm.

As Lebel approached, Savary paused, leaning on the skip, wiping his face with a rag. "Hey, Pierre, I'm getting old. What about a job in the kitchen or even the library. I'm not fussy."

"Nonsense," Lebel said. "Look what magnificent shape you're in for a man of your age, all thanks to regular exercise and hard work." He turned to Brosnan and took a paper and pen from his pocket. "You've got a visitor due on the morning boat, my friend. Are you willing to receive him?"

Brosnan paused, leaning on the sledgehammer. "Who is it?"

Lebel looked at the paper. "Monsieur Charles Gorman. Solicitor, Lincoln's Inn Fields, London." He looked puzzled. "Solicitor?"

"What the English call their lawyers, Pierre," Savary advised him.

"Reason for visit, legal business." Lebel repeated the question. "Will you receive him?"

"Why not?" Brosnan said.

Lebel held out the paper and pen. "Then sign in the appropriate section." Brosnan complied and handed them back. "Okay," Lebel said. "Back to work," and he folded the document and stuck it in his pocket. "I may have a treat for you tonight. Another body. They're expecting some old guy up in the infirmary to die any minute."

"So kind of you to think of us." Savary picked up another rock as Lebel walked away. "Interesting, Martin. You didn't tell me your lawyer was coming to see you."

"What's even more interesting is that he isn't my lawyer," Brosnan said. "I've never heard of Charles Gorman in my life."

He brought the hammer down with all his strength and split the rock that was his target in half.

It was dark when Barry turned the Land Rover into the farmyard and braked to a halt. As he switched off the engine, a woman screamed. Barry jumped to the ground. The front door was flung open, light flooding into the yard. Jenny Crowther almost made it, and then Varley had her.

Her dress was torn, one shoulder bare, and Varley laughed drunkenly and tried to kiss her. She tried to pull away, disgust and loathing on her face as her hands clawed at him. Barry moved in fast and punched Varley in the kidneys, then grabbed him by the collar and pulled him back.

Varley cried out in pain and went down on one knee. He stayed there for a moment, shaking his head, then looked up at Barry. He got up slowly, shook his head again as if to clear it, then charged, hands reaching out to destroy.

Barry moved to one side, grabbing for the right wrist, twisting it around and up in an armlock, and, using Varley's own momentum, ran him into the wall. Varley, on his knees for the second time that night, tried to stand, and Barry kicked him in the stomach.

Varley lay on his back, groaning, and Hedley Preston standing in the doorway laughed drunkenly. "I told you he could take you apart any time he wanted, Sam. You should have listened. I'm always right, never wrong." He raised his glass. "To you, Mr. Sinclair, and all who sail with you."

Barry said, "You could have stopped this, you bastard. I told you to keep him in line." His right hand swung up, the Ceska coughed once, and Preston dropped his glass and cried out, clutching his neck.

He leaned against the doorpost, blood oozing between his fingers. Barry tapped him gently between the eyes with the muzzle.

"Don't worry, Preston. Just a scratch, that's how good I am with one of these things. Next time, old son, you're dead."

He turned, took the girl by the arm, and pushed her toward the Land Rover. "I'll take you down to Salter's place. In fact, I'll stay there again tonight myself." She was trembling and clutched his arm, and once again, he was aware of that strange surging excitement. "It's all right," he said as they drove out of the farmyard, and he reached across and took her hand. "It's all right."

Later that night, standing at the window of his bedroom, smoking and looking down into the yard, he saw her come out of the kitchen with the light and cross to the barn. Barry opened the door and went downstairs quickly.

When he went into the barn, she was filling a basket with wood. "Here, let me do that," he said.

"That's all right, I can manage," she replied in a low voice without turning around.

He lit a cigarette, aware of a sudden unbearable tightness in his chest that threatened to choke him. She had changed out of the torn cotton dress, and the black one she now wore, like the other, was too small and stretched tightly across her buttocks and thighs.

She stood up and Barry dropped his cigarette and moved close, his arms sliding about her, pulling her against him. He held her for a moment, his lips against her neck, and then pushed her gently forward and down into the hay.

And then she truly did come to life, her hands tightening in his hair, her mouth fastening on his with great, bruising kisses that were almost frightening in their intensity.

SEVEN

It was Lebel's duty, as the officer on Brosnan's tier, to take him down to the visitors' room on Tuesday morning. When he opened the door and ushered Brosnan in, Devlin was standing with his back to them, peering out of the window. Brosnan had received no greater shock in his life than he did when the small man turned to face him.

"Ah, Mr. Brosnan. My name is Charles Gorman. My firm has been retained by the Brosnan Corporation in Boston to discuss certain legal matters affecting your future. There is also the matter of an appeal for clemency on your behalf to the President of France. Your mother feels. . . ."

"My mother," Brosnan said, "is wasting her time, Mr. Gorman. The only way she'll ever get me off this rock is in a box."

"Monsieur Gorman, please," Lebel said, "you and your client must sit on either side of the table, but you will be alone. As his legal adviser, you are entitled to this. I will lock the door. When you are ready to leave, please ring the bell."

"Can we smoke?" Devlin asked.

"But of course, Monsieur."

Lebel went out, the key turned in the lock. Brosnan reached across the table, and Devlin took his hand and held it for a long moment.

"Cead mile failte," he said in Irish. "A hundred thousand welcomes."

Devlin smiled. *"Go raibh maith agat,"* he replied. "My thanks. Let's stick to the Irish, just to confuse the buggers if they happen to be listening in." He sat down, lit a cigarette, and pushed the pack across. "Good to see you, Marteen."

It was the affectionate diminutive of the name that normally would be used with a child. In the old days, Brosnan had not cared to be called Little Martin by a man considerably smaller than himself. And then, of course, he had come to know Devlin rather better.

"You look well, Martin, considering."

"Never fitter. I work in the quarry most days. You look good yourself. Still at Trinity?"

"They keep me out of kindness. I was invited as visiting professor at Yale this year."

"God help them."

"Came to nothing. The State Department refused me a visa."

Devlin glanced about him, his face somber. "Was this what it was all about—truly?"

Brosnan said, "They closed down Devil's Island, but they still had this in reserve. Tell me, Liam, how you've been? Did you ever find those Plains of Mayo you were always looking for? Remember Blind Raftery's poem?"

Devlin said, "Once, a thousand years ago. November, nineteen forty-three to be precise, at what you might call the hour of maximum danger."

"The Churchill affair?"

"A lovely ugly little peasant," Devlin quoted, "who turned my heart not once, but twice. She was seventeen and I was thirty-five."

"And too old?"

"Not for that one. But there was a problem. I was the enemy."

"So, what you're trying to say is that you found your Plains of Mayo thirty-six years ago?"

Devlin smiled with infinite sadness. "And lost them again in the finding. Now wouldn't that make you laugh all the way to hell and back?"

"Not really. What's all this about?"

"It's simple enough. How would you like to get out of here?"

Brosnan didn't take it seriously for a moment. "Well, a little divine intervention would be divine because that's what it would take. Even my mother, formidable lady as she is, discovered a long time ago that neither lighting a candle, saying her prayers, nor offering large sums of money would do any good."

"Has she been to see you?"

"Once, four years ago. I saw her then only to make it clear I wouldn't see her again."

"And Anne-Marie?"

Brosnan paused and went very still. "What about Anne-Marie?"

"I left her in St. Denis this morning. She begs you to see her."

"No," Brosnan said in a low voice. "I will not do it."

He jumped to his feet and went to the window, reaching for the bars, his cheek to the stone. After a while, he turned.

The rusting barred window had no glass in it, and wind whistled through. Devlin shivered. "God save us, *avic,* but I hate to see you in this place."

Brosnan came back to the table, helped himself to another cigarette and sat down. "All right, Liam, what are you after?"

Devlin grinned crookedly. "Just consider me that divine intervention you were looking for, shut your mouth, and listen."

When he was finished, Brosnan sat back in his chair, brooding, the gray eyes giving nothing away.

"Well?" Devlin said.

"I don't know," Brosnan told him. "I used to be big on slogans like Ireland must be free. It came naturally from a love of literature, a joy in words, but then you discover that the reality is that you must be prepared to walk over corpses to achieve your end."

"And it isn't worth it?"

"I'm beginning to wonder whether any cause is worth the loss of a single human life."

"I know, Marteen, your revolutionary ardor has cooled a little. So has mine, and I was at it longer than you."

Brosnan got up and went to the window and held the bars again, looking out. "Suddenly, I feel old, Liam. Really old, you know what I mean? I can't get worked up about things anymore. Not even Frank Barry and the KGB and Ferguson and D15 and the stupid senseless bloody games they're all involved in."

"Not even to get out of here?"

"There's no way Ferguson can get me out of this place," Brosnan said flatly.

"Ferguson thinks he can."

Brosnan didn't reply, so Devlin came to the one issue he had been avoiding, no help for it now. "Martin, you heard what happened to Norah?"

Brosnan nodded without turning around. "I heard. She died about eighteen months ago."

Devlin cleared his throat. "But the way that she died, that's the thing."

Brosnan turned, his face blank, the eyes very dark. "You've something to tell me?"

Devlin said, "It's difficult to know where to begin, Marteen."

Brosnan was across the room in three quick strides, had him back across the table, his hands on his throat. "Tell me!" he said in a low hoarse voice. "Tell me!"

* * *

Afterward, he sat at the table, his head in his hands for a long time without saying anything. Then suddenly he stood up, went and rang the bell.

He turned to Devlin. "I need to think. I'll speak to you again later." Before Devlin could reply, the key turned in the lock, and Lebel appeared. "Mr. Gorman has papers for me to sign. I'd like some time to think about it. Can I go back to my cell for an hour?"

Lebel turned to Devlin. "You have no objection, Monsieur?"

"None at all."

"Then please wait here. I shall return and take you to the officers' canteen. A little refreshment might be in order while you wait."

Savary had just been returned to the cell for the noon break. He was lying on his bed smoking a cigarette, when the door was unlocked and Lebel ushered Brosnan in.

"An hour, then," the prison officer said and departed.

"How did you get on?" Savary started to say, and Brosnan waved him to silence, listening at the door.

"So, a mystery?" the old man said as Brosnan came and sat on the other bed facing him. "Oh, I get it," he added shrewdly. "This Gorman—someone you knew after all?"

"Just shut up and listen," Brosnan said. "I haven't got much time."

When he was finished, Savary sat there, clenching and unclenching his hands in excitement. "For God's sake, seize this chance with both hands, Martin. Go!"

Brosnan reached across and put a hand on his shoulder to still him. "No, Jacques, listen to me—just a little while longer. In the first place, I don't believe Ferguson can swing this thing with the French authorities. I'm not some little thief—some cat burglar or confidence man. I killed a policeman, and you know how they look at that sort of thing at the Palais de Justice. In the second place, even if Ferguson could arrange it, it would take time—too much time to suit me."

"So what's your alternative?"

"I'm crashing out," Brosnan said simply.

"But Martin, this is impossible. No one has ever escaped from this damn rock."

"I've always known I could get outside the walls via the sewer. I told you that," Brosnan explained. "But that gets you nowhere because you're still on the island. And then, while we were on the burial detail with Lebel the other night, I saw it. We break into the storage hut, steal a couple of life jackets each, and enter the water from the burial rock."

Savary gazed at him in awe. "We? You said we?"

"Sure, the both of us, Jacques. Stay on this

rock, you'll end up in the sea in a canvas bag sooner or later, so why not take a chance on the sea while you can still fight?"

"But the Mill Race," Savary said. "It would be the death of us."

"Or the saving of us, don't you see?" Brosnan said. "That current runs up to ten knots, curving toward St. Denis. Now, if a boat was waiting in the appropriate area . . ."

Savary broke in, shaking his head. "No fishing boat is allowed within a four-mile radius of the island. You know that."

"The current would take us that far in half an hour."

"But such a boat would never find us. Be reasonable, Martin. That sea out there and at night."

"I've thought of that," Brosnan said. "All we need is one of those electronic homing beacons. They're standard issue in all air forces now. Pilots have them stitched to their life jackets so when they ditch at sea the rescue craft can home in on them."

"And if they missed us?" Savary whispered. "Or if your heart gave out, or you couldn't stand the cold?"

"All right, all right." Savary waved a hand. "You've infected me with your own madness. When do we go?"

"I don't see any reason to hang about. We can get everything we need right here except that homing device. They're only the size of a cigarette pack. Devlin will have to get hold of one and smuggle it in to me. I don't see any problem there."

"And the boat?"

"I was thinking that was where that son of yours could come in."

"Jean-Paul?"

"If the *Union Corse* can't organize a fast run by night in a trawler out of St. Denis, they must be slipping."

"But of course." Savary was laughing now, excitement boiling over. "Jesus, Martin, but I feel alive again like I haven't done in years."

He embraced Brosnan enthusiastically, kissing him on both cheeks. Brosnan turned and hammered on the cell door. "Come on, Pierre!" he called. "Let's be having you."

Anne-Marie, sitting on the balcony of the hotel in St. Denis, had seen the prison supply boat enter the harbor so she was not surprised when Devlin appeared on the adjoining balcony twenty minutes later. He clambered over and sank into the wicker chair opposite her.

"You saw him?" she asked eagerly.

"Oh, yes, I saw him."

"And he was well?"

"Never fitter. In fact, fighting fit."

Her face clouded. "What happened?"

"It's simple, really. At first, when I outlined the deal, he wasn't particularly interested, and in any case he didn't believe that Ferguson could get him out. And to be frank with you there, I'm inclined to agree with him."

"So?"

"I told him about Norah." He shook his head. "He took it hard. If Frank Barry had been within touching distance, Martin would have broken him in his two hands."

Anne-Marie got up and poured him a whisky. She came back to the table. "And that changed his point of view?"

"You could say that." Devlin swallowed a little whisky. "God, I needed that. Now, he intends to break out within the next two or three days in company with his cell mate, a man called Savary."

"But how can this be done?" she asked.

So Devlin told her. When he was finished, he poured himself another whisky. "As harebrained a scheme as I'd ever heard of."

To his astonishment, Anne-Marie got up and stood at the rail, looking out to sea to where Belle Isle crouched behind the horizon. "Oh, I don't know. I can see the logic of it. It's so beautifully simple. He could be right. It could work."

"It could just as easily go the other way." Devlin moved to the rail beside her. "I was talking to the captain of the supply boat coming over. He tells me that some nights that thing they call the Mill Race out there is like a river in flood."

"So, what did you tell Martin? That you would help?"

"I didn't have much choice. He said if I didn't have something working by Thursday night, he'd take to the water anyway and take a chance on floating the ten miles to St. Denis."

"Not possible." She shook her head. "The cold would have killed them by then. Tell me, this Savary you mentioned? Would that be Jacques Savary, the gangster?"

"That's right, and apparently he has a son, Jean-Paul, who's following enthusiastically in his father's footsteps. I'm supposed to contact him as soon as possible at a nightclub called House of Gold."

"Oh, yes," she said. "The most notorious establishment in Marseilles. It will be interesting to see how you get on there. With your accent, my dear Liam, I think you may well need the services of an interpreter."

He frowned and put a hand on her arm as she turned away. "Are you sure about this? If it goes wrong, if your involvement became public, you could end up in prison yourself."

"Liam, dear Liam." She kissed him gently. "Such a clever, devious human being and such a child. Is there any possible way you could keep me out?"

It was raining again as Frank Barry and Jenny Crowther walked along the track through the reeds at Marsh End. The two boats swung on their lines beside the jetty. It was the *Kathleen*, Salter's own craft, that Barry boarded now, lugging the case he carried over the rail.

He went into the gleaming wheelhouse and examined the interior carefully, going down on his hands and knees until he found what he wanted. Under the instrument panel there was a large inspection flap, which gave access to the electric system. When he pulled the release catch, it swung down on hinges.

Barry said to Jenny, "Keep a weather eye out for Salter, there's a good girl, just in case he decides to show up."

He took from his pocket several items he had purchased that morning at the local general store—a screwdriver, screws, a bradawl, and a small hacksaw. There were also a number of brackets of the type used to secure tools at some convenient spot on a wall.

He neatly and methodically bored the necessary holes in the flap and screwed the brackets into place. Then he opened the case, took out one of the Sterling submachine guns, loaded it, then slipped it into place, held by the brackets. Then he carefully loaded one of the Smith and Wessons and positioned it underneath the Sterling. He pushed the flap up, the catch clicked into place.

Jenny, standing outside in the rain watching the shore, had been keeping one eye on him also. "What's all that for then?" she asked, and her voice was totally different, like that of a new person.

"What I call an ace in the hole."

He took out the other Sterling and quickly removed the end of the firing pin with the hacksaw. Not too much, just enough, and he fired it up into the air to make sure, a round up the spout. Then he did the same with the other Smith and Wesson.

He put them back in the case with the gas canisters and turned to Jenny who was staring at him curiously. "Now they won't shoot."

"That's it, darling." Barry moved out in the rain and slipped an arm around her waist. "I'm very ordered, you see, Jenny. I always like to know exactly where I am."

She held on to him tightly, her face glowing, and he kissed her. "I love the rain. It makes me come alive in a way nothing else does. A fine day, thanks be to God." He smiled down at her. "And with the rest of it stretching before us, I suggest you take me into the thriving metropolis you call Ravenglass and show me the sights."

Twenty minutes later and five miles out of Marsh End on the way into Ravenglass he pulled onto the side of the road and braked suddenly.

"What's wrong?" she said.

"That place over there? What is it?"

There was a watch tower, several decaying

hangars, and an overgrown runway crossed by another. The fence around the place was rusting.

"Tanningley Field," she said. "The RAF built it in the war. Someone tried to run a flying club there a few years ago, but it didn't work. It hasn't been used for years."

"Is that so?" Barry said. "Now that is really very interesting."

He started the engine and drove away.

The Maison d'Or was in the old quarter of Marseilles and could be approached only on foot, along a narrow cobbled street, lined with houses four or five stories high, with small iron balconies and shuttered windows. In spite of the new and stricter laws the police were supposed to invoke, prostitutes sat outside most of the doors, dressed in a myriad different ways to attract clients, most of them holding cheerful conversations with each other across the narrow alley.

As Devlin passed, Anne-Marie on his arm, they were the target for a number of humorous remarks, mainly vulgar. He was astonished at the cheerful ease with which Anne-Marie handled the situation and at the fluency of her own gutter language when she replied.

He said, "One thing's for sure, the oldest profession is anything but oppressed. How does that sit with your women's struggle?"

"That women have a choice, a free choice, is

all I ask," she said. "What they do with that choice is their own affair."

The door of the Maison d'Or was locked, and Anne-Marie rang the bell. A panel slid back instantly, and a pair of hard blue eyes inspected them.

"We're looking for a little fun," she said.

"Aren't we all, sweetheart. Are you members?"

"No, from out of town, but I promised my friend here a good time." She made an obscene gesture with the fingers of one hand.

The door opened to admit them. The doorman looked as if he'd been a useful middleweight prizefighter in his day, his eyes swollen with scar tissue. He looked Anne-Marie over approvingly and whistled.

"You look such a nice girl, too."

The foyer was decorated in scarlet and gold. The two girls behind the cloakroom counter wore elegant black dresses, and one of them came forward to take their coats.

"I told you the Maison d'Or was special," Anne-Marie said.

In the ornate mirror, Devlin was aware of a young man who had appeared from a small doorway almost hidden beside the gold-draped entrance to the club itself. He was enormously attractive, with dark hair that curled slightly and black eyes that moved over everything with a kind of amused contempt. The badly broken nose for some reason fitted perfectly with the elegant Yves St. Laurent suit in dark-blue flannel. He watched them for a moment, a Gauloise dropping from the corner of his mouth, then came forward.

"Monsieur," he said to Devlin. "You will permit me?"

Devlin raised his arms, smiling slowly, and the young man ran hands over him expertly.

"What is this?" Anne-Marie demanded indignantly.

"Hush, girl," Devlin told her. "No problem. I'm clean."

"No offense, Monsieur," the young man said at last, satisfied.

"None taken," Devlin said cheerfully. "It takes one to know one. We'd like to see Monsieur Savary."

"That isn't possible," the young man said. "Monsieur Savary isn't here. I could take a message."

"I don't think so," Devlin told him. "He'd prefer to receive it himself. It's from his father."

The doorman said, "Heh, what the hell is this?"

The young man waved him down, the slight smile still fixed firmly in place, but the eyes had stopped smiling. "A large claim, Monsieur."

"Yes, well, when Savary comes in, maybe you could mention it to him. We're in no hurry."

Devlin took Anne-Marie by the elbow and headed for the draped entrance to the club. The young man snapped his fingers and a headwaiter materialized from nowhere to lead them to a table.

"Champagne," Anne-Marie said. "Irish whisky for the gentleman."

"You wouldn't happen to have a bottle of Bushmills available?" Devlin said.

"But of course, Monsieur," the headwaiter replied. "We pride ourselves at Maison d'Or on our ability to provide all our customers' requirements."

"And I expect that covers a wide field," Devlin said and looked around him.

It was typical of such establishments the world over. A trio playing intimate music, a small dance floor, tables crowded together, and a gaming room through an archway. In this case, the only surprise was the decor, for everything, wall coverings, curtains, carpets, and furniture, was in excellent taste.

The headwaiter returned with their drinks himself. "Something to eat, perhaps?"

It was Anne-Marie who answered him. "Later. For the moment, we wait for Monsieur Savary."

The headwaiter shrugged and walked away. Devlin said, "Do you get just the slightest impression we're not wanted?"

He toasted her, she sipped her champagne. It was too early for the club to be busy, that curious half-way point in the life of such establishments, a kind of lull before the real action of the night takes place.

The doorman was leaning against the bar, a

glass in his hand, watching them closely. He emptied his glass and moved toward them.

"Get ready," Devlin muttered. "Unless I miss my guess, this is battle station alert."

The doorman said, "Look, Monsieur Savary isn't coming in tonight, so I'd drink up and move on if I were you. Of course the *poule* can stay." His hand dropped to Anne-Marie's shoulder, the broad fingers sliding inside the open neck of her shirt.

She didn't even flinch. "Could I have some more champagne?" she asked Devlin.

"Of course." He reached for the bottle. "And by the way," he said to the doorman, "you'd oblige me by not doing that. I mean, she doesn't know where you've been, does she?"

Very slowly, the doorman released his grip. "You little jerk," he said. "You know what I'm going to do with you?"

"No," Devlin said. "Do tell me."

He was in the act of pouring Anne-Marie's champagne and, in an almost casual gesture, he reversed his grip and smashed the bottle across the side of the doorman's head. The man cried out, going down on one knee, clenching at the tablecloth, glasses bouncing to the floor.

There was immediate consternation, diners crying out in alarm. The band stopped playing, and several hard-looking specimens in dinner jackets moved in fast. There was a sudden shouted command as the young man with the broken nose appeared, waving his arms.

Everyone backed off. The doorman stood up, shaking his head like a bull, holding a napkin to the blood mingling with the champagne. "You were right, boss," he said. "Not what he seems, this one."

The young man inspected the damage. "Not too bad, Claude, you've known worse. Go and get yourself patched up."

Already half a dozen waiters were tidying things up. The young man turned. "Very good, Monsieur . . . ?"

"Devlin."

"I like your style."

"And I yours," Devlin said. "You are Jean-Paul Savary?"

"Guilty." Savary gave them a mock bow.

"Then why the performance?"

"Because I recognized Mademoiselle Audin here." He took her hand and kissed it gallantly. "You have no greater admirer of your work. Anyway, it gave me pause for thought. I don't like to jump straight in, I like to think." He sat down and snapped his fingers for the head-waiter. "Now, a message from my father, you say? How can this be?"

"He shares a cell at Belle Isle with a friend of mine."

"Prisoner 38930—Martin Brosnan," Savary said.

"That's right." Devlin frowned. "You even know his number?"

"There is nothing affecting my father and Belle Isle that I do not know, and on the rock a man's number stays with him till death. They make certain by tattooing it on the right forearm."

Anne-Marie said, "He's been there a long time, your father, I'm surprised the *Union Corse* hasn't managed to do something about it."

"If it had been any other crime than the one he is in for." He shook his head. "He tried to knock off de Gaulle. Not only that, he came damn close. They'll never forgive him." There was a sudden savagery in his voice.

Anne-Marie continued. "And you've never tried to break him out?"

"Of Belle Isle?" he laughed incredulously. "No one has ever escaped from that damned rock. No one."

Devlin said carefully, "Well, Thursday night, Martin Brosnan and your father are going to attempt to break the record, with your help or without it. That's the message I bring from your father."

Jean-Paul Savary sat there, hands flat on the table, staring at Devlin. He turned slowly to Anne-Marie. "This is true?"

"Absolutely."

He took a deep breath and stood up. "Then I suggest we adjourn to my private suite upstairs and discuss the matter."

*   *   *

It was very warm in the comfortable sitting room. Anne-Marie opened the windows to the balcony and went outside to look at the harbor below. After a while, she went back in.

Devlin and Jean-Paul had their jackets off and leaned over the table which was covered by a large-scale chart of the Belle Isle area.

"Could it work?" Devlin asked.

"In theory. The homing system Brosnan mentioned is no problem. I have heavy connections with the smuggling business in this area. We often recover stuff dropped over the rail of a passing ship at sea using just such a device. And the boat is no problem. We took over a fishing company on the docks last year. We own six trawlers. I can have one at St. Denis tomorrow."

"In other words, there's no technical reason why it shouldn't work."

"True, but it's still a hell of a thing to step off the rock in that sea and take a chance that I would put at no better than fifty-fifty."

"You seem cheerful enough about it."

"He's been in a stone tomb for fourteen years, Mr. Devlin. This is the only chance he'll ever get to beat the game. Who am I to refuse him that? But there are other things to consider. Many important points which do not seem to have occurred to you."

There was a knock at the door and Big

Claude, the doorman, looked in. "Doctor Cresson is here."

"Good, show him in."

Anne-Marie said, "What do we need a doctor for?"

Jean-Paul lit a Gauloise and smiled. "You'll see, *cherie*. You'll see."

André Cresson was a large, fat man with dark, sad eyes and a double chin. His tan gabardine suit looked as if it hadn't been pressed in months, and he smoked incessantly, lighting one cigarette from the stub of another, his black shirt smothered with ash.

He said, "You say they intend to come out through the sewers?"

"That's right," Devlin told him.

Cresson made a face. "Not good. Sewers are a bad scene at the best of times, but in a place like Belle Isle . . ." He shrugged. "Probably the original tunnels from the eighteenth century. The effluent of years."

"What are you saying?" Jean-Paul demanded.

"Well, there are often pockets of CO_2 and methane. The first will suffocate. The second will not only suffocate, but will explode from a spark if conditions are right. But that's just a chance they have to take."

"The point is, no candles or matches?" Devlin said.

"Exactly. You will be seeing this man Brosnan again before the attempt, Monsieur?"

"That's right. I saw the assistant governor and made it clear there were further matters of business to iron out before I could finalize them with my client. There was no problem. I see Brosnan Thursday morning."

"Then I suggest a small pocket flashlight might be in order. A thing perhaps difficult to come by in prison. You see, the main danger would occur if they were to fall in the effluent. Nausea, vomiting and a rapid death within a few hours can occur due to a gutful of human pathogenes. There is also the possibility of viral hepatitis."

There was a profound silence. It was Anne-Marie who said, "And what can be done about all this, Doctor?"

"Oh, immediate drug therapy the moment they are retrieved." He smiled sadly. "If, indeed, they are retrieved. The waters of the Mill Race, my friends, even on a calm night, will reduce body temperature rapidly. This would particularly affect my old friend Jacques who is not, to be frank, as young as he was."

Jean-Paul said, "All right, then you come with us on the trawler to administer whatever drugs are necessary the moment we have them over the side. Naturally, I'll see that you're well taken care of for this service."

Cresson shook his head. "No, Jean-Paul, your father and I go back more years than I care to remember. He was always my good friend. This one, I do for him."

Jean-Paul smiled. "Then, in his name, I gratefully accept."

Devlin said, "Let's assume it works like a charm, and they make it. What happens next?"

"As I told you," Anne-Marie said. "I have a small farm in the hills above Nice. I use it when I want to get away from things. It's very remote and up high. You can see anyone approaching for miles. They can go there during the recovery period."

"What about your staff?" he asked.

"No problem. I only keep sheep there, a Spanish mountain variety. One shepherd, Old Louis, and he's away up in the hills most of the time."

"Sounds good to me."

Jean-Paul said, "I appreciate the offer, but I'll take care of my father."

"They'll need to lie low for some time," Devlin pointed out. "This thing will cause one hell of a stink. We'll have every cop in France looking for them and Interpol on the alert."

"True," Jean-Paul said. "But let's look at it another way. What if the sea claimed them? What if they died from exposure, and the Mill Race carried them in to the rocks outside of St. Denis?"

There was a long silence. Anne-Marie said in a low voice, "If you're implying what I think you are, there is the obvious problem that the bodies would not be Jacques Savary and Martin Brosnan."

"And wouldn't stand up to any kind of forensic examination," Devlin added.

"Battered beyond recognition, wearing prison uniforms, stenciled with their own numbers, floating in on stolen prison life jackets?" Jean-Paul shook his head. "I would think it unlikely that they would take the examination any further than that." He eased his back, staring down at the chart thoughtfully. "I make a considerable amount of money from the operation of gambling casinos. We always win because the odds favor the house. I'll make you a prophecy on this one—a gambler's hunch. I think that if the authorities recover those two bodies, they'll dispose of them as quickly as possible and simply announce that prisoners Brosnan and Savary have died, either from natural causes or perhaps in an accident at the granite quarry."

"What you're saying is that they would kill the escape story altogether?" Devlin said. "In other words, it never happened."

"Eminently sensible, if you think of it. That way the authorities are not left with egg on their face, and Belle Isle's reputation for being escape-proof is left intact."

Anne-Marie said, "He could be right. It makes a great deal of sense."

"Perhaps," Devlin said. "Only time will tell on that one. So, what's the next move?"

Jean-Paul turned to Cresson. "We're in your hands now, André. Scour the city. Mortuaries, undertakers, all the usual places. The trawler leaves for St. Denis tomorrow afternoon. When it does, I want two suitable bodies in its cold storage."

André Cresson lit a fresh cigarette from the stub of the one he was smoking and took a pen and a small leather-bound notebook from his pocket. He said to Devlin, "I know where I am where Jacques is concerned. I was his doctor for years. Perhaps, Monsieur, in the interests of accuracy, you'd care to give me a description of your friend Brosnan?"

EIGHT

Frank Barry lay in bed smoking, staring up at the ceiling. It was seven o'clock in the morning, and cold November rain drifted against the window. Jenny Crowther slept beside him, breathing gently, her lips slightly parted. She looked, in repose, incredibly innocent, even childlike. He considered her dispassionately, his mind busy on important things.

He slid from between the blankets, padded to the chair on which he'd left his clothes, and pulled on slacks and an old sweater. He ran fingers through his hair and picked up his suitcases.

Jenny stirred and sat up. "You're going?" she said, and there was alarm in her voice.

He put the cases down and came to the bed. "No, you stay where you are. I don't want you up at the farm today, understand?"

She gazed at him searchingly. "You'll be back?"

"Later," he said.

She flung her arms around his neck and kissed him passionately. It had no effect on him at all, and he was conscious of a strange feeling of regret.

"Be a good girl," he said, and he picked up his suitcases and went out.

There was a smell of bacon cooking. He found Salter in the kitchen at the stove.

"Ah, Mr. Sinclair," he said. "Can I offer you a little something?"

"Not really." Barry poured himself a cup of tea and drank it quickly. "I always prefer to work on an empty stomach."

Salter stopped smiling. "This is the big day then?"

"I'd have thought a devious old sod like you would have learned by now that the less you know the better off you are." Barry picked up the suitcases and went to the door. "I've told Jenny to stay away from the farm today. That applies to you as well."

The threat was implicit. Salter stood there clutching the frying pan, looking thoroughly alarmed. Barry went out and crossed the yard to the barn.

Fifteen minutes later he parked the Land Rover at the end of the jetty. The rain was fine and soft in the mist and, as usual, there wasn't a soul about. He slipped over the rail of the *Kathleen* and went into the wheelhouse. First, he dropped the inspection flap under the instrument panel to check that the Smith and Wesson and the Sterling were still there. Satisfied, he went outside. *Kathleen*'s tender, a yellow inflatable with an outboard motor, swung at the stern on a line. He pulled it into the jetty, clambered down and cast off. The outboard, like everything else about Salter's boat, was brand new. It started with no trouble at all, and he headed away along the creek toward the sea.

He turned into a side channel, followed it for a while, then tried another, for some twenty minutes beating back and forth, even turning toward the land again, before he pushed through a bank of reeds and found what he wanted. It was a pool, roughly circular in shape, perhaps sixty or seventy feet across. It shelved steeply toward the center and at that point was about fifteen feet deep.

It was as if he were the first person to enter that place. There wasn't a sound, only the rain, and he shivered, remembering stories he'd heard as a child back home in Ireland of fairy pools and the like. Strange, but it was as if it had been waiting for him. As if he had been there before. Nonsense, of course, but in any case, it would suit his purpose admirably. He started the tender's engine again and made his way back to the boats.

Hedley Preston stood in front of the wardrobe mirror and adjusted the blue army beret to a suitably rakish angle. The camouflaged battle dress gave him a sinister appearance. He adjusted the webbing belt at his waist.

"Well, now," he said softly. "Who'd have thought it."

He went downstairs and found Varley, similarly attired, standing at the fire, a glass in his hand. Varley glanced over his shoulder and said sourly, "Look at you. Quite the hero."

"One thing's certain," Preston told him cheerfully. "You won't be if Sinclair finds you with that in your hand."

"Stuff Sinclair," Varley said, but at the sound of steps in the passageway he hurriedly put the glass on the mantelpiece behind a photograph.

Barry appeared in the doorway, one of the suitcases in his hand. The uniform suited him. He looked a soldier down to the last inch, and the Browning in the webbing holster at his waist fitted the picture perfectly.

"So, here we are," Preston said. "Now we get to know what it's all about."

"Just as much as you need to."

Barry put the brown suitcase on the table, opened it and took out a map of the area, which he unfolded. "One truck, possibly two, passing this point on the road to Wastwater. Half a dozen soldiers in one for certain. They'll also have an escort. I shan't know how many until later."

"Soldiers?" Varley said. "Here, what is this?"

"Don't wet yourself," Barry said. "They don't let armed soldiers go racketing around the countryside in Britain, so you've nothing to worry about. We block the road with the Land Rover to stop them." He took one of the gas grenades from the case. "Lob one of these in the back of the truck. The gas it contains works instantly. They'll be unconscious for an hour."

"And what about us?" Preston asked.

"All catered for." Barry held up a small khaki colored gas mask with a green canister dangling from it.

"So, they're all sleeping like babies," Preston said. "What do we do?"

"Off-load what we find in the truck into the Land Rover. Thirty minutes back to the coast where I've got a boat waiting. We load up, and you two are finished. You can get the hell out of it."

"With another five thousand pounds each," Preston said. "Let's not forget the most important item."

Barry took the Sterling submachine gun and the Smith and Wesson from the suitcase. "Both these are loaded for bear in case anything goes wrong, but no shooting, not unless I give the word. Understood?"

"Perfectly, Mr. Sinclair." Preston picked up the Sterling lovingly. "A thing of beauty is a joy forever."

Varley handled the Smith and Wesson gingerly, then slipped it into his webbing holster. "One thing I'd like to know," he said belligerently. "What's in this bloody trunk that's so important?"

Barry closed the suitcase and stood looking at them, holding it against his leg. There was a long moment before he said, "Right, let's get going."

He walked out. "Now look here," Varley began, and Preston choked him off instantly.

"Cool it, Sam, understand? Everything comes to him who waits, as I've already told you, so for the moment let's just do as the man says." He picked up his Sterling and followed Barry out.

The funeral parlor was on one side of a small, cobbled square in the old city. When Jean-Paul Savary, Devlin, and Anne-Marie approached there was a horse-drawn hearse outside, a splendid baroque creation in black, with weeping golden angels at each corner and black plumes stuck up between the horses' ears.

"Ostrich feathers," Jean-Paul said. "Actually, it's illegal now, but when people are as conservative as they are around here it's difficult to break such ancient customs."

He pulled on a bell rope at the side entrance. It was opened immediately by a tall, thin old man in a rusty black suit. "This way, Monsieur Savary," he said.

They followed him along a dark passage. The smell of incense and wax candles filled the air, heavy and oppressive. There were chapels of rest on either side of the passage, most of them with a corpse lying in state in an open coffin so that the relatives and friends might visit.

Devlin said, "Thank you very much, but I'd rather go some other way."

"Does it really matter?" Anne-Marie asked. "When you're dead, you're dead." They paused in a doorway to look at an old man propped up in a coffin lined with black satin. He wore a blue suit, collar, and tie, his hair was neatly combed, and his face had been colored with stage make-up, the lips vermilion. "What can it possibly matter to him that they've made him into a waxworks freak."

"As long as it comforts his old mother, you mean?" Devlin shivered. "No thanks. As a bad Catholic I think I'll stipulate cremation."

The old man opened a door at the end of the passage and stood to one side. The room they entered was the preparation room, where bodies were washed, or embalmed if required, before actual burial. Dr. Cresson, the eternal cigarette in his mouth, was standing by a stone sink talking to a tiny, rat-faced man who wore a shiny blue suit and carried a black bag in one hand.

Cresson turned to greet them. "Ah, there you are."

There were two stone mortuary slabs in the center of the room, a body on each covered by a sheet.

"Everything going according to plan?" Jean-Paul asked.

"I think so. Both these individuals died in automobile crashes."

"Can we have a look?"

"I wouldn't advise it. Not unless you actually enjoy that kind of thing. They don't look too good."

"Will they pass?" Devlin asked.

Cresson nodded. "I think so, after I've done a little more work on them." He beckoned the rat-faced man over. "Jean-Paul, this is the tattooist I mentioned, Mr. Black. English, but he's been in Marseilles some time now."

Jean-Paul took the little man's hand. "I am grateful for your help in this matter. The *Union Corse* does not forget its friends, believe me."

"A pleasure, Monsieur. May I start now?" Black said.

"But of course." Jean-Paul turned to Cresson. "You have the numbers?"

"Yes."

"Then all that remains is to make sure the right one goes on the right corpse."

Anne-Marie and Devlin watched, fascinated, as the little man opened his bag, produced a battery-operated tattooist's needle and a bottle of dye, and went to work.

"An extra, but essential touch," Jean-Paul said.

As they watched, the little man neatly tattooed Brosnan's number on the forearm of the taller corpse. He rubbed in the dye, then swabbed the flesh and held the forearm up.

"Satisfactory, Monsieur Savary?"

"Beautiful," Jean-Paul said. "You are a true artist, my friend. And now my father, 28917."

"Very well, Monsieur."

Jean-Paul turned to Anne-Marie and Devlin. "The rest, I think, is in the hands of fate."

From a vantage point among trees at the side of the road two hundred yards north of Brisingham airfield, Barry watched through binoculars as they unloaded the Luftwaffe transport plane. He could see only two vehicles, a large three-ton truck and a jeep. As he watched, the Bundeswehr soldiers loaded three crates into the back of the truck and then climbed in after them.

Their officer stood talking for a while to a young man in the uniform of a captain in the British army. After a while, they got into a jeep which moved off across the runway, followed by the truck. Barry waited until both vehicles were turning out of the gate into the road, just to make sure, then he jumped into the Land Rover and drove away.

The rain had increased into a solid, driving downpour since Barry had gone, and it was not too pleasant crouching out of sight behind a graystone wall in the trees at the side of the road. Varley had a half bottle of Scotch from which he took frequent swallows.

Preston said, "You really are a daft bastard, aren't you?"

"Mind your own sodding business," Varley snarled. "Nobody tells me what to do. Not you and certainly not Mr. God-Almighty Sinclair." He emptied the bottle and dropped it to the ground. "I'll fix him when I'm good and ready." He put a finger to his nose. "You see if I don't."

Preston shook his head in disgust. Varley was a liability, not only now but for the future, so much was obvious. On the other hand, who needed him? Preston caressed the barrel of the Sterling and stiffened, suddenly alert at the sound of an engine.

"Here, I think he's coming."

A moment later the Land Rover appeared. Barry turned it across the road, got out, and moved through the trees to join them.

"Everything all right?" Preston asked.

"Fine," Barry told him. "Two vehicles. A jeep leading that's got three in it, followed by a three-ton truck. The driver and a sergeant in the cab, half a dozen Krauts in the back. That means three grenades. I'll slip the first one into the jeep when I go talk to them. You and Varley take the truck, one in the cab, another in the back."

"Fine by me, General." Varley saluted drunkenly.

Barry bent down and picked up the empty whisky bottle and threw it from him with a curse. He grabbed the big man by the front of his battledress. "Spoil this for me, you drunken pig, and I'll blow your head off. That's a promise."

There was no time for more, for suddenly there was the deepening note of an engine as a vehicle started up the hill.

"All right," Barry said. "Get your masks on," and he turned and ran down to the road. He opened the door of the Land Rover, got his gas mask, and slung it around his neck and stood there waiting.

The German artillery major was in the rear seat of the jeep, while the young English captain sat up front beside the driver, half turned toward him while they spoke. He didn't see Barry until the driver drew his attention to him and slowed.

The captain said, "I wonder what this is all about?" He wound down the window. "What's going on?" he demanded as Barry approached.

"Change of plan, old boy, didn't they tell you?" Barry said. "Well, isn't that bloody typical?"

He pulled the pin and lobbed the gas grenade through the open window, turning away instantly to pull his mask up over his face.

Preston and Varley ran out from the trees, Preston cutting across the road to the rear of the truck, tossing his grenade over the tailgate.

It was Varley who fouled things up. He pulled

the pin of his grenade as he ran forward, tripped and went sprawling, the grenade rolling away from him in a curl of white smoke.

The truck door swung open and a big sergeant of Artillery jumped to the ground. Barry, having no option, drew his Browning and shot him twice as the sergeant launched himself at Varley. In the same moment, Barry picked up the smoking grenade and threw it into the cab, where the driver still sat behind the wheel.

It was suddenly very quiet. Preston came around from the back of the truck, and Barry pulled Varley to his feet and shook him in anger, his voice muffled inside the gas mask.

He turned and hurried around to the back of the truck, let down the tailgate and clambered over the inert bodies of the German artillery men and examined the three green containers he found there.

Preston and Varley joined him. It took them exactly four minutes to move the containers across to the Land Rover. Within five, they were driving away, leaving the two army vehicles silent in the rain at the side of the road.

Jenny Crowther walked along the path beside the estuary in the rain, a forlorn-looking figure in the head scarf and old raincoat. Her life until Barry had been nothing, one gray day after another. Now, he circled in her brain so constantly that she could think of nothing else.

She moved along the jetty and stood, hands

in pockets, looking at the two boats. After a while, she stepped over the rail of the *Kathleen* and went into the wheelhouse. She sat on the bench, her back against the bulkhead, staring at the instrument panel. Finally, she reached underneath and dropped the inspection flap. The Sterling and the revolver hung there, neat and deadly in their brackets. She touched them gingerly, then pushed the flap back up into place and went out again.

She moved along to the *Jason* next and stood looking at it, wondering what it was all about, a slight, puzzled frown on her face. She stepped over the rail and went into the wheelhouse and stood there undecided, not certain what she was doing there at all. Suddenly, in the distance, she heard the sound of an engine.

By the time she got out on deck it was very close. She hesitated, then went down the companionway quickly and closed the door.

The Land Rover braked to a halt at the end of the jetty. Barry got out and went around to the rear, where Preston and Varley sat with the three containers.

"All right, let's have these on board the *Jason*, quick as you like," he said. "Pass me the first one. I can manage it on my own."

"Anything to oblige," Preston said, then pushed it across.

It was comparatively light. Barry had no difficulty in negotiating the rail and the companionway. Jenny, hearing him coming, moved to the other end of the cabin and hid in the toilet.

Barry got the door of the cabin open and went in with the container. He put it down on the floor, and Preston and Varley appeared carrying the second, which was larger.

"Good," Barry said. "One more and we're done, and you two can be out of it."

Varley gave Preston a sly glance, but they went back up the companionway, Barry after them. When they reached the Land Rover, he stood watching them manhandle the third container out. As they started back along the jetty, he reached under the driving seat, found the briefcase, and followed them.

It would be interesting to see when they made their move. The only certainty was that Preston would make a drama out of it. He went and stood by the stern rail, put the briefcase on the ground at his feet and unclipped the holding strap of the webbing holster. He could hear the rumble of their voices in the cabin below, took out the Browning quickly, cocked it, and replaced it in the holster. He lit a cigarette and waited.

They came back on deck and Preston said, "You've got money there, I hope?"

"That's right."

"Yes, well we'd like to talk to you about that. About what's below in those containers and how much there really is in that briefcase."

"In other words, clever bastard," Varley cut in, "we want it all."

Barry turned, a slight smile on his face, the cigarette hanging from the corner of his mouth. Preston had him covered with the Sterling, and Varley drew his Smith and Wesson.

"Do I walk away from this?"

"I'm afraid not, Mr. Sinclair." Preston shrugged. "You lose, all the way around."

"A crying shame." Barry tossed his cigarette over the side. "And to think you could have had your wages and been away."

His hand dropped to his side, reaching for the Browning, and Preston pulled the trigger of the Sterling. There was only the mechanical chatter of the bolt reciprocating. Preston stopped smiling, as in that final dreadful moment he saw it all.

And as Barry fired, Jenny erupted from the companionway. "No!" she cried, flinging herself at Preston and the bullet caught her full in the back, driving her against him.

Preston held her as a shield, trying to back away. Barry shot him through the head, fragmenting the top of his skull, punching him back against the wheelhouse, still clutching the girl.

Varley was firing his Smith and Wesson frantically, one metallic click after another. With a desperate cry, he flung the useless weapon at Barry and turned to run. Barry shot him twice in the back, shattering his spine, and Varley fell to his knees and hung across the rail.

Birds drifted up from the reeds, circling in panic, the air filled with their cries and the beating of their wings. Barry holstered the Browning, dropped on his knees and cradled Jenny Crowther in his arms. She was quite dead, her eyes wide, staring. He closed them gently.

"Poor, stupid little bitch," he said and kissed her on the forehead. "There was no need—no need at all. I had it all sewn up."

He picked her up in his arms, went down the companionway and laid her on one of the benches. Then he went back on deck and knelt beside Preston, opening his shirt and searching him quickly. As he had expected, Preston was carrying the five thousand pounds on him, as was Varley. He tumbled them down the companionway one after the other, then retrieved his briefcase, went over the rail, and hurried along to the *Kathleen*.

He went into the wheelhouse and looked about him. Simplest places were always the best, or so he'd found. There was a bench against the wall. The padded leather top lifted easily enough. There was an accumulation of rubbish inside, ropes, oilcans, plastic bags. He concealed the briefcase under the plastic bags and went outside.

Next, he untied the *Kathleen*'s tender and hauled it along the side of the jetty and attached it to the *Jason*'s stern. Then he went back on board and cast off, hurried into the wheelhouse, and started the engine. Ten minutes later he was nosing through the great bank of reeds to enter the pool he had discovered earlier that day.

He switched off the engines. The *Jason* glided to a halt. He went down the companionway, ignoring the bodies, and worked his way from the prow to the stern, opening the sea cocks. The *Jason* was already beginning to settle as he went out on deck. He hauled in the tender, dropped into it, and pulled away to the side of the pool.

The *Jason* was sinking fast now, the water almost at deck level. He lit a cigarette and waited, and then, with a final sudden rush, she dipped beneath the surface and settled on the bottom. Only then did he start the outboard and push his way back through the reeds to the estuary.

Henry Salter was sitting in the kitchen drinking tea. His nerves were bad, and his hand shook a little as he added a tot of brandy. Wind rattled the window, and rain slapped against the pane. He hated the winter. It worried him, filled him with unease, but not as much as Barry did. He could hear him moving about upstairs now and, a moment later, descending the stairs.

When Barry came into the room, he was

wearing the dark raincoat he had arrived in and carried one of the brown leather cases. He sat in the chair opposite and put the case on the table.

"Well, that's that. I've cleared up at the farm. You wouldn't know anyone's been there."

"And Preston and Varley?"

"Couldn't wait to get their hands on the cash and away. And speaking of cash," he opened the case, took out Preston's five thousand pounds and pushed it across. "As promised."

Salter was sweating a little, as he reached out to touch. "I've been listening on the radio, Mr. Sinclair. There hasn't been any mention of any untoward incident on the local news."

"And why should that sort of thing concern a respectable man like you, Mr. Salter?"

"Of course," Salter said. "Why indeed? You're leaving in the *Jason* now?"

"The *Jason* has already left, old son." Barry smiled. "All taken care of. I'm very organized, you see." He reached in the case and produced Varley's money and tossed it across the table, packet by packet. Salter watched, fascinated. "A bonus, Mr. Salter. You've been more than helpful, you see, and I always say the laborer is worthy of his hire. I expect to be back this way again very soon. Nothing too demanding this time, but it would be nice to think that you were here, ready and waiting to take care of my requirements."

"Of course, Mr. Sinclair. Anything you say," Salter muttered.

"Good, I'll be off then."

Barry picked up his case and moved to the door. Salter said, "One more thing, Mr. Sinclair. What about Jenny?"

Barry turned slowly. "You've no need to worry about Jenny any longer, Mr. Salter. She's my concern from now on."

"I see." Salter nodded knowingly. "I'm hardly surprised. Very fond of you, that girl. A love match, eh?"

Barry managed a smile. "Well, as they say, that's what makes the world go round."

He went out. Salter sat there listening. Only when he heard the rented car drive away did he start to count the money with trembling fingers.

NINE

By the time Barry reached Manchester airport, his hair was again soaked in brilliantine and neatly parted, and he was wearing the thick horn-rimmed spectacles. He made the Jersey plane with only twenty minutes to spare and sank into his seat with a certain amount of relief, for there wasn't another until the following day.

He ordered a large Scotch from the pretty British Airways stewardess in her blue uniform, lit a cigarette, and sat looking out of the window, going over it all in his mind, giving particular attention to Belov.

"Poor Nikolai," he said softly. "You certainly are in for one hell of a shock, old son."

His Scotch came, and he sipped it slowly with conscious pleasure. Things were going well, very well indeed.

One hour later he was walking out of the main entrance to Jersey airport to hail a taxi to take him down to the harbor, and it was here that he ran into his first snag. According to a notice chalked up on a blackboard, there was no further sailing to St. Malo that day.

Barry went into the shipping office and spoke to the clerk who exhibited the usual competent indifference that such people do. "Technical trouble, I'm afraid, sir. No problem with the morning sailing. They'll have another craft over."

And Barry, bowing to the inevitable, walked back along the quay into town and booked himself a room for the night at the Royal Yacht Hotel.

Sitting on the balcony of the hotel room at St. Denis, Anne-Marie searched the horizon for Belle Isle. It was a calm day, with excellent visibility. She found it at last, a shadow, no more than that, even when she focused the binoculars.

Devlin came out of his room in a bathrobe, toweling his hair dry from the shower. "If you're interested, the trawler docked an hour ago at the fish pier."

"Is Jean-Paul on board?"

"No, he comes tomorrow afternoon with Cresson. He'll phone me here after I've visited the island again, just to make sure everything's all right."

"You'll be going with them tomorrow night?"

"Yes."

"Can I come?"

She wasn't pleading, she wasn't that sort. Devlin said, "What a scoop this all would have been for you! What pictures! Another prize!"

"Bastard," she said amiably.

He said seriously, "You've considered the worst implications. The fact that we may miss them altogether. . . ."

"Or that they may be dead when we haul them aboard?" She nodded gravely. "Whichever way it goes, I'd like to be there, Liam."

"And why not?"

"Thank you."

"Thanks is it?" he said. "God save us, and what for? Anyway, I must away out of this and take care of a phone call I've been avoiding making for twenty-four hours at least."

"Important?"

"Ferguson," he said.

Ferguson had been called away at a moment's notice by the Director General. When the phone rang at the Cavendish Square flat, Harry Fox was sitting at the desk in the study working on some papers.

"Brigadier Ferguson, please?"

"Not here, I'm afraid. Can I help?"

"Harry, me boy. It's your long lost Uncle Liam."

Fox was immediately alert. "For God's sake, professor, where have you been? Ferguson's been kicking the furniture to pieces. You were supposed to keep in touch."

"Jesus, Harry, do you think you could stop calling me professor? Makes me sound like some old character actor playing Einstein in a bad television play. Tell Ferguson I've been working like a dog."

"So what's happened? You saw Brosnan?"

"I did indeed and didn't get very far until I mentioned Norah. That set him alight with a vengeance."

"So he's willing to play along?"

"In a manner of speaking. Look, Harry, Ferguson isn't going to like this, but the truth is Martin doesn't rate his chances of getting him out very highly, so he's taking care of it himself."

"He's what?" Fox was shocked, and it was clear in his voice. "That's madness. It can't be done."

"He thinks differently. You're getting all this down on your little recorder, I trust."

Fox laughed in spite of himself. "Of course. Is Miss Audin with you?"

"She is indeed. I'll be off now."

"Just a minute." Fox cried. "Where can we get in touch with you?"

Devlin chuckled. "Don't call us, we'll call you," he said and replaced his phone.

It was half an hour later that Ferguson appeared. He looked tired and went to the sideboard to pour himself a brandy. "What a day."

"Did the Director General want you for anything special, sir?"

"Had us all in, Harry, all department and section heads. Nasty little fracas up in the

Lake District earlier today. A West German artillery team were on their way to the Wastwater proving ground by road to demonstrate this new antitank rocket of theirs. Somebody walked all over them on one of those country back roads. Very professional. Gas grenades in the back of the vehicles, ours, apparently. Type the SAS use on those smash-your-way-in jobs."

"Any shooting, sir?"

"One death—artillery sergeant. Apparently the characters involved were in combat uniform, gas masks, the lot. Took the rocket pod, of course, and away."

"Anything in it for us, sir?"

"I'm not sure. Strictly speaking it's a job for the local police. Special Branch is assisting, naturally, and I've sent Carter up there with them, just in case. In view of the delicacy of the situation, the Director General has managed to get a security clampdown placed in force. Not a word to the media. The West Germans aren't going to like this one little bit."

Fox said, "Devlin telephoned in, sir."

Ferguson's eyes gleamed. "Did he, by God! What's he been up to?"

"I think you'd better hear for yourself, sir." Fox turned on the recorder.

Ferguson sat listening, his face darkening. When the tape was finished, he jumped up and paced angrily across the room.

"Damn you, Devlin!"

"Frankly, sir, I don't really see how Devlin's had much to do with it. It's Brosnan's choice, after all."

"Madness," Ferguson said. "If by some miracle he does escape it would cause an absolute sensation in France. The man would become a folk hero. The authorities would be bound to turn the country upside down to find him as an act of self-preservation."

He stood at the window fuming. Fox said carefully, "You could stop it, sir, very simply."

"By alerting the governor of Belle Isle? Could you do that, Harry?"

"No, sir, not really."

"Neither can I, and Devlin knows that damn well, otherwise he wouldn't have told us." He shook his head. "I don't know. Is the Audin woman still with him?"

"Apparently so, sir. What would you like me to do?"

"Nothing much you can do, Harry." Ferguson frowned suddenly. "No, there is. I want you to put together a brief account of this affair so far. The salient facts, who's involved, what we've done. Everything except the business about Norah Cassidy."

Fox was surprised. "May I ask why, sir?"

"I'll explain later, Harry. One copy for my personal file and one for the eyes of the Prime Minister only."

"Shall I send it around to Number Ten, sir?"

"Not yet. I'd like to be prepared. That's all.

She might send for me at any time. You never can tell. A mind like a Swiss watch, that lady. Security One, needless to say. Tell Meg Johnson she does this one herself. No one else touches it."

Meg Johnson was a formidable, gray-haired lady in her late fifties, widowed since 1951, when her husband had been killed in Korea. She had been Senior Secretary of Administration in Ferguson's department since its inception.

The report on the Brosnan affair that Harry Fox had dictated to her fitted neatly onto a single sheet. It was typed exquisitely, the margin size exact. If it was for the Prime Minister's eyes, then it had to be perfection. Nothing less would do.

She took it in to Fox who read it quickly and nodded his approval. "Excellent, Mrs. Johnson. You've excelled yourself. One copy, please, for the Prime Minister, which for the moment will be held with the original in Brigadier Ferguson's Red file."

She went back along the corridor to her office, reading the report again, strictly in the interests of accuracy. Its contents did not concern her. She never allowed the details of any report to sink in. That, she had found over the years, was the best way.

Satisfied, she opened the door to her office, which communicated with the copying room. The woman on duty was Mary Baxter, senior secretarial assistant. They were old friends and had worked together for years.

Mrs. Johnson said, "Hello, Mary, what are you doing here?"

"Young Jean was taken ill at lunchtime. I'm just filling in."

Meg Johnson passed her the report. "One copy, please."

As Mary Baxter started to feed the page into the machine, she saw *For the eyes of the Prime Minister only.* She took in only that much before the phone started to ring in Meg Johnson's office. Meg hurried in to answer it.

It was a routine matter taking only three or four minutes to handle. As she was writing a memo, there was a nervous cough, and she looked up to find Mary Baxter standing there holding the report.

"One copy, you said?"

"Thanks, Mary. Just put them on the desk," Meg Johnson replied, still concentrating on her memo.

The other woman did as she was told and went out. Back in the copying room, she closed the door carefully, then took out the two extra copies of the Brosnan report she had made. She folded them neatly and slipped them into the pocket of her tweed skirt. She checked her watch. Almost time to go home. She switched off the light and went out.

* * *

Mary Baxter was of impeccable background. Her father had spent his entire career as an army doctor, and, as her mother had died when she was five, she had spent all her impressionable years at a succession of boarding schools.

A plain, rather ugly girl, she had few friends. She had entered the civil service as a ministry secretary to start with. Her total reliability had led to promotion, then, after a while, a transfer to D15, once her security clearance had gone through.

She had money left her by her father, a good apartment in St. John's Wood, and very little else. She was forty-two, still plain, her hair drawn back in a tight bun, and the tweed suits and sensible flat shoes she wore did little to enhance her appearance.

And then she had met Peter Yasnov. She'd had an invitation to a cultural evening at the Brazilian embassy, the sort of thing that came up occasionally. Usually, she didn't go to such affairs, but for some reason this time she had, and that's where she'd met Yasnov.

He'd been more than attentive—had stayed with her all evening—had not only taken her home, but had arranged to squire her to a concert at the Albert Hall the following week.

His slow insistent seduction had finally taken her to bed where she had discovered the delights of sex for the first time in her life. By the time she also discovered that he was a commercial attaché at the Soviet embassy, she was hooked, she didn't care. Anything he wanted she gave him and that included any information of value that she came across in the office. Usually her access to the interesting stuff was limited, but this was really something special.

She wasn't supposed to see him for another four days, an eternity of waiting, and he had always forbidden her ever to call at his flat. But for this. . . .

She had only taken two copies to make sure she got a good one. She slipped one into her dressing table drawer, put the other in her handbag, and went out.

Peter Yasnov had been commercial attaché at the Soviet embassy in London for two years. A captain in the KGB, his previous posting had been at the Paris embassy where, under Nikolai Belov's tutelage, he had made remarkable progress. A handsome, dark-haired, and elegant young man, he was particularly attractive to women, a circumstance that had its uses and explained why his masters had thought it worthwhile to indulge him in the small townhouse in Ebury Court, not far from the Palace of St. James.

He emerged from the shower, humming softly to himself, pulled on a robe and went into the living room to get a cigarette. He was standing at the window, looking down idly into the court, when Mary Baxter came around the corner, passed the two telephone repairmen with their green tent over the manhole in the pavement, and walked toward the house. Yasnov cursed softly and went downstairs.

The main function of the Special Branch of the Metropolitan Police based at Scotland Yard is to act as the executive arm of the security services. Surveillance forms a large part of Special Branch work, and the two detective sergeants posing as telephone workers in their tent in Ebury Court had been watching Peter Yasnov in one way or another for a month now.

Mary Baxter rang the bell and turned, looking back along the court while she waited, enabling the SB man with the camera to take several excellent photos.

"I haven't seen her before, have you?"

"Hardly his style, I would have thought," his colleague said. "She's no dollybird."

The door opened, and Yasnov appeared in his white bathrobe. Mary Baxter flung her arm around his neck and kissed him. The sergeant's camera clicked again.

"Now that is interesting," he said as she passed inside and the door closed. "He didn't look pleased at all. You'd better follow the lady, George, when she comes out. Find out who she is. There could be something in this one."

*   *   *

Yasnov was thoroughly angry, as he made clear. "I told you never to visit me here." He shook her by the shoulders. "Are you trying to ruin everything?"

"Please, Peter, I didn't mean any harm."

There were tears in her eyes, and he was filled with disgust, but he made a brave effort to conceal it and held her close to him for a moment.

"All right, I lost my temper, but you must understand my position."

"I know, Peter, I'm so sorry." She got her handbag open. "But I felt sure you'd be interested in this. I thought you might want to see it."

For the eyes of the Prime Minister only. The moment Yasnov saw that, his stomach tightened with excitement, and the paper trembled slightly in his hand as he took in the contents. He turned away from her and walked to the fireplace. *The biggest touch he'd ever had by far.* It was inconceivable that this block of wood in the tweed skirt had come up with such a thing.

She approached him hesitatingly. "Did I do right? Is it what you wanted?"

He turned with a dazzling smile and pulled her close. "For an exceptionally good girl, an exceptional kiss," and he crushed his mouth on hers.

She clung to him, trembling. "Oh, Peter, I'd do anything for you. Anything."

He cradled her head in his shoulder and

checked his watch. Fifteen minutes was all it would take, and if it kept her happy—he put an arm around her. "Come upstairs, my darling," he whispered and led her out of the room.

Mary Baxter left half an hour later. She had never felt so alive. It was as if something that had been locked up inside her for years had been released. She felt so full of energy that she walked a considerable part of the way home before taking the subway, totally unaware of the man following her.

Yasnov left his house an hour later and walked a couple of streets before hailing a cab. He alighted in Kensington High Street and went the rest of the way on foot to the Soviet embassy in Kensington Palace Gardens. Five minutes later, he was closeted with his immediate superior, Colonel Josef Golchek.

Golchek read the report through twice and nodded. "Very interesting," he said. He lit an American cigarette. "Of course, it isn't going to prevent the start of the Third World War or anything. Its real importance lies not in the substance of this report but in the implication that the woman Baxter can actually get her hands on a report intended for the eyes of the British prime minister only. The possibilities for the future would seem to me to be fantastic."

"And this report. What do I do with it?" Yasnov demanded.

"Send it to Nikolai Belov in Paris. Code Three, for his own eyes. He'll know how best to handle it."

"Very well." Yasnov moved to the door.

As he opened it, Golchek said, "One more thing, Peter."

"What's that?"

"You'll have to continue to keep her happy."

"For that," Peter Yasnov said with feeling, "I should be made a Hero of the Soviet Union."

It was nine o'clock that night when Mary Baxter was led by a woman detective sergeant of Special Branch into Charles Ferguson's office. He nodded to the detective sergeant and she went out, closing the door.

"Sit down, Miss Baxter."

She did as she was told, suddenly tired. She was not afraid. The shock of her arrest had had a numbing effect so that she was not really capable of taking anything in. It had never occurred to her, not for one moment, that this kind of thing might happen.

"You know why you're here?" Ferguson said.

"I've no idea. If there has been some mistake in my work."

He pushed the surveillance photos across the desk. She looked at them blankly, then picked up the one that showed her kissing Yasnov in the doorway. "You've no right . . ." she began.

"We have every right," he said gently. "You

work for the British Security Service. All right, in a minor capacity perhaps, but that makes your association with a man like Yasnov very suspect."

"All right," she said, "so he's a commercial attaché at the Soviet embassy."

"And also, Miss Baxter, a captain in the KGB."

She gazed at him incredulously. "I don't believe you."

"I have a photo of him here in uniform. Excellent likeness, don't you agree?"

There was a knock at the door and Harry Fox entered, face grave. He glanced at Mary Baxter, then put the second copy of the Brosnan report she had made on the desk in front of Ferguson.

"I found this, sir, in one of her dressing table drawers," he said grimly.

"Dear God Almighty." Ferguson got up, beckoned to Fox, and went out into the corridor. "Watch her," he said to the detective sergeant, and she went into the office and closed the door.

"Well, sir?" Harry Fox said. "What do we do?"

"What can we do, Harry, except hope and pray Devlin calls us again. This could give him real problems."

"What about the Baxter woman?"

"Let's see, shall we?"

They went back into the office, and the detective sergeant stepped out again. Mary Baxter sat holding the photo of Yasnov in uniform in her lap. She had stopped crying, there was something close to anger on her swollen face now, and Ferguson seized on that fact instantly.

"He certainly made a bloody fool out of you, didn't he?"

"He told me he loved me," she said bitterly. "All lies. Nothing but lies." She tore the photo into several pieces. "I could kill him."

"Much more sensible to pay him back in his own coin." Ferguson gave her a cigarette and a light.

"What do you mean?" she asked.

"You could go to prison," he said. "For a long time. On the other hand, it does seem rather a pity when there's another way of handling this matter." He held up the copy of the report. "This, after all, is past history. Not much we can do about it now."

"What exactly do you mean?"

"Simple enough. You continue to see Yasnov as if nothing had happened. Feed him the information I give you."

She shook her head, shocked. "I don't think I could do that."

"Why not?" Ferguson demanded. "He used you for his own purposes, didn't he? I should have thought it truly poetic justice for you to use him for yours."

She was like a different person now, her face hardening. "You know, I think I'd rather enjoy that, Brigadier." She stood up. "Do you think I could wash my face?"

"Certainly." Ferguson indicated the door. "Bathroom through there."

"My God," Fox said after she'd gone out.

"I know, Harry, I warned you just how dirty a business it was. You can tell that girl from Special Branch to clear off. We shan't be needing her."

In Paris, the coding machine chattered in the radio room of the intelligence section of the Soviet embassy. The woman operator watched the message appear line by line on the display screen. When it was finished she removed the tape which had recorded it and summoned the supervisor.

"A Code Three from London for Colonel Belov's eyes alone. It also includes as ancillary information three photos over the wire. Here are the serial numbers."

"He's-in Berlin," the supervisor said. "Due back tomorrow afternoon or evening. Hold it till then. You can't do anything with it anyway. It requires his personal key to decode. I'll get those photos from the wire room. You can hold those too."

She walked away, and the operator placed the tape in her data drawer, locked it, and returned to work.

*   *   *

It was almost midnight and chilly on the balcony of Anne-Marie's hotel room at St. Denis. She went inside and returned, putting on her sheepskin jacket. She sat down beside Devlin again.

"This time tomorrow night, it could be all over."

"True." Devlin's cigarette glowed in the dark.

"How will I find him, Liam?"

"Changed, girl, and considerably. Be prepared for some big differences."

"I don't mind that. An essential requirement for any human being is to grow or change or learn how to become reconciled to their limitations."

"Ah, you're talking about the rocky road to maturity" Devlin shook his head. "I mean something else. He's not the wild man who saved you in that swamp in Vietnam, and he isn't the brave soldier who stood at my side in Ulster in sixty-nine. To be honest with you, if he's learned anything at all it's that he's been used too much for other people's purposes. I don't think he believes in anything anymore."

"I can't accept that."

Devlin said, "Girl, dear, don't try to make him into some mythological hero. Whatever else he is, he is not that. I'm turning in now. The supply boat leaves at seven."

He swung a leg over the balcony rail and went into his room, leaving her there, staring out into the darkness.

TEN

When Lebel opened the door of the interview room and ushered Brosnan in, Devlin was standing by the window, peering out through the bars.

He turned, smiling. "Ah, there you are."

"Mr. Gorman." Brosnan shook hands and sat down, and Devlin took the chair opposite.

"If you need me, Monsieur, remember the bell." Lebel went out, locking the door.

They spoke in Irish. Devlin said, "Will he search you before taking you back to your cell?"

"Pierre?" Brosnan shook his head. "All for a quiet life, that one. What have you got for me?"

Devlin opened his briefcase. "Have a cigarette." He pushed a pack across and followed it with another. "One contains the homing device, the other a pocket flashlight. I wasn't sure if you could lay your hands on one. I was thinking of the sewers."

"We've got candles and matches."

"Holy Mother of God," Devlin said. "The worst thing you could do! You'd blow yourself to hell. Now listen to me."

211

He went over everything thoroughly. When he was finished, Brosnan nodded. "You've certainly got it all wrapped up, but then you always were the organizing type. I like the touch with the two corpses. That should amuse Jacques. Obviously his son takes after his father."

"What time will you be leaving?"

"We're locked up for the night by eight-thirty. It's dark by then, at the moment anyway, so we might as well make our move straight away. There isn't another check until midnight."

"So they'll discover you've gone then?"

"Not the way Lebel checks the cells. With luck, the first they'll know is at seven o'clock in the morning."

Devlin nodded. "How long in the sewers?"

"There's some climbing to do first. I'd give it an hour. With luck, we'll be at the funeral rock by nine-thirty. The current should have us outside the four-mile limit by ten-fifteen."

Devlin sat there frowning. "This is a desperate ploy, you know that?"

Brosnan said, "Of course I do."

Devlin got up and rolled a small plastic ball across the table. "When you peel the skin off, it's luminous inside. A signaling device we used in the war. My own life was saved by one once. I know there are lights on the lifejackets, but. . . ."

He shrugged and went to the window and

peered through the bars. The Mill Race was clear to see, flecked with whitecaps in spite of the calm weather.

Brosnan clapped him on the shoulder. "Don't worry, Liam, Jacques Savary and I know what we're doing. We all come to a box in the end, anyway. The important thing is to go kicking like hell."

The hydrofoil from Jersey to St. Malo took around an hour to complete the journey. Frank Barry spent the time working his way through all the English national newspapers that he'd purchased before leaving St. Helier.

There wasn't a mention, not even a hint, of the Wastwater affair in any of them, which was interesting. On the other hand, it made a great deal of sense. Not exactly the sort of thing that even the West Germans would want to advertise.

He passed through customs using the French passport, experiencing no difficulty at all, and immediately went to a telephone to call Belov at his Paris apartment.

The phone was answered by the Russian's personal secretary from the embassy, Irana Vronsky. She told him that she'd just been speaking to Belov in East Berlin and that he wouldn't be back until the flight arrived at midnight.

Barry said, "If he speaks to you again, tell him that I'll be back in touch in the morning."

He picked up his suitcase and left the booth.
The train for Paris departed in twenty minutes.
On the other hand, there was no reason to
hurry. He had most of the day still before him,
and a fine soft day it was and to be enjoyed.
He walked across the parking lot to the rental
car company on the other side, and fifteen
minutes later drove out into the main road in a
Peugeot coupe with the top down.

It was dark, and the trawler was slipping out
through the harbor entrance at St. Denis when
Devlin followed Jean-Paul Savary down the
ladder into the fish hold. The door to the cold
storage locker was open, and Dr. Cresson and
Big Claude from the club stood inside at the
slab on which fish were usually gutted, cutting away the plastic bags that contained the
two corpses.

From what Devlin could see in the shad-
owy light, the faces were disfigured beyond
recognition.

"Jesus," he said.

"The force of the Mill Race pounding in on
the granite rocks along the shore outside St.
Denis," Jean-Paul said. "It is not unreasonable
to expect such a result."

Devlin touched the leg of one of the corpses.
It was like marble. "If there ever was an
autopsy, it would indicate entirely the wrong
time of death, wouldn't it?"

"Keeping the bodies frozen as we have done

takes care of that to a certain degree," Cresson said. "It considerably arrests the process of decay. But frankly, my friend, if this is to succeed at all, it will be because the authorities accept these two gentlemen at face value."

"Or without it," Devlin said.

He followed Jean-Paul back up on deck, and they went into the wheelhouse. The captain was older than Devlin had expected, with a weather-beaten face beneath the peaked cap. He wore a black oilskin. The cheroot he was smoking smelled foul, and Devlin stayed in the doorway.

"Now then, Marcel," Jean-Paul said. "What's the score?"

"Not good, boss," the old man said. "A bad blow forecast, winds seven to eight. Not enough to blow anyone's roof off, but for men out there in the waters of the Race. . . ." He shrugged.

Jean-Paul turned to Devlin, his face pale in the dim light. "Don't worry, this old sea rat is the finest skipper on the coast. If anyone can bring this off it's him—with the help of this gadget, of course." He tapped the gleaming blue box on the chart table. "The very latest thing. I had it installed yesterday. Microchip and digital read-out, so it really thinks for itself. Once locked onto the wave-length of that homing device, it will give us a course straight to it, whatever the weather."

"Fine," Devlin said, "but if you've got any candles handy, I'd like to light a couple, just in case."

Jean-Paul returned to the charts, and Devlin went out on to the bridge where Anne-Marie stood at the rail, muffled in her sheepskin jacket. Whitecaps stretched into the darkness, and spray scattered across the deck as the trawler dipped its prow into the waves.

"It's not good, is it?" she said.

"Not from the sound of it." He grabbed the rail tightly. "You might as well know it all. The captain thinks it will get worse before it gets better."

"Enough to put them off?" she said. "Martin and Savary, I mean?"

"I can only speak for Martin, but in my opinion nothing could stop him entering the water if he makes it outside those walls, no matter how bad the storm. He's prepared to die if necessary, you see. That's the important thing."

"My God," she whispered and then suddenly clutched his arm as the wind carried a strange roaring sound from the far distance.

"Did you hear that, Liam? What is it?"

"Why, from the sound of it, I'd say that must be the Mill Race."

She didn't say a word. He slipped an arm about her shoulders, and together they stood there at the rail listening.

Pierre Lebel pulled back the flap on the spyhole of the cell on the upper tier. Brosnan and Savary sat opposite each other with a wooden box between them. Savary had a pack of tarot cards in one hand and was laying out the wheel of fortune.

"This gives an answer to a specific question," he said, "and the outcome of events in the immediate future."

"Really?" Brosnan said. "You amaze me. Do I cross your palm with silver?"

"I've told you before, I've got gypsy blood."

Lebel called. "You should be in bed you two. Lights out."

The cell was plunged into darkness. Savary called, "God bless you, too, Pierre, and thanks for everything. You've been swell."

"Idiot!" Brosnan whispered.

Lebel checked the next cell; they listened as his footsteps worked their way along the landing. The barred gate at the end clanged, he descended the iron stairs, and the footsteps faded.

"Switch on the flashlight," Savary said. "I just want to see what I've laid out." Brosnan produced the small pocket flashlight Devlin had given him. It had a surprisingly powerful beam. Savary turned over the first card. It showed death, a skeleton on horseback riding across a field of corpses. Savary gathered up the cards and put them on the shelf. "Now that I can very definitely do without. I'm not looking anymore. Let's get moving."

Brosnan turned over his mattress, slid his hand through the seam at one side, and pulled out a coil of nylon rope and a sling with snap links at the end, items he had frequently used at the quarry when placing dynamite charges in the cliff face. He also produced a narrow-handled screwdriver and a pair of twelve-inch heavy-gauge wire cutters, which Savary had obtained from a convict who worked in the machine shop. They each arranged their beds with extra clothes, a few books, a pillow to give the appearance of a human form.

"Do you think it will pass?" Savary asked.

"With Lebel? Most nights, he doesn't even look in, and I reckon that will be good enough if he does. Now let's get moving. We've got a tight schedule."

They pulled on their heavy reefer coats, prison issue for those working outside in bad weather, and leather and canvas gloves. Brosnan picked up the rope, and Savary knelt at the door with a spoon. There was a slight click, and he stood up. "That's it, Martin, let's go."

They moved outside, and he closed the door carefully behind them. They stood in the shadows of the wall for a moment, then moved quietly to the end of the landing.

The central hall was illuminated by a single light, and music drifted up from the radio in the duty officer's room. The roof and the dome were shrouded in darkness. Brosnan climbed on the rail and scrambled up the steel mesh curtain to the roof of the cell block. He hooked the snap links of his sling into the wire to hold himself secure and took out the wire cutters.

It took him no more than five minutes to make a hole about three feet across, through which he pulled himself. Once on the other side, he stepped onto one of the steel support girders. He looked down at Savary, his face pale in the darkness, and beckoned. The Frenchman followed him.

They balanced together on one girder and held onto another. Brosnan hooked a line to the sling around Savary's waist and touched him briefly on the shoulder. There was no need to say anything, for they had discussed in detail the route and what to expect.

The difficult part came now, for the grill he needed to reach was thirty feet up in the darkness and the girder curved out, following the line of the wall. Brosnan slipped his sling around it, fastened the links at his waist, and started to climb, bracing himself against the girder, using a well-proven climbing technique.

It was now that his strength and excellent physical condition stood him in good stead. He heaved himself up inch by inch, until he reached his objective, a large ventilation grill.

It was held in place by four screws, and he took out his screwdriver, braced himself against the girder, and set to work. The screws were brass and came out easily enough, but he left the one on the bottom left-hand corner partly in position so the grill swung down, no longer obscuring the entrance, but still held securely.

So far so good. He looked down at Savary, waved and tugged on the line, and the Frenchman secured himself to the girder with his sling and started to climb.

Brosnan kept the tension on the line, giving Savary all the help that he could. It went well enough for a while, and then a door clanged far below. Savary, shocked by the unexpected noise, lost his hold and slipped.

Brosnan clenched his teeth and leaned back against the girder, a foot on the wall, and held on, the line cutting into his back and shoulder. Savary hung there, while below, a prison officer crossed the hall and went into the office. There was a rumble of voices, laughter.

Savary swung back against the girder and started to climb again and finally reached Brosnan.

They poised there for a few moments, and Brosnan whispered, "Okay, Jacques, you first."

Savary unhooked himself from the beam, leaned forward and went head first into the shaft. Brosnan coiled the line neatly about his waist and went after him.

Clouds of dry dust filled his nostrils, and he took out the flashlight and switched it on, the spot traveling ahead of Savary, picking out the dirt-encrusted metal sides of the shaft. The Frenchman started to pull himself along, no room to crawl, and Brosnan followed. Then there was a distinct current of air, a low, humming sound far below, and the shaft emerged into a sort of central chamber, the dark mouths of other shafts at intervals around it.

The noise came from a hole about three feet in diameter in the center of the chamber, and Brosnan crouched beside Savary and shone his torch down.

"This is it," he said. "I saw the plans for the ventilation system of this place two years ago when I was working with the heating engineer's detail at the hospital. From what I remember, this shaft goes down sixty or seventy feet to the boiler room. How are you doing?"

"Fine," Savary said. "Don't worry about me. I haven't felt so good in years."

Brosnan examined the interior of the shaft with his torch. The circular metal sheets were held in place by steel stays.

"Good footholds," he said. "If you get tired, just wedge yourself against the sides for a few moments. I'll go first, then if you fall you can drop on me."

Savary's teeth gleamed in the darkness. "Good luck, Martin."

Brosnan started down, holding the flashlight in one hand. It was easy enough, far easier than the earlier climb up the girder in the central hall. The hum of the generators increased as he got closer to the bottom of the shaft. There was light down there, shining up through a grill. He braced himself against the sides of the shaft and tried to peer through. All he could see was the boiler room floor. Usually, there was no one on duty at this time of night and if there was, it was likely to be a trusty anyway. Not that he had much choice.

He shined the flashlight up and found Savary poised just above him. "Hang on," Brosnan whispered. "I'm going through."

He slipped the flashlight into his pocket, braced himself against the sides, then stamped on the grill with both feet. It buckled, started to give, and at the third attempt gave way completely and crashed to the floor eight feet below, followed by Brosnan himself.

He got up, shaken but unhurt, and looked about him. The boiler room was in semi-darkness, the only light a small bulb that hung over the dials on the instrument panel on the far wall. Most important of all, there was no one there.

He called up the shaft, "Okay, Jacques, let's be having you. Just let yourself go," and a moment later caught the Frenchman as he dropped through.

They moved to the door at once. Brosnan opened it and peered outside. Rain fell heavily, bouncing from the cobbled courtyard.

"The manhole cover is over there," he said. "To the right of the hospital entrance. Keep your head down, and let's go."

He kept to the shadows of the wall, working his way around the courtyard, Savary at his heels, until he reached the manhole cover and crouched down. He got the screwdriver out and cleaned the dirt from the iron handles that were set into the cover, but when he heaved it refused to budge.

"What is it, for God's sake?" For the first time there was panic in Savary's voice.

"Nothing," Brosnan said. "Probably hasn't been up in years. I'll fix it, don't worry."

He worked the screwdriver around the edge of the manhole cover methodically, stifling an insane desire to laugh. There had been a notice on the command board at Khe Sahn. *For those who fight for it, life has a flavor the sheltered never know.* Whoever wrote that had certainly known what he was talking about.

He tried again, exerting all his strength, Savary wrapping his hands around him to assist. The manhole gave suddenly and easily, so that Brosnan lost his balance and they fell together.

The stench was immediate and appalling, accentuated by the freshness of the rain. Savary said, "Oh, my God, I didn't realize."

"The only way, Jacques," Brosnan said. "Down you go."

Savary disappeared into darkness and Brosnan followed, descending a short iron ladder, pausing only to slide the manhole cover back into place. When he switched on the flashlight, he found Savary standing in three feet of stinking water and excrement. The Frenchman leaned against the wall and vomited.

He turned, his face pale. "I can't take much of this, Martin."

"You don't have to," Brosnan lied. "A couple of hundred yards, that's all, I promise you."

The tunnel was six feet high and very old, the brickwork crumbling, and as they advanced the flashlight picked out rats by the dozen, scampering along the ledges on either side. Fifty or sixty yards further on, the tunnel emptied itself into a pool over a concrete apron. It was obviously the main catchment chamber for the entire system, several other tunnels emptying into it.

Brosnan slid down the apron, holding the flashlight high, and found himself almost chest deep. Savary came after him, lost his balance and went under. Brosnan pulled him up by the collar, and the Frenchman surfaced in a dreadful state, his face smeared with filth. He was badly shocked.

Brosnan said, "Come on, Jacques, keep going. Just keep going."

He worked his way across the pool and pulled himself up on a concrete ledge, heaving Savary up behind him. He followed the ledge and came to an iron ladder, the water with the sewer cascading down beside it for some thirty feet.

They descended the ladder and moved on, negotiating two more before the walkway ended.

"We must be close to the shoreline now," Brosnan said. "It can't be much further."

He eased himself down into the water, and

Savary followed him. The water rose higher and higher as Brosnan advanced. There was a ground swell now, and the stench was not so apparent. Then suddenly, a yard or two ahead, the tunnel simply disappeared.

Savary said, "Now what?"

"The outfall must be under the surface," Brosnan said. "I hadn't counted on that."

"So what do we do?"

"Swim for it."

"Under water?" The Frenchman shook his head. "I don't think I can."

Brosnan gave him the flashlight. "Hang onto this and I'll take a look."

He took a couple of deep breaths, went under, and swam forward, sliding against the roof of the tunnel. Ten feet, fifteen, twenty and he was through and immediately surfaced in a channel among rocks at the foot of the cliffs.

It was dark, rain falling, a heavy swell running. He floated there for a moment, took a breath, and went down into the mouth of the tunnel again. The return journey was more difficult, but he surfaced beside Savary a few moments later and braced himself against the tunnel wall, gasping for breath.

"Bad?" Savary asked.

"Twenty feet, Jacques, that's all, and you're out."

"I can't," Savary said.

Brosnan was untying the line from about his

waist and he snapped it to the link on Savary's sling. "You want to go back?"

"No, I'd rather die."

"Good. I'm going to swim out again now. When you're ready, pull twice on the line and hold your breath. I'll haul you through."

He didn't give Savary time to think about it, simply dived under the water again and swam back along the tunnel. He surfaced and floated for a moment in the pool and then found that his feet could touch bottom and that it was no more than five feet deep. He pulled in the slack on the line until it was tight and waited. The tugs, when they came, were quite distinct. He started to haul in with all his strength, pulling steadily, never stopping until Savary surfaced beside him, gasping for air.

Brosnan held him for a moment, then said, "Okay, let's get out of here," and together they waded out of the water and scrambled up the hillside, the walls of Belle Isle towering into the night above them.

Lightning flickered on the far horizon as they crouched at the door of the hut while Savary worked the lock. Finally, it clicked open. They moved inside, Brosnan closed the door and switched on the light.

"All right?" he said to Savary.

The Frenchman nodded, nervous, excited. The sea had washed the filth from his body and he seemed to have recovered his spirits. "We beat the bastards, eh, Martin?"

"Not yet," Brosnan told him. "Get ready, quick as you like. Two life jackets, remember, not one. We'll need all the flotation we can get out there."

Five minutes later, they were ready. Brosnan took the homing device Devlin had given him, activated it, then strapped it to one of his life jackets.

He said to Savary, "Let's go," and he switched off the light, opened the door, and they left.

The rain hammered down, and when the sheet lightning crackled they saw waves lashing into foam stretching as far as the eye could see. They descended the cliffs, following the course of a ravine that finally emptied itself into the water.

The funeral rock towered into the night above their heads, and Savary looked up at it. "Maybe we're just saving Lebel a job."

Brosnan uncoiled the line and secured it, first to Savary's sling and then his own, leaving an umblical cord perhaps six feet long between them.

"Together, or not at all?" Savary said.

"Exactly."

They shook hands, then made their way to a ledge on the outer reaches of the rocks where the sea roared by. Brosnan turned inquiringly, Savary nodded, and they jumped, committing themselves to the waters of the Mill Race.

*   *   *

They were carried along at a terrific rate, for
the current was running at nine or ten knots
and the distance they were covering was quite
phenomenal. Strangely enough, it didn't seem
particularly cold at first, but that would come
later. The clothing helped there, of course,
and the heavy reefers.

There was no real sense of passing time.
Just the sea and the roaring and the tug of the
line at Brosnan's waist as Savary pulled at it.
Occasionally lightning flickered again, but all
it illuminated was the sea, a waste of broken
water in which they were quite alone.

After fifteen or twenty minutes Brosnan did
begin to feel the cold. He wondered how Savary
was doing, tugged on the line and a moment
later got a response. Belle Isle was so far back
there in the darkness that there seemed no
longer any need to fear detection and he
switched on the light on his life jacket. A moment later, Savary did the same, and they
continued on, dipping over the waves like two
will-o'-the-wisps in the darkness.

On the bridge of the trawler, Anne-Marie and
Devlin stood at the rail as the ship plunged
into the waves. They both wore oilskin coats
and sou'westers, and water streamed from them.

As lightning flickered, illuminating the size
of the seas breaking, the white carpet of foam,

Devlin said desperately, "This is no good—no good at all."

And then Jean-Paul leaned out of the wheelhouse, his voice full of excitement. "We've got them!" he cried exultantly.

Anne-Marie and Devlin hurried into the wheelhouse. Jean-Paul and Claude bent over the blue box on the chart table. Lines moved across the screen, there was a rhythmic pinging sound, and the red illuminated figures on the digital read-out altered with incredible rapidity and finally stopped.

Jean-Paul made a quick calculation. "That's it," he said to old Marcel at the wheel. "They're about a mile to the northeast. Steer two-four-two." As they altered course, he said to Devlin, "When the regular beat of that signal becomes continuous and high-pitched, we're there."

Anne-Marie held Devlin's hand, and together they stood there watching the screen.

Brosnan was cold, and his face and eyes were sore from the salt water. He was tired, completely at the end of his tether. When Savary's light went out, he tugged on the line, but got no response and when he tried to haul the Frenchman in to him, realized he didn't have the strength.

A few moments later, the light on his own life jacket went out. So that was it then, and now that it had come it didn't seem to matter. He floated, eyes closed, head back, and was lifted high on the crest of a wave. He opened his eyes and saw the lights of a ship to the right of him.

It was enough, and as he went down into a trough he opened his mouth and yelled at the top of his lungs. Yet, in the roaring of the sea, he couldn't even hear himself.

He lifted on another wave, Savary trailing behind him. The ship was closer now, close enough for him to see that it was a trawler, her lines plain in her deck lights. He shouted and waved, all to no purpose, went down again, and then suddenly remembered Devlin's parting present at the prison, the signaling ball.

He felt for it in his right hand pocket, got it out, desperately clutching it in numb fingers, and tore at the plastic covering with his teeth. The phosphorescence dazzled him with its beauty, shining in the night like a glowworm, and he cupped it in his right palm and held it aloft.

It was Big Claude who caught sight of the light to port and ran to the wheelhouse instantly. Marcel cut back the engines and brought the trawler around, curving in. Devlin and Anne-Marie ran to the port rail where Jean-Paul and Claude were throwing a boarding net over the side.

"What do you think?" Devlin demanded.

"It's got to be them. Must be," Jean-Paul said savagely.

He took the spotlight Claude passed him, switched it on, and played it across the water.

"Nothing!" Anne-Marie said. "Not a damn thing!"

And then Brosnan rose high on the crest of a wave, arm raised, Savary trailing behind him.

ELEVEN

Brosnan coughed as the whisky caught at the back of his throat. He looked up at Devlin sitting on the edge of the bunk. "Bushmills?" he asked hoarsely.

"What else? I brought the bottle specially. And now that you're back in the land of the living, there's someone to see you. I'll see how Savary's getting on."

He moved out of the way, and Anne-Marie sat down. She still wore the oilskin and pushed damp hair back from her forehead in an inimitable gesture.

"Here we are again then," Brosnan said.

"So it would appear." She reached over and touched his face briefly. "You're still cold."

"Frozen to the bone. I'll have nightmares about the Mill Race for the rest of my life. How's Jacques?"

"Dr. Cresson is working on him in the next cabin."

"You mean he's still unconscious?"

"I'm afraid so."

Brosnan sat up, pulling the blanket around him. "Show me."

She led the way to the next cabin. Jacques Savary lay on the bunk swathed in blankets, his face white and shrunken, eyes closed. Jean-Paul watched anxiously with Devlin while the doctor worked over his father.

"He's cold," he said. "Too cold. At his age. . . ." He filled a hypodermic and injected the contents into Savary's right forearm. "The most powerful stimulant I dare use." He turned to Jean-Paul. "The pulse is very weak. He needs hospitalization as soon as possible."

"Who the hell says so," said Jacques Savary in a low voice.

His eyes were open, he smiled weakly, and Jean-Paul seized his hand and dropped to one knee beside the bunk. "What were you trying to do, scare the hell out of me?"

"Something like that." Savary's eyes sought Brosnan and found him. "We showed the bastards, eh?"

"Definitely," Brosnan said.

Cresson said, "Everybody out. He needs sleep."

Savary grabbed Jean-Paul's coat as he got up. "I'm not going back to that place, not ever. You understand?"

"Sure, Papa."

"So now we're out, the most important thing is dumping those bodies in the right place. Get on with that, and never mind about me. Lots of time to sleep later."

Brosnan went back into the other cabin, followed by Devlin and Anne-Marie. He sat on the bunk. "What happens now?"

"The captain is going to land us at St. Denis about an hour from now. Jean-Paul has his own plans for his father. We three will move on to Anne-Marie's farm in the hills above Nice."

"And Barry?"

"Plenty of time for him when you've rested a few days. Now I suggest you lie down again and get a little shut-eye before we land."

"He's right, Martin," Anne-Marie said. "We'll leave you for a while."

They went out, and Brosnan pulled the blanket around him, lay back, and closed his eyes; but there was no comfort there, simply a distorted pattern of images, waves breaking in the darkness, and his eyes were sore from the salt. But he was free, that was the amazing thing. Free again after four years in one of the grimmest prisons in Europe, and the strange thing was, it had no effect on him at all.

He slept for a short while in the end, came awake suddenly, and realized that the trawler had virtually stopped. He lay there for a moment thinking about it, then got up and dressed in the clothes which had been provided—jeans, a heavy fisherman's sweater, and a reefer.

When he went out on deck it was still raining, but the sea was calmer as they rode in the lee of the shore. Anne-Marie stood at the rail watching while Devlin and Jean-Paul lowered one of the corpses over the side to Claude in a dinghy. The other lay on the deck on its back. The face was bound with a cloth to mask the mutilation, and it had been dressed in Brosnan's prison uniform, reefer, and the two life jackets.

"Your other self." Devlin knelt down and pushed up the sleeve, baring the tattooed prison number.

"You think of everything," Brosnan said.

"Jean-Paul, not me. I can see why that boy is such a successful crook."

They picked up the corpse between them and lowered it over the side to Claude and Jean-Paul, who had joined him. Brosnan said, "Roped together, don't forget that. The authentic touch."

"I won't." Jean-Paul started the outboard and turned the boat toward the shore.

The three of them leaned on the rail and watched it go. "And how does it feel, attending your own funeral?"

"Like Lazarus, risen again," Brosnan told him. "Washed clean."

"What for?" Anne-Marie said. "A reprise of the old life? Or a fresh start?"

"After I've dealt with Frank Barry, perhaps."

She shook her head. "There's the smell of death on you, Martin, do you know that? You'll never change."

She turned from the rail and went below. Brosnan said, "What's wrong with her?"

"Well, if you don't know, son, I can't tell you," Liam Devlin said.

There was considerable activity on the fish pier at St. Denis, as more than twenty trawlers unloaded their catch. Jacques Savary sat in the back of a black BMW limousine with Cresson. He looked much more his old self. He wore a cashmere sweater and an expensive sports jacket. Jean-Paul leaned in to tuck a traveling rug around his father's knees.

Brosnan, Devlin, and Anne-Marie stood watching, and as Jean-Paul stepped back Brosnan leaned in the car and took Savary's hand. "Maybe we can do it again some time?"

Savary held his hand for a moment and then, in an excess of emotion, pulled Brosnan close and embraced him.

Brosnan turned away, and Jean-Paul took his hand, his face serious in the yellow light of the lamp bracketed to the wall of the warehouse above their heads.

"To repay what you have done is an impossibility, but just remember this. We of the *Union Corse* can accomplish most things." He took out his wallet, extracted a card and passed it across. "My private numbers." He smiled crookedly. "All four of them. If there is ever anything you need, and I do mean anything. . . ."

He embraced Brosnan, holding him for a moment, shook hands with Devlin and Anne-Marie, got into the BMW, and nodded to Claude who had the wheel. The big limousine moved away along the wharf.

Brosnan watched it go, suddenly tired, at the end of things in some strange way. He turned to Devlin and Anne-Marie. "Now what?"

Anne-Marie took his arm. "Come on, soldier, from the looks of you I'd say you need to sleep for about a week."

She took the wheel of the rented Citroën, Devlin beside her, leaving Brosnan on his own in the back. "How long?" he asked as she drove away.

"This time in the morning, three hours if we're lucky. Go to sleep."

He closed his eyes, leaning back against the seat. At first there was only the Mill Race, the waters passing over him, his head filled with the stink of it, and then, suddenly, darkness.

It was just after six o'clock, dawn touching the horizon with light, as Pierre Gaudier left his cabin in the sand dunes a mile outside St. Denis. A packer on the day shift at the fish pier, he always started the day at first light, scavenging the beach before anyone else got there.

The handcart he pushed in front of him sported old automobile tires which moved well over the wet sand, and he paused every so often to pick up driftwood. When his cart was almost full, he was at the end of the beach where the final kick of the Mill Race hammered in across jagged black rocks. He paused to light a cigarette before turning back, and then noticed a flash of orange in the rocks up ahead. He flicked his match away and walked forward.

One of the bodies was draped across a rock, the other floated beside it in a pool, and the waves broke across both of them constantly. Gaudier crossed himself, then waded into the water, caught hold of the body in the pool and tried to pull it back to the beach. It was only then that he became aware of the line that held them together.

He scrambled up to the body on the rocks and fumbled at the line to untie it and immediately saw two things. The legend, *Department of Correction—Belle Isle,* stamped on the life jacket and the prison number stenciled in white across the back of the coat.

"My God," Gaudier said, crossing himself again, and he tried to turn the corpse over.

He saw the face then, or what was left of it, and staggered back in horror, losing his balance and falling into the pool beside the other body. He pushed it away from him with a hoarse cry, scrambled out of the water, and ran back along the beach to St. Denis.

It was just after nine o'clock, and Pierre Lebel sat in the anteroom of the governor's office at Belle Isle, totally crushed. What had happened was so unbelievable that he had been unable to take it in. His discovery of the empty cell on the upper tier at seven o'clock had coincided with the phone call from the chief of police in St. Denis to the governor.

How it had happened, how Savary and Brosnan had managed to achieve the impossible, was not relative now. The only important thing was the consequences. For Lebel, they could only lead in one direction. Instant dismissal, twenty-five years of service down the drain, and no pension.

The door opened and the governor beckoned to him. Lebel went in and stood at the desk while the governor lit a cigar and went to the window and peered out. What he said next was a total surprise.

"To enter such a sea as was running last night—quite incredible." He shook his head. "Magnificent idiots, that's what they were, Lebel. Why would they do such a thing, risk everything?"

Lebel amazed himself by saying, "To get off the rock, sir."

The governor was still looking out to sea. "Yes, well, we'd all like to do that, wouldn't we?"

There was a knock at the door, and the chief officer appeared. "The bodies have arrived from St. Denis, sir."

"Good," said the governor. "We'll take a look, shall we?"

* * *

It was cold in the mortuary, bitterly cold, and the two bodies dripped seawater as they lay on the slabs, still wearing the clothes and life jackets. The governor pushed back the sleeve of first one corpse and then the other and examined the tattooed numbers. He lifted the sheets to peer at the faces and replaced them hurriedly.

"So, that's what the Mill Race and those rocks at St. Denis do to a man." He turned to the chief officer. "Pity we can't show photos to every convict in the place."

"Yes, sir." The chief officer hesitated. "What happens now, sir?"

"I've spoken to the Minister of Justice in Paris. The story will be released to the press. No reason not to. All it proves is what we've known all along. That nobody escapes from Belle Isle."

"And the bodies, sir?"

"Disposed of in the usual way, exactly according to regulations, and today. I don't want any nonsense with relatives trying to claim them, particularly that son of Savary's. He's as big a crook as his father was." He turned to Lebel. "As for you, taking all the circumstances into consideration, I don't think you were really to blame for any of this. On the other hand, I must do something, if only for the records, so I'll fine you a month's salary."

Lebel, overcome with joy, could hardly speak. "Thank you, sir," he stammered.

The governor went out, and the chief officer said, "You're a lucky man, Pierre."

"You don't have to tell me," Lebel said fervently.

"Just as I don't have to remind you you've still got the funeral detail, so get on with it."

He went out, and Lebel turned and found old Jean, the mortuary orderly, standing between the two slabs. "Jacques Savary and Brosnan, eh?" He shook his head. "Who'd have thought it?"

He leaned down and examined the number on the forearm of the body on his right, then turned to the other. "Strange," he said.

"What is?"

"Savary's number. The seven is done the way the English do it."

Lebel put on his reading glasses, raised the arm and checked the number. The old man was right. The figure seven was plain, no line across the stem in the continental manner.

The old man gazed at him searchingly. "Maybe the tattooist made a mistake?"

Lebel put his glasses away and said quietly, "Bag them up, Jean, now. And this one, we do together. Okay?"

The old man smiled and shuffled away to his post.

They took them out through the main gate and pushed the handcart up the winding road to the funeral rock. Lebel got the necessary weights from the store, and they threaded them through the straps, taking one body each, not speaking.

It was a fine day, no rain now, only the sea stretching to a gray horizon where the sun was trying to come through. They pushed the cart to the outer edge of the rock, tipped it, and slid both bodies off together. They plunged into the swirling waters below and disappeared instantly.

Old Jean said, "The only way anyone gets off Belle Isle."

He turned and walked away, pushing the cart in front of him. Lebel said, "That's right," and then he added softly, "and good luck, you bastards, wherever you are."

Ferguson was working at his desk at Cavendish Square when the phone rang.

Harry Fox said, "Bad news, sir, just over the wire from Paris. Not had time to make the papers yet. Brosnan and Savary were drowned last night trying to escape from Belle Isle."

Ferguson put down his pen. "Are you sure about this, Harry?"

"No doubt about it, sir. The bodies were found on the beach outside a place called St. Denis this morning."

"So that's that," Ferguson said.

"Afraid so, sir. Any word from Devlin?"

"Not a thing."

"I should think he'll probably phone in any time now, sir, in view of what's happened."

"Very probably. Carry on, Harry. I'll see you later."

Ferguson replaced the receiver and sat there brooding for a moment, then got to his feet and stood at the window.

"Damn you, Brosnan," he whispered. "Why couldn't you have waited?"

Nikolai Belov's plane had been delayed for fourteen hours in Berlin because of fog, and he didn't arrive at Charles de Gaulle Airport until noon. He drove straight to the Soviet embassy and was taking off his overcoat, when Irana Vronsky came in with a cup of coffee.

She was a handsome, full-bodied woman of thirty-two, with calm eyes, black hair tied back with a velvet bow. The neat gray skirt, white silk blouse, dark stockings, and good shoes only accentuated her undeniable attractiveness.

She had been Belov's secretary for eight years, and he had seduced her within a month of her taking up the appointment. She was totally devoted to him and brushed aside his affairs with other women as being of no consequence. She was the one certainty in his life and was content.

There was nothing that went on in the office that she was not fully conversant with, and he had already spoken to her on the telephone the previous night.

"A bad flight, Colonel?" She always addressed him formally in the office.

"I prefer to forget the entire experience. That airport really is appalling, but never mind that now. Has Barry been in touch again?"

"Just over an hour ago. He said he'd ring back."

"And gave no explanation why he didn't make the rendezvous with the Northern Fleet trawler?"

"None, Colonel."

"Have you checked the British papers?"

She nodded. "Not a word of anything remotely similar to what Barry intended. There is an urgent communication from our London embassy, marked for your eyes only, Code Three. Perhaps that contains relevant information."

"Let's go and see."

Belov went out, and she followed him down to the coding room where she went to get the tape and the photos. The operator inserted it into the machine, Belov keyed it to his personal code. The machine chattered briefly, and the decoded information appeared on a printout sheet, which Irana tore off and handed to him.

The message gave Belov the fullest briefings on the Brosnan affair and also contained a full profile of Devlin and Anne-Marie Audin, illustrated by the photos he held in his hand.

He handed the lot to Irana. "What do you make of that?"

She read the report and frowned. "But there's

something about this in the latest edition of the morning paper, Colonel."

"Are you sure?"

"I'll show you." They went back along the corridor to her office, which was next to his. The Paris morning papers were on her desk. She hunted through them and finally said triumphantly, "There you are. Stop Press. Prisoners drowned trying to escape from Belle Isle prison. Martin Brosnan and Jacques Savary."

Belov took the paper from her, sat on the edge of the desk and read it. "This man, Savary, was quite a character," he said. "I thought his name sounded familiar."

"And Brosnan must have been a handful too," she said.

"Yes, it could have developed into a troublesome situation if it had come to anything."

The phone rang on her desk. She picked it up, spoke briefly then turned to Belov. "Barry."

Belov took the phone and didn't waste any time. "You're in Paris?"

"So it would appear," Barry said cheerfully.

"My apartment in thirty minutes," Belov said and put down the phone.

Barry stood at the railing of the terrace of the apartment on the Boulevard St. Germain and looked out across the river. "They really do you very well, your people," he said as Belov came through the open window and handed him a Scotch and soda.

"Never mind that sort of nonsense. Explanations, Frank, that's what I want. What went wrong over there?"

"Not a thing." Barry helped himself to a cigarette and sat down in a wicker chair. "Couldn't have gone better."

Belov was astonished. "You mean you actually did the job? But that's not possible. There hasn't been a word in the English newspapers."

"Security clampdown," Barry said, "which makes sense if you think of it. Anyway, all that's important is that I do have that rocket pod."

"Then why didn't you make the rendezvous with the Northern Fleet trawler?"

Barry chuckled. "Nikolai, this may come as a shock in view of our long relationship, but I don't trust your lot, and it occurred to me that if I once boarded that trawler with that very valuable piece of merchandise I might very well never get off again. You do follow me?"

"Nonsense." Belov was genuinely angry. "Haven't I always treated you fairly? When have I ever let you down?"

"Not you, old son, the sods back at headquarters I'm thinking of," Barry said. "This one is big, Nikolai. The biggest thing you've ever handled. You said that yourself. Maybe too big."

Belov took a deep breath. "What do you want?"

"A plane ready and waiting whenever I need

it. A Cessna will do. I'll fly her myself, of course."

"Where to?"

"Back to the Lake District. No problem. I'll find some suitable abandoned strip near where I want to be. I'll leave the plane there."

"And what about British air traffic control? They like to know who's flying in their air space."

"Oh, I'll be long gone by the time they discover where I put down."

Belov nodded reluctantly. "All right. There's a small flying club near Croix, just outside Paris. We've found it useful in the past. I'll see a suitable plane is ready and waiting for you. Now, what other nasty surprises have you in store for me?"

"Number one, the exchange takes place in Ireland, south of the border, of course." Belov started to explode, and Barry shook his head. "I won't have it any other way. Anything I've ever done can be construed as political, so I can't be extradited. I'm safe there. An old aunt of mine has an estate ten miles outside Cork, on the coast. Very suitable place to do business. I'll let you have details, naturally."

Belov put up a hand. "I wouldn't dream of disagreeing. Just tell me the rest and let's get it over with."

"Two million," Barry said. "That's what it's going to cost you."

Belov looked horrified. "Two million. You must be crazy."

"No, just thinking of retiring. I'm not getting any younger, old son." There was a heavy silence. He said, "I have got it, Nikolai, believe me. No matter how much of a security clampdown exists, your contacts in West Germany should be able to confirm what happened for you."

"True." Belov said. "I'm not able to speak on the money, though. I'll have to consult Moscow. I'll let you know."

"By tomorrow morning," Barry said. "I don't want to hang about."

Belov said wearily. "You're a bastard all the way through, Frank. I've always treated you fair and you do this to me. I should have known."

Barry helped himself to another whisky. "You learn something new every day."

Belov went into the living room and returned with the transcript of the message from London. "Better read that."

Barry finished reading and smiled. "Well, would you look at that now?" he whispered.

Belov said, "Have you seen the Paris papers this morning?"

"No, should I have?"

Belov tossed a newspaper across. "Noon edition. Makes interesting reading."

The story was there in full, together with photos of Savary and Brosnan. Barry read it through quickly. "Brosnan dead? That doesn't seem possible."

"It comes to us all."

"Not Martin Brosnan. You didn't know him like I did. Tried to kill me once."

"What for?"

"Oh, let's say he didn't approve of the way I carried on our particular war at that time."

Belov shrugged. "Old history, none of which has any relevance now that he's dead."

"But Devlin isn't," Barry said.

Belov frowned. "You think he's a threat?"

"He could give the Devil points, that one." Barry got up and walked to the railing. "I wonder what he's up to right now, or what's more to the point, where is he?"

"Somewhere in the area of St. Denis last night, waiting to receive Brosnan—must have been," Belov said.

"That's right, and the Audin girl with him. So where are they now?"

"Back in Paris, perhaps."

"Easy enough to find out. She must be in the phone book."

Five minutes later, the phone rang in Anne-Marie's Paris apartment. Her daily maid, who was in the kitchen, dried her hands and went to answer it.

The voice at the other end spoke excellent French, with a slight accent. "Mademoiselle Audin?"

"No, Monsieur, she isn't here. Who's speaking?"

"*Paris-Match*," Barry said smoothly. "It's important I get hold of her. Do you know where she is?"

"But of course, Monsieur. She phoned me here only an hour ago to say that she would be spending a few days on her farm."

"Farm?" Barry laughed warmly. "Sounds very unlike Anne-Marie."

"Oh, it's just a small place, Monsieur, near Vence, in the hills above Nice. A village called St. Martin. One old shepherd, a few sheep. Mademoiselle Audin uses it to get away from things. That's why she hasn't a telephone there."

The maid was the kind of woman who obviously couldn't stop talking, and Barry cut her off. "Never mind," he said. "I'll wait till she gets back," and he hung up.

"So what do you intend to do?" Belov demanded.

"I think I'll take a plane down to Nice. After all, it only takes an hour. Scout this place of hers out. See if she's got Devlin there with her."

"Why not let it go, Frank? As soon as I get your money confirmed from Moscow, you can be away. Why bother with this Devlin?"

"Old scores to settle there," Barry said. "And in any case curiosity was always my besetting sin. You might say I have a compulsion to find out what the bastard's up to."

"Have it your own way," Belov said wearily.

"I usually do, hadn't you noticed? One thing you can do is give me an address in Nice where I can pick up a little muscle if I need it. Nothing fancy, no nonsense about using their brains. Fist and boot men, that's what I want. Can you handle that?"

Belov nodded. "Yes, as it happens we have excellent connections in Nice. I can give you a suitable address."

"Great, I knew I could rely on you. I'll be in touch as soon as I get back." He grinned and slapped Belov on the shoulder. "Cheer up, old son. It might never happen."

TWELVE

The small farm high on the hill above St. Martin
looked rather medieval. It had a tower at one
end, and a roof covered in red pantiles, faded
by the sun. Devlin looked down to the village,
far below in the valley, the single ribbon of
road that zig-zagged up the hill to the farm.
The heat of the afternoon sun was warm on
his back, and he stretched lazily, turned back
to the farm, and went into the kitchen.

Anne-Marie stood at the wood stove, prepar-
ing dinner. She wore a tweed cap, open-necked
shirt, and overalls tucked into boots.

"How do you like it?" she demanded.

"A man could be happy here or go stark,
raving mad." She laughed, and he said, "What
about Martin?"

"Still fast asleep when I looked in." She put
the pan on the stove. "I'd like to have taken a
picture, but I didn't want to risk waking him.
He looked different."

"How different?"

"I don't quite know how to put it. Very
young."

Devlin lit a cigarette and sat down, shaking

his head. "Sure and you're kidding yourself there, girl dear. There are no young men, not in Martin's generation or yours, for that matter. All the hopes, all the aspirations disappeared a long time ago, swallowed up by the swamps of Vietnam and the brickfields and back alleys of Ulster."

She wiped her hands on a cloth and said gravely, "Yes, I'm afraid you're very probably right. The belief that life is a romantic affair is an essential ingredient missing in our generation. We learned, too young, that dishonesty is necessary for survival."

"What's that, the thought for today?"

Brosnan stood in the doorway wearing a woolen shirt and jeans. He badly needed a shave and his hair, still almost shoulder length, was tousled.

Anne-Marie said, "You look like a. . . ."

She searched for words, and he laughed. "Like what? A thoroughly dangerous convict on the run?"

"No chance." Devlin threw a newspaper across to him. "Anne-Marie's been down to the village store. Noon edition just in from Nice. You're dead and that's official."

Brosnan read the item through and showed no particular emotion. Anne-Marie said, "Don't you feel anything?"

"Not really." He ran his hands over his face. "What I could do with is some fresh air and a sense of space. How about a look over this sheep farm of yours?"

She turned to Devlin. He nodded. "Go on, get out of it," he said, "the both of you. I'll make myself a cup of tea and read a book or something."

Brosnan and Anne-Marie went outside, and he looked up toward the high hills, shielding his eyes from the sun. "Those sheep up there?"

"That's right. Spanish mountain sheep."

"A hell of a pull up those slopes to reach them."

"Oh, Old Louis, that's my shepherd, doesn't mind. He's been doing it all his life. I'm a little more up-to-date myself though."

She opened the barn door, and Brosnan saw a motorcycle up on its stand. "You mean you go up there on that?"

"That's what it's made for. It's Spanish as well. Montesa dirt bike. They'll do half a mile an hour if you want over rough ground in bottom gear. On the other hand, I usually do go rather faster than that."

"Okay," Brosnan said. "Show me."

"If you like."

She pushed the bike off its stand, wheeled it outside and mounted, kick-starting expertly. The engine roared, and he climbed on the pillion and put his hands round her waist.

"Okay, let's see what you can do."

She let in the clutch and they roared away.

*   *   *

The Montesa did everything she said it would, taking the slopes with a satisfying growl as she opened the throttle. When they ran out of track, she took to the hillside, climbing higher and higher until they went over a ridge and found sheep before them, scattered across the parched grass, grazing peacefully.

Finally, she braked to a halt beside a small whitewashed cottage, with a roof of red pantiles, in a slight depression surrounded by olive trees. To one side a wild and beautiful ravine dropped steeply.

"Old Louis uses this as a base when he's up here. Sometimes stays for weeks. He doesn't like it down there." She nodded to the valley, far below, St. Martin drowning in the late afternoon heat.

"I know what he means," Brosnan said.

She tried the door, and they went in. There was a living room and kitchen combined and a bedroom. The floors were stone flagged, the walls crudely plastered, but inside it was cool and dark as it was intended to be.

"He must be farther up," she said.

She lifted the wooden lid of a water cooler, took out a bottle of white wine, and found two glasses. They went back outside and sat on the bench against the wall. From somewhere lower down, there was the hollow jangle of a bell, remote, far away.

"That's the oldest ram, Hercules," she said. "Leader of the pack, or should I say the flock?"

She filled his glass and her own and stood there, looking down at the valley. "My favorite time of day. Everything seems to hang fire."

She turned briefly to him and smiled, and he realized, with a sense of discovery and as if it were the first time, that she was beautiful.

"People lived here once," he said. "In another world. Now they don't. Some of that lingers on. I suppose that's what your Old Louis is trying to recapture."

She sat down on the grass in front of him, ankles crossed. "What happens now, Martin?"

"To us, you mean?"

She shook her head with a kind of impatience. "No, to you."

"Well, first there's Frank Barry to take care of. The object of the exercise, after all."

"Let him go, Martin. There's no profit in it. He's a walking dead man. Next week or next year," she shrugged, "somewhere, someone's waiting for him. He must know that himself."

"Very probably, but I'd prefer to be that someone myself." Brosnan was quite calm, no evidence of emotion at all on his face. "This is personal, but then you know that?"

"Norah?" She shook her head. "You used to talk about her a lot, remember? From the sound of her, the last person to want you to pursue this thing."

"Perhaps," Brosnan said, "but then Norah was always too good for this life. She never made that most important discovery of all."

"And what would that be?"

"That it's not just a matter of the bastards like Frank Barry. Most people let you down, one way or the other in the end. A fact of life." There was an edge of bitterness in his voice when he said that.

She said, "Like me, you mean, or Liam, or Jean-Paul?" She put her glass down carefully, trying to control her anger. "And what about Martin Brosnan, who hauled an old man out of Belle Isle with him when it would have been a damn sight easier to do it on his own?"

"I owed him," Brosnan said. "We shared a cell for four years. He sustained me with his wit and his humor and his wisdom." He laughed harshly. "That's ironic, isn't it? A gangster who's spent most of his life on the wrong side of the law and still he has real virtues."

She got up and walked to the edge of the ravine and looked down into the valley again. When she turned, she was calmer. "All right, let's move on from Frank Barry. After that, what happens?"

"I don't know," he said. "Ireland, I suppose. The only place left where I'm safe."

"Back to that struggle of yours that was so important? My life for Ireland. Thompson guns by night and never wanting it to stop?"

"The only game we've got, you mean? When I picked up a rifle that night in Belfast, that first night, I was trying to stop people killing other people. Afterward, I found myself on a course there was no turning back from. Remember what Yeats said? Too long a sacrifice can make a stone of the heart." He shook his head. "Too much blood, my love, too many dead. Nothing's worth that. No more causes for me."

"So what will you do?"

"The Brosnans came from Kerry, remember? I bought a farm there a few years ago. Sheep mostly, just like this place." He laughed. "I like sheep. They don't take life too seriously."

"So you'd like to go back there?"

"It's quite a place. Sea and mountains, green grass, soft rain, fuschia growing in the hedges, glowing in the evening. *Deorini Dei*—the Tears of God, they call it." He laughed softly. "And the prettiest girls in all Ireland."

He had stood to stretch himself and found her watching him, the shadow of pain in her eyes. He moved close and reached for her hand. "You'd fit into the scene admirably."

He pulled her to him and kissed her on the mouth. Her lips were soft and dry, and he was trembling slightly, his stomach hollow with excitement. For a moment she responded, and then she took a deep, shuddering breath and pushed him away.

"No, Martin, I'm not starting that again. You see, in spite of what you've said, I don't think you've changed. I think you'll always be the movement's official undertaker. Now let's go."

She turned and walked back to the motorcycle.

* * *

Frank Barry alighted from the Paris plane at Nice airport at four-thirty. He picked up a Peugeot from one of the rental firms, checked on the location of St. Martin, and drove straight there. It only took him an hour. A drink at one of the village's two cafes and a talkative waiter gave him the location of Anne-Marie Audin's farm. By six o'clock he was crouched behind a wall in an olive grove on the other side of the valley, examining the farm through binoculars.

The only sign of life was the smoke from one of the chimneys rising in a straight line in the still air. He lit a cigarette and waited. About fifteen minutes later, the door opened and Liam Devlin strolled into the yard.

"Well now," Barry said softly. "Would you look at that?"

He became aware of a humming sound somewhere in the distance, realized that it was an engine moving closer, swept the hillside above the farmhouse with his binoculars, and found the motorcycle.

It looked like two men at first glance, Anne-Marie had the peak of her cap low over her eyes. He couldn't make out the face of the man behind. The motorcycle entered the yard and came to a halt. As Devlin moved toward them, Anne-Marie took off her cap, shaking her hair down, and Brosnan paused to light a cigarette, giving Barry a clear look at his face.

Barry laughed, a feeling of intense pleasure

coursing through him that he couldn't explain, even to himself. "God save us, Martin," he said softly, "but you've done it again, you bastard."

The three of them went into the house. Barry waited for a while, then walked back down the track to where he had left the Peugeot.

"What's our next move?" Brosnan asked Devlin.

It was after dinner, and they sat in the lamplight by the fire smoking. Through the half-open door Anne-Marie could be heard working in the kitchen.

"There is only one possible move," Devlin said. "Barry's KGB contact in Paris, this fella Belov."

"We can't exactly go knocking at the door of the Soviet embassy."

"No need. Ferguson supplied me with his address. He has an apartment on the Boulevard St. Germain."

"That's it, then," Brosnan said. "We start for Paris tomorrow."

Anne-Marie walked in with tea and coffee on a tray in time to hear his words, and Devlin's reply, "Jesus, Martin, would you give us time to catch our breath?"

"I don't see any point in hanging about," Brosnan told him.

"He can't wait to get to the funeral, you see," Anne-Marie said and went back into the kitchen.

Devlin said, "Since there's no help for it, I'd better get you tooled up."

He went out. Brosnan poured the tea and drank it with conscious pleasure. A luxury denied him on Belle Isle. He was pouring a second cup when Devlin returned with a small suitcase which he placed on the table and opened.

"A parting gift from Jean-Paul Savary. I didn't bring any hardware through from London with me. Couldn't take a chance on the customs."

There were two Brownings, a short-barreled Smith and Wesson revolver, and a sinister-looking Mauser with the bulbous silencer.

"Very interesting," Brosnan said and picked up the Mauser.

"That takes me back," Devlin told him. "Model 1932. Specially developed for German counterintelligence operatives. Ten-round magazine."

Brosnan reached in the case and took out a sleeveless vest whose nylon surface gleamed in the lamp light. "Flak jacket?"

"What we call the up-market model for the man who has everything," Devlin told him. "Manufactured by the Wilkinson Sword Company. Nylon and titanium. Jean-Paul tells me they can stop a .44-magnum bullet at point-blank range."

"Very impressive," Anne-Marie said from the doorway. "You're going to war again then?"

Brosnan said evenly, "I think I'll get some

sleep now. Let's get an early start in the morning."

"All right," Devlin said.

Brosnan brushed past Anne-Marie without speaking to her. After he had gone, she came to the table, shut the lid of the case angrily, and sat down.

"I told you not to try and make him into something he isn't," Devlin said.

She shook her head. "He's changed, Liam. Different from what I expected."

"Girl, dear, he was never what you thought he was in the first place. The dark hero who came headfirst out of the reeds in Vietnam to save you was a man, just as ill-formed and fallible as the rest of us. Those photos you took over the years showed only the surface of things. The danger in your profession."

"I never truly understood him," she said. "I see that now."

"A good feature for the center page," Devlin said. "And the camera likes him. You always made him look good."

"Him and his damn roses," she said bitterly. "Something else I never understood. Getting into the GOC's office at Army headquarters in Lisburn that time and leaving a rose instead of a bomb, as if to say Brosnan was here. Games for children."

"Oh, I don't know," Devlin said. "That's partly the poet in him, I suppose. The lover of what you French call the *beau geste*. But there's more to it than that. The Plains Indians in America, the Sioux and the Cheyenne, had an interesting variation on the war theme. The bravest thing a warrior could do was get close enough in battle to touch the enemy with a stick. That was the real measure of a man's bravery, not whether he'd killed his enemy or not."

"And you think that's what he was doing with his roses? Saying look how brave I am?"

"No," Devlin said gravely. "I think what he was really saying was, I could have killed you but I didn't, so perhaps we should think again. Find another way."

"I don't know, Liam." She stood up wearily. "Too complex for me, and so is he. I'm going to bed."

She kissed him on the forehead and went out.

Behind the golden façade of the Côte d'Azur, the underworld of Nice was as tough and as ruthless as that of Paris or Marseilles, Barry knew that. The address Belov had given him turned out to be a small back street nightclub not far from the harbor, run by a man named Charles Chabert.

He was a small man, a surprisingly civilized-looking individual with a mustache and gold-rimmed glasses. His dark suit was of excellent cut and as sober as his general image. His cognac was excellent, too, and Barry sipped a little and smiled his appreciation.

"Muscle," he said. "That's all I need. My contact in Paris assured me you were just the man to provide it."

Chabert nodded. "I have a certain reputation, Monsieur, that is true. How many men would you need?"

"Three."

"To go up against?"

"Two."

Chabert looked surprised. "With you, that makes four. Is that necessary?"

"To take care of the two I have in mind it is."

"I see. Formidable?"

"You could say that. I need them first thing tomorrow. A morning's work only. I'll pay you twenty thousand francs."

"Would there be the possibility of a little shooting?"

"Definitely."

Chabert nodded. "I see. Then in that case, the price will be thirty thousand. Forty," he added, "to include my fee."

"Done." Barry smiled cheerfully and held out his hand. "One thing, I'm in sole charge. You make that clear. No cowboys."

"But naturally, Monsieur. These are my own people. They do as I say." He picked up the internal telephone and said, "Send Jacaud, Leboeuf, and Deville to my office."

"They sound like a cabaret act," Barry said.

"In a way, that's what they are. Excellent

professional performers. Let me give you another cognac."

A moment later, there was a knock at the door.
It opened and three men filed in. They stood
against the wall, waiting. In spite of the good
suits, Barry had only to look at the faces to know
they were exactly what he was looking for.

"Satisfied, Monsieur?" Chabert asked.

"Perfectly."

"Good, then perhaps you would be kind
enough to settle now. Cash in advance is the
one policy I always strictly adhere to. Life,
after all, is an uncertain matter, and we are all
vulnerable—even you, my friend, particularly
when involved in an affair like this."

Barry, who had come prepared, courtesy of
Belov, laughed and took a thick wad of notes
from his inside pocket.

"You know, I like you, old son, I really do,"
he said, and started to count out the agreed fee
in thousand-franc notes.

Devlin usually woke at dawn, the habit of years,
but that following morning he overslept and
discovered, when he opened his eyes, that it
was eight-thirty. He got up quickly, had a
shower, and then dressed.

He hesitated, looking at the bulletproof vest,
then decided to try it and put it on under his
shirt. As it weighed sixteen pounds he knew
he was wearing it, but it fitted snugly enough
and was not particularly uncomfortable.

When he went into the kitchen, Brosnan was sitting at the table eating scrambled eggs. Anne-Marie turned from the stove. She looked tired, dark circles under her eyes, as if she had slept badly.

"There you are. What would you like, eggs?"

Devlin shook his head. "I haven't eaten breakfast in years. A cup of tea would be fine." He sat down opposite Brosnan. "And how are you this beautiful morning?"

"Couldn't be better," Brosnan said. "The first time I've done this in years." He reached across and opened Devlin's shirt, disclosing the vest. "You've got a button undone. What are you wearing that for?"

"Oh, I thought I'd give it a try," Devlin told him. "You should try yours. It's fun." He swallowed the tea Anne-Marie gave him and stood up. "When are we leaving?"

"Whenever you like. How are we going, by road or air?"

"By road will take forever. On the other hand, it might be safer. There's that face of yours to consider."

"I'm dead, Liam," Brosnan said. "Nobody will look at me twice, and that picture in the paper was five or six years old. Another thing, I had short hair then. A pair of sunglasses, and I'm laughing."

"All right," Devlin said. "Air it is. You get ready. I'm just dropping down to the village to make a telephone call."

"Ferguson?"

"He might just have something to say that's worth hearing."

"If it's about Barry, I'll buy that."

Devlin turned to Anne-Marie. "I'll take the Citroën if I may."

She handed him the keys. "One thing, Liam, when you go it's without me."

"I see." He glanced at Brosnan who continued to eat stolidly. "Whatever you think best, girl dear." He held her hand for a brief moment, turned, and went out.

Barry had driven up from Nice in the Peugeot, followed by the three hoods in a small van with the name of a well-known Nice electrical contractor on the side panel. They drew into a rest stop just outside St. Martin, and Jacaud got out of the van and pretended to be tinkering with the engine. Barry drove into the village. He was not sure of his next move. It certainly wouldn't do to just drive up to the farm. On that narrow road, they would be seen coming all the way up from the village.

In any case, the situation was taken out of his hands for as he pulled in beside the church, he saw Devlin at the wheel of the Citroën getting gasoline at the filling station further along the street.

Barry got out the Peugeot and dodged into the church, leaving the door slightly open, and watched.

                    *   *   *

Devlin pulled out of the filling station, turned across the street, and parked under a tree. He got out and walked over to the cafe. A young woman was washing the half-dozen tables and chairs that stood outside.

"Morning, Monsieur," she said. "You would like coffee?"

"Never touch the filthy stuff," Devlin told her, "but if you've got a cup of tea, that would be fine after I've used the telephone."

"My father's using it at the moment, Monsieur, phoning our weekly order to the wholesaler in Nice. He shouldn't be long. I could get you the tea while you wait."

"And why not?" Devlin lit a cigarette, sat down, and turned his face to the morning sun.

It was very quiet in the church, winking candles and incense heavy on the cold air, and down by the altar the Virgin seemed to float out of darkness, a slight, fixed smile on her face. No one waited by the confessional boxes. The place seemed quite empty, and then Barry saw that there was a young boy at the altar, kneeling in prayer. He stood up, crossed himself, and walked to the door.

"Are you looking for the *curé*, Monsieur? He's not here. He's gone to Vence."

He was only nine or ten, and Barry ruffled his hair and smiled. "No, I'm watching a friend of mine. See, the man over there at the cafe?"

"I see, Monsieur."

"I tell you what," Barry said. "Let's play a trick on him."

"A trick, Monsieur?"

"That's right. You go over and tell him the priest wants to see him. Then when he walks in, he'll get a big shock when he sees me." He took out his wallet and produced a ten-franc note.

The boy's eyes went round. "For me, Monsieur?"

Barry slipped it into his pocket. "Off you go now, and mind you don't give the game away."

Devlin's eyes closed as he turned his face to the sun, and he was not aware of the boy's approach until he tugged at his sleeve.

"Monsieur?" the boy said timidly.

"What is it, son?"

"The priest, Monsieur, in the church." He waved vaguely. "He asked me to get you."

"The priest?" Devlin smiled good-humoredly. "But I don't know him. There must be some mistake."

"Oh, no, Monsieur, he pointed you out to me. He said the gentleman at the table, and you are the only one."

Devlin looked around him. "So I am, that's a fact. All right, let's see what he wants."

He tried to take the boy's hand, but he turned and ran away. Devlin shrugged and walked across the street, passing the Peugeot, and went up the steps. He paused, the innate caution

that was the product of years of living danger-
ously sending his hand into his pocket to feel
for the butt of the Browning.

It was dark in the church after the bright
morning sunshine. He stood just inside the
door, waiting, and someone said in French in a
hoarse whisper, "Over here, Monsieur Devlin."

He was aware of the cassock, the figure in-
substantial in the gloom. "What is it?" he demanded and stepped forward.

"A message from Jacques Savary, Monsieur.
Please—in here."

The priest moved into the confessional box,
drawing the curtain, and Devlin went into the
other side and sat down. The whole thing made
perfect sense now, of course. Savary and his
son, after all, were the only people who knew
where they were.

There was a movement on the other side of
the grill, and the voice said, "Have you anything to confess, my son?"

"Well, I've sinned most grievously, Father,
and that's a fact, but what about Savary?"

"He can roast in hell as far as I'm concerned,
Liam, me old son, along with you!"

The Ceska in Barry's right hand coughed
twice, ripping through the grill, slamming into
Devlin, hurling him back against the side of
the confession box. There was a fractional moment when he fought for air and then total
darkness.

Barry opened the curtain and looked down

at him sprawled in the corner. "All debts paid, Liam," he said softly.

He pulled the cassock he had borrowed from the vestry over his head, flung it into a pew, closed the curtain on Devlin again and went out.

Unlike Devlin, Brosnan put the nylon and titanium vest on over his shirt. It didn't look too bad after all. In fact it went quite well with his jeans. He pulled on the reefer and slipped one of the Brownings into his righthand pocket. The Mauser went into his belt at the rear, snug against his back.

He smiled, remembering that it was Devlin who'd taught him that. He took the Smith and Wesson with the short barrel, hefted it in his hand, and went into the bathroom. He found a roll of surgical tape in the cabinet over the washbasin, tore a couple of lengths off and taped the Smith and Wesson to the inside of his left leg, just above the ankle, covering it with his sock.

When he went into the kitchen the radio was playing, but there was no sign of Anne-Marie. He found her sitting on a bench outside in the morning sun, eyes closed. He strolled across and paused, uncertain what to say. Below him he could see the Citroën coming up the winding road.

"Liam's coming," he said.

"Is he?"

He leaned on the wall. "Do you still paint?"

"Yes," she said, "only in watercolor now. I've given up oils."

"Devlin once told me that any fool could paint in oils, but that it took a real painter to master watercolors."

Behind him Devlin's Citroën moved into the courtyard and still she kept her eyes closed. "Go away, Martin, just go away."

"All right, if that's the way you want it," Brosnan said and turned toward the Citroën. It took a moment for him to see that the man leaning out of the window of the car, Jacaud, was holding a revolver and that it was pointing straight at him. Suddenly Frank Barry, who had been hidden from view, sat up in the rear seat and kicked the door open. When he got out, the Ceska in his hand was pointing at Brosnan, too.

The van drew into the yard, and Leboeuf and Deville got out. "Shall I see if he's carrying a gun, Monsieur?" Jacaud asked.

"Oh, I think we can take that for granted."

Jacaud found the Browning in Brosnan's righthand pocket. "Where's Liam?" Brosnan demanded.

"In hell, I shouldn't wonder. When last seen, he looked very dead indeed."

Anne-Marie said, "No, not that."

Brosnan took a step forward, hands coming up. "You bastard!" he said.

Jacaud slashed him across the kidneys with

the barrel of his gun, and Brosnan cried out and went down on one knee.

"The right place for you." Barry said and nodded to Jacaud. "Frisk him again. He always was a tricky one. Favored the back of his belt as I remember."

Jacaud found the Mauser and passed it across. "Nasty," Barry said and gave it back to him. "A bit old-fashioned for me. Now let's have the girl."

She tried to run and Leboeuf and Deville grabbed her between them and rammed her against the car. Brosnan, fighting for breath, looked up. "What do you want with her?"

"You can think about that in hell, Martin."

Jacaud said, "Do we kill her?"

For a second, Barry seemed to see Jenny Crowther stagger forward as his bullet struck her in the back. He said savagely, "No, you bloody well don't. I'll take care of her myself."

He took a black plastic case from his pocket, opened it and produced a disposable syringe, ready filled. "I don't mind you keeping Devlin company, Martin, but your girlfriend here—now that seems an awful waste."

Anne-Marie cried out as the needle went in. Within seconds, she was collapsing, and Barry pushed her into the rear seat of the Citroën and tucked a traveling rug across her.

"She'll sleep like a baby, all the way to Paris."

"Drugs," Brosnan said through clenched teeth. "Just your style."

Barry frowned. "Come off it, me old son. She'll sleep like a baby for ten hours and then wake without even a headache."

He got into the Citroën and started the engine. Jacaud said, "What do we do with him?"

"Officially he's dead already," Barry said. "So I suppose the answer is obvious."

"Haven't you got the stomach to do it yourself, Frank?" Brosnan said. "Look me in the eye while you pull the trigger, or maybe you'd prefer me to turn my back?"

Jacaud and Deville held him down as he struggled, and Barry laughed. "You used to despise me, Martin. I wasn't good enough for you and your bloody cause. In the end, you're the one on his knees in the muck, and that's how I want to remember you. Not even worth the killing myself."

He drove away, and Jacaud and Deville hauled Brosnan to his feet and took him between them into the barn followed by Leboeuf. They sent him staggering forward with a vicious push that put him on his knees again.

Leboeuf moved across the barn to examine an old cart. "What a dump," he said.

Deville leaned against the wall by the door and Jacaud came forward, the Mauser in his hand. Brosnan got up, staggered to an old bench against the wall and slumped down.

"This is it, then?" he said.

Jacaud shrugged. "You should have stayed home, my friend."

"So it would appear."

Brosnan leaned over, groaning in pain and got his right hand to the butt of the Smith and Wesson he had taped so carefully to the inside of his left leg. He groaned again and sank to one knee. Jacaud moved in close, grabbed Brosnan by the hair, and yanked his head back just as Brosnan tore his Smith and Wesson free and in the same motion fired straight at Jacaud's heart.

The force of the shot at such close range lifted Jacaud off his feet, slamming him into the ground. In the same instant, Brosnan shot Leboeuf in the back before he could turn, the bullet shattering his spine, driving him head-first into the cart.

At the door, Deville screamed, trying to draw his gun, already too late as the Smith and Wesson arced toward him. Brosnan's third bullet caught him in the center of the forehead, and Deville went backward into the yard.

There was silence and Brosnan stood there for a moment, quite still, legs apart, perfectly balanced, the Smith and Wesson ready. He was like a different man, another human being altogether.

After a moment, he slipped the Smith and Wesson into his pocket and retrieved the Mauser and the Browning from Jacaud. Then he crossed to the Montesa, shoved it off its stand, kick-started it savagely, and roared out across the yard and down the road toward St. Martin.

THIRTEEN

The old priest couldn't tell at first whether the man lying there was drunk or very ill. "Monsieur," he said in his querulous voice, shaking Devlin, "are you all right?"

Devlin opened his eyes slowly.

"Thank God," the priest said.

Devlin saw the old priest bending over him. He felt as if he'd been kicked very hard several times in the body, and he ran a hand over the general area of his heart and through a rent in his shirt found one of the bullets Barry had fired at him embedded in the vest.

"Have you been drinking?" the priest demanded.

"Not at all, Father." Devlin managed to smile. "You can smell my breath. A touch of malaria, that's all."

"Malaria?" the priest said, astonished as Devlin painfully got up and righted the chair.

"Picked it up in the tropics years ago. Still get a touch now and then in the most unexpected places."

He walked to the door and found that it hurt him to breathe so that when he went outside, he leaned against the wall at the top of the steps for a moment. Brosnan arrived on the motorcycle at that precise moment and braked to a halt beside the Citroën, which was parked at the bottom of the steps.

Devlin said, "How in the hell did that get there? I left it under the tree by the cafe."

"Frank Barry took it to drive up to the farm. I thought it was you, Liam. He took us completely by surprise."

"No more than he did me. Shot me smack in the center of my chest." Devlin pulled the round out of the vest and held it up. "Jesus, Martin, but these things are a wonderful invention. All it did was knock me cold for a while. I'll see that bastard in hell yet."

"Not if I see him first," Brosnan said. "He's taken Anne-Marie."

"He's what?" Devlin was shocked. "Then how come he left you in one piece?"

Brosnan explained. When he'd finished, Devlin said. "So, he came down here, transferred her to his own car, and cleared off. Come to think of it, there was another car here when I walked across to the church."

"Can you remember what it was?"

"A Peugeot, I think. A sedan."

"Right, let's get after him."

Brosnan started down the steps, and Devlin lurched after him. "Just a minute, Martin, where to?"

"Paris. When he gave her that shot in the

arm he said it would keep her quiet all the way to Paris."

"All right, so which way has he gone? Five miles north of here, you have a choice of three separate routes through the Alps to Lyons. On the other hand, maybe he's cut down toward the coast to take the route from Cannes to Avignon, or would you like me to make a few more suggestions?"

Brosnan kicked the side of the car in frustration. "Why in hell did he take her? What for?"

"The whim of the moment. Maybe he just wanted you to know that he had her when you died. Like pulling the wings off flies. There is only one real certainty in this whole business. He's going to Paris, and Paris means Belov. Now, if we caught a plane from Nice, we'd be there before him. He has to drive all the way, can't do any other with Anne-Marie in the car."

"By God, you're right," Brosnan said. "Let's get moving."

"Not just yet." Devlin tried to ease his sore ribs. "One puzzle remains. How in hell Frank Barry knew we were here. Just give me five minutes to phone Ferguson."

It was Harry Fox who picked up the telephone. He listened for a moment, then turned to Ferguson. "Devlin, sir."

"Give it to me." Ferguson snatched it from

him. "For God's sake, Devlin, where have you been?"

"Never mind that now. Can you explain to me how Frank Barry managed to trace Brosnan and me to the Audin girl's farm at St. Martin?"

"Brosnan?" Ferguson said in astonishment. "But I thought he was dead."

"Well you shouldn't believe everything you read in the papers. But what about Barry? The bastard just tried to shoot me dead. Now he's gone haring off to Paris with Anne-Marie Audin."

Ferguson said, "Look, Devlin, it's a tricky one to explain. There was a leak here, I'm afraid. Someone passing on information to the KGB in London."

"About our little affair?"

"I'm afraid so. I should imagine details were passed to Belov in Paris, and, naturally, he would have alerted Barry."

"Well thanks very much," Devlin said. "Nothing like efficiency. That's what built the Empire. You'll excuse me if I ring off now."

"But Devlin," Ferguson said hastily, "what are you going to do?"

"Well, we don't exactly have a choice, do we? Go to Paris to see Colonel Nikolai Belov."

He left the cafe and got into the passenger seat of the Citroën. "What did you find out?" Brosnan asked.

"Nice airport, quick as you like," Devlin said. "I'll tell you on the way."

*   *   *

Barry took the scenic route through the High Alps. At Grenoble, he took the road for Lyons and stopped a few miles further on at a small roadside garage to fill his tank. Anne-Marie slept peacefully in the rear seat.

The old man at the pumps said, "Madame looks as if she's enjoying herself."

The traveling rug had slipped, and Barry reached over and tucked it around her tenderly. "Yes, we're on our way to Paris. The best way to pass the time on these long trips. Can I use your telephone?"

"But of course, Monsieur. In the office."

"Thanks," Barry said. "If you could check the oil, water, and tires, I'll be obliged."

When he dialed Belov's special number at the embassy, it was Irana who answered. "Barry here. Is he there?"

"Just a moment."

"How did things go?" Belov asked.

"Couldn't be better. You may be surprised to know that both the gentlemen in question were still around."

"Is that so? Presumably you took care of that?"

"Oh, yes. You might say I closed the books. Have you any news for me?"

"Yes, the business deal we discussed? I'm assured there will be no cash-flow problem. You may proceed with the arrangements as soon as you like."

"Good, then I'd like the transportation you promised arranged for tonight. Any problems?"

"None that I can see."

"I'll see you at Croix, then, round about midnight."

As the old man came into the office, Barry put the phone down. "What's the damage?"

"Two-fifty, Monsieur."

Barry paid him and slapped down an extra fifty-franc note. "That should cover the phone call."

"Monsieur, please, it's too much," the old man said.

"Nonsense," Barry said. "Things are going rather well for me at the moment. I'd like you to share my good fortune."

He got behind the wheel and turned for a quick look at the girl. She still slept peacefully, all lines gone, no strain there at all. He smiled, patted her face and drove away.

Brosnan and Devlin arrived at the Nice airport to receive their first major setback. The departure schedule board indicated delays on all flights to Paris.

"I'll see what the problem is," Devlin said.

He left Brosnan by the newsstand and approached the Air France ticket counter where a couple of charming and imperturbable young women were doing their best to placate a queue of very angry passengers.

When it was Devlin's turn he said, "What's the trouble at Paris?"

"The firemen are on strike at Charles de Gaulle. That means the guys at Orly and Le Bourget back them in the interests of union solidarity."

Devlin said, "And how long will the comedy continue?"

"I honestly don't know. Last time it was twenty-four hours, but they like to keep everyone guessing. You know how it is, Monsieur?"

"Indeed I do." Devlin turned and hurried back to Brosnan.

"Could be tomorrow."

"To hell with that," Brosnan said. "Tomorrow could be too late. The train schedule from Nice is no damn good. We'll just have to go by road and step on it, that's all."

He took Devlin's arm and hurried him out of the entrance and across the concourse to the parking lot.

Croix was exactly what Barry had expected, a small airfield with a control tower, two hangars, and three Nissen huts, headquarters of a flying club according to the sign on the gate.

The doors to one of the hangars were open, and the Cessna 310 stood outside. There was a dark BMW sedan parked beside it, and when Barry braked and switched off his engine he heard voices. Belov and Irana Vronsky walked out, a small, dark man in white coveralls following them.

Barry got out and went to meet them. "Is this it?" he asked, nodding at the Cessna.

"That's right. The best Deforges could do at such short notice. He's my man here."

"Perhaps we could go to my office and discuss the destination?" Deforges said.

"Fine." Barry opened the rear door of the car, leaned inside, then stood up holding Anne-Marie in his arms. "Have you got a couch or something handy in there? My friend here is still sleeping it off."

Deforges glanced at Belov as if for guidance, then shrugged. "I suppose so."

He led the way into the hangar, and Barry followed, Belov and Irana walking beside him. "The Audin girl? This is crazy. What do you intend to do with her?"

"Take her with me."

They had reached a glass-walled office, and Deforges opened another door and showed him into a tiny room with a washbasin and a small bed covered with army blankets.

"You can have this."

He went out and Barry laid Anne-Marie on the bed. Irana leaned over her and put a hand on her forehead. "How long will she be out?"

"Another hour."

"But what are you playing at, Frank?" Belov demanded.

"Well, it was either kill her or bring her

along, and I've never been very good at knocking off women."

"You're mad."

"So they tell me."

"Haven't you enough on your hands without this woman?"

"You let me worry about that." Barry pushed him and Irana out and closed the door. "Now, what about this plane?"

"It's outside on the runway," Belov said.

"All right," Barry said. "The English Lake District, that's my target, particularly the coastal area."

Deforges rummaged through his chart drawer and finally found what he was looking for. Barry ran his fingers down the Cumberland coast. "Ravenglass. There should be an old RAF station a few miles south. Yes, there it is. Tanningley Field."

"It's marked as no longer operational," Deforges pointed out.

"That's right, but the runway is perfectly usable. I've seen it. How long should it take me in the Cessna?"

"Well, its cruising speed is a hundred and sixty, but it all depends on the weather. I'll call Orly and find out."

He went into the other office and picked up the telephone. Barry lit a cigarette and said, "I've been thinking, Nikolai, it would be very unfortunate if I arrived to find anyone wait-

ing for me. That young fellow who met me on
Morecambe pier last time, remember?"

Irana flushed angrily, opened her mouth to
speak, but Belov cut her off. "Frank, why must
you talk like this? We have a deal. I accept
your terms. I want no further trouble or
difficulty. All I want is that rocket pod."

"Good," Barry said, "so there's nothing to
worry about then."

Deforges came back. "There's a head wind
and a low coming in from the Irish Sea that
could bring heavy rain by morning. Even a
chance of fog. In the circumstances, I'd allow
four and a half hours flight time. Possibly five,
and you'll need light to land on such a field."

"What time is dawn?"

"Just after seven."

"All right, I'll leave about two-thirty in the
morning."

"One problem," Deforges said. "You'll have
to be officially routed both for leaving France
and entering English air space."

Barry nodded. "So where do you think I
should be going?"

Deforges looked at the map for a few moments.
"Ronaldsway Airport on the Isle of Man. Only
fifty miles from your final destination on the
English coast. At the last moment, tell the
Ronaldsway air traffic control people that you
are diverting to Blackpool. Then I suggest you
make an approach across the sea to Tanningley
at under six hundred feet. At that height, you

won't show up on any radar screens. Of course, someone may see you land, but at that time of the morning there shouldn't be too many people around."

"It doesn't matter, anyway," Barry said. "I'll be out of it again before you know it. You get things moving then. I've got a telephone call to make."

Deforges went out, and Barry went into the other office, closed the door, and picked up the phone. Irana and Belov watched him through the glass.

"I don't trust him, Nikolai," she said. "He's made a fool of you once. He could do it again."

"I don't really have much choice, my love. I must get my hands on that rocket pod. . . ."

"So they can pat you on the head, promote you to general, and transfer you to Moscow?" she said. "To be perfectly frank, Nikolai, I'd rather stay in Paris."

He frowned impatiently. "I've warned you before about talking like that. One of these days you'll forget yourself and do it in the wrong company."

"I only do it out of concern for you."

"I know." He kissed her on the cheek with genuine affection. "No point in you hanging on here any longer, particularly as you have your own car with you. Go on back to the apartment."

"What about you?"

"I'll see Barry off, then I'll join you."

She squeezed his hand, picked up her fur

coat, and went out. Belov lit a cigarette and watched Barry, who was now engaged in conversation with someone.

At Marsh End, Henry Salter was just about to go up to bed when the phone rang. He answered it without hesitation, for in the funeral business one got used to the fact that people died at any hour of the day or night.

"Henry Salter."

"Is that you, me old son? Sinclair here."

Salter's stomach turned hollow, and he pulled a chair forward and sat down. "What can I do for you, Mr. Sinclair?" he asked, voice shaking.

"How are things with you since I left? Any problems?"

"A lot of police activity about twenty miles up the dale from here toward Wastwater."

"Oh, yes. What happened?"

"Nobody seems to know."

Barry laughed. "That's really very good. When we parted, I said I'd be back and I will. You know the old airfield at Tanningley?"

"Yes."

"I'll be landing there in a light plane a bit after seven in the morning. Meet me in the Land Rover."

"But it hasn't been used for years, that airfield," Salter said.

"Five thousand pounds, in cash, for your very valuable assistance. I'll be away again within a couple of hours. How about it?"

Salter struggled against his natural greed and lost. "I'll be there, Mr. Sinclair."

"See that you are," Barry said and put down the phone.

Devlin and Brosnan reached Paris just after one and went straight to the address on the Boulevard St. Germain. Belov's apartment was on the top floor of a luxury building of some distinction.

"What do we do if he isn't in?" Brosnan asked.

"How would I know, boy? Wait for him. Try picking the lock. We'll see."

They walked along the carpeted corridor and paused at the door numbered thirteen. "Unlucky for some," said Devlin and punched the bell.

There was a pause and then the door was flung open, and Irana Vronsky said, "What kept you, darling, I. . . ."

The smile faded from her face. Brosnan moved fast, his hand on her jaw, holding the mouth closed so that she couldn't scream, ramming her back into the apartment. Behind him Devlin closed the door.

Brosnan threw her on the couch and produced the silenced Mauser. "This thing doesn't make a sound. Any trouble, I'll blow your head off. Now, where's Belov?"

Irana took a deep breath to pull herself together. "Go to hell!"

She wore a superb black silk dressing gown

that gaped as she tried to get up, revealing black silk stockings and a hint of garter belt. Brosnan shoved her down again.

Devlin said, "Dressed like that, I think we can safely assume the lady is expecting the colonel at any moment. All we have to do is wait." He sat down opposite her, helped himself to a Russian cigarette from a box on the table and sniffed it. "Bolshevik firecrackers. I had a friend once who smoked these things. Picked up a taste for them in the Winter War, but that was before your time. Would you by any chance know who I am?"

"You take a very good photo," she said calmly.

"And my friend?"

"Mr. Brosnan looks extremely healthy for a dead man."

Which was a bad mistake, and Devlin seized on it at once. "So, you've either seen or been in touch with Frank Barry."

She sat there, glaring at him, furiously angry with herself for being so stupid. "What do you want?" she demanded.

"Well, a nice cup of tea would do for a start," Liam Devlin told her.

Anne-Marie opened her eyes, stretched, and lay there, staring up at the light bulb above her head. Her mind was blank, and she wondered where on earth she was—and then she remembered the men at the farm, Martin on his knees. She sat up and found Barry sitting on the end of the bed watching her. Amazing how calm she was, no headache, no after-sleep drowsiness.

"Where are we?" she asked.

"A little airport outside Paris." There was a pot of coffee and a couple of cups on a tray beside him. He filled one and passed it across. "Drink this." She hesitated, and he smiled and sipped some himself. "Satisfied?"

She took the cup, and the door opened and Belov entered. "Ready to go whenever you like, Frank. Deforges has got the engines turning over." He glanced at Anne-Marie. "Does she still go with you?"

Barry looked at her inquiringly. "Well?"

"Do I have a choice?"

He laughed and turned to Belov. "She goes."

Belov shrugged and went out. Anne-Marie said, "Is it permitted to ask the destination?"

"The English Lake District. You'll enjoy that. Lovely at this time of the year. Afterward, if you're a good girl, Ireland. If you behave yourself, I'll let you go there."

"Unexpected generosity, surely. Why take me along in the first place?"

"Oh, I've a lovely nature when you get to know me, and in Ireland, you see, I'll be safe. Neither the British nor the French nor anyone else can extradite me. I'm a political offender, a most useful profession on occasion. The Irish government won't like it, but you can scream the rooftops down once we're there, and it still won't change the situation."

She lay there, propped up on one arm, staring at him. "Did you really kill Liam?"

"Yes," he said. "In the church at St. Martin."

"And Brosnan?" There was a silence between them. "Why not me, too?"

He said, "My friend who looked in a moment ago thinks I should."

"Why don't you?"

"We all have our blind spots, my love, even a bastard like me. I don't kill women." He hesitated, remembering Jenny Crowther. "Not by intention, anyway."

"Oh, I see," she said. "Not by intention? That really is a great comfort."

He stood up, took the Ceska out, cocked it, then put the safety catch on, and replaced it in his pocket. "The choice is yours."

Which was no choice at all, as they both knew. "Oh, I wouldn't miss it for anything." She got to her feet. "When do we leave?"

"Marvelous," Barry said. "I knew you'd see sense, and just think what a feature you could get out of it all. Now hold out your hands." He produced a pair of handcuffs and snapped them into place, clamping her wrists together in front of her. "The world's a deceitful old place, and I like to be as certain as possible about things."

"The only certainty at the moment is that you haven't killed me yet, Mr. Barry," Anne-Marie said.

"Oh ye of little faith."

He opened the door and ushered her through.

There was fog heavy on the damp air, and although Deforges had switched on the landing lights it was not possible to see to the end of the runway. Belov watched the Cessna turn and pause. As Barry boosted power, it rolled forward, the roaring of the engines filling the night. It started to lift off and was swallowed up by the fog instantly.

Deforges came across from the hangar, head turned to catch the muffled beat of the engines as Barry started to climb. "Is he any good?"

"Oh, yes," Belov said. "He has the Devil on his side, that one. Good night, Deforges," and he walked away to his car.

Barry climbed to six thousand feet, took a course direction from the air traffic control at Orly that turned him toward the Channel coast. He switched to autopilot and turned, pushing his headphones down around his neck.

Anne-Marie sat amidships, strapped in, her wrists still handcuffed in front of her. "Four and a half to five hours. You can be sensible and comfortable or just plain uncomfortable. The choice is yours."

She held up her wrists without a word, and he produced the key and unlocked them. "Good girl," he said. "There's coffee and sandwiches and even a couple of half-bottles of booze in the case at your feet. Feel free."

He turned away, switched from autopilot, and took control again.

It was three in the morning when Belov reached the apartment on the Boulevard St. Germain. He was tired and cold, and the prospect of Irana waiting filled him with a conscious pleasure. He got out his key, opened the door, and Irana called in Russian, "Run, Nikolai!"

Belov found himself staring into the barrel of a gun. And then Brosnan had him by the collar, kicked the door shut, and pushed him into the living room.

Irana sat on the couch, Devlin standing behind her. Belov stared at him in astonishment, as Brosnan ran his hands over him expertly, finding the Walther PPK in Belov's pocket and removing it.

Devlin said, "You look surprised, Colonel Belov, as well you might be, knowing who we are."

Belov tried to bluff it out. "I don't know what you want, and I certainly don't know who you are. If it's money, there's about four thousand francs in my wallet."

"You can save it," Devlin said. "Your lady friend here has already spilled the beans. She was surprised to see us because she thought we were both dead. That can only mean one thing. You've either spoken to or heard from Frank Barry. Where is he?"

Belov took a Russian cigarette from the box on the coffee table. "You don't really expect me to answer that."

"When last seen, he had a friend of ours with him, a lady named Anne-Marie Audin. We're very concerned about her, Colonel," Devlin said. "I think I may go as far as to say that my friend here is feeling rather upset about the whole business, and when he gets angry, he becomes very unpredictable."

Belov glanced at Brosnan's hard, implacable face. "I can't help that."

Brosnan slid open the windows to the terrace. He moved close to Belov and hit him under the breastbone, knuckles extended. The Russian went down on his knees.

Brosnan said, "I don't give a damn who you are. I don't even care which side you're on. I'm only interested in saving that girl. You've got a minute—one minute to start talking. If you don't, I'm going to throw you off the balcony."

Irana cried out and tried to get to her feet. Brosnan pushed her down and said to Devlin, "Keep her quiet."

He shoved his foot into Belov's rear, sending him sprawling toward the terrace, and Irana looked up at Devlin and said desperately, "Stop him! For God's sake, stop him! I'll tell you what you want to know."

Belov half-turned toward her on his hands

and knees, shaking his head, and Brosnan kicked his legs from under him, reached for his collar, and started for the open windows.

"No, please don't let him!" She grabbed at Devlin's coat.

"The whole truth," he said. "Everything."

"I promise."

He called to Brosnan. "Okay, Martin, take him into the bathroom and let the poor fellow clean himself up."

Belov stood at the washbasin examining his face in the mirror. His nose was bleeding, and he sponged it carefully with a washcloth.

"You play rough, Mr. Brosnan."

"It worked, didn't it?"

"Oh, yes," Belov said. "The old ploy. One guy's reasonable, the other is nasty. It never fails. I've used it myself many times." He sighed. "Only poor Irana didn't know that."

"All Irana knows, if you want my opinion, is that she loves you."

"Yes," Belov said soberly. "So it would appear."

The door opened, and Devlin said, "You can come out now."

Irana got to her feet and ran into Belov's arms. "I'm sorry, Nikolai, but I wasn't prepared to see you killed."

"That's all right." He smoothed her hair with one hand. "Actually, I'm rather flattered."

Devlin turned to Brosnan. "He left a small

airport outside Paris at about two, taking Anne-Marie with him. He's flying himself in a Cessna 310."

"What's the destination?"

"The English Lake District. I'll explain it all later. Watch these two while I call Jean-Paul. Not Ferguson, right?"

Brosnan smiled. "Why bother the man? This isn't Ferguson's business anymore."

In Marseilles, at the Maison d'Or, Jean-Paul Savary was counting the evening's take from the casino with the assistance of the club manager, and it was he who picked up the phone when it rang. He listened, then held it out to Jean-Paul.

"For you, boss. A Monsieur Devlin."

Jean-Paul took it instantly. "Savary here."

"How's your father?"

"Sunning himself in Algeria. And you and Martin?"

"Things could be marginally worse, but I doubt it. You said anything at any time."

"And meant it. What do you need?"

"We're in Paris. We need a light plane and the kind of pilot who doesn't ask questions to drop us at an unused airfield in the English Lake District."

"When do you want to go?"

"Right now."

"Give me your phone number. I'll call you back."

"You can fix it?"

"My friend, the *Union Corse* can fix anything, except perhaps the Presidency."

Jean-Paul put the phone down, took a small black book from a drawer in the desk, and checked through it. He picked up the phone again and dialed a Paris number.

Leaning against the window, smoking a cigarette, Devlin said, "I've been thinking about this whole business, Colonel, and it seems to me Barry's made a right old mug out of you."

"Yes," Belov said evenly, "I'm inclined to agree with you. So where is this conversation leading us?"

"I'd have thought it was obvious. You've promised him two million, and you'll take delivery of this rocket pod in Ireland. Now from something the lady here let drop when she was being so informative, I understand the Germans have been rather reluctant to let their American allies have a look at this wonderful new weapon. Understandable, as feelings have not been exactly cordial there for some time."

Belov said carefully, "So what are you suggesting?"

"I wouldn't want to spoil your evening, but if Frank Barry can get two million from you, I should have thought it likely that the CIA would give him five. Or do you think I'm being unreasonable?"

Belov sat there staring at him, and Irana

hugged his arm. "I warned you," she said. "I told you what he was like."

"All supposition."

The phone rang, and Devlin picked it up. He listened for a few moments then said, "God bless you, Jean-Paul." He turned to Brosnan. "Small airport about half an hour's drive out of Paris, near a place called Brie-Comte-Robert."

"I know where that is," Brosnan said.

Belov said, "You intend to take up the chase by plane?" He shrugged. "Too late, my friend. Barry will have at least two hours' start on you."

"We'll see," Devlin told him.

Brosnan said, "What are we going to do about these two?"

"A point." Devlin stood looking down at them, hands in pockets. "I suppose you could try phoning this man Salter, tell him to warn Barry we're on our way in spite of what I said to you?" Belov didn't reply, but the look in his eyes said it all. "I thought so. Have a look in the kitchen, Martin. Find some rope." Brosnan went out and came back with a ball of twine and a clothesline. "Fine." Devlin turned to Irana, "What time does the maid get in? Seven? Eight?"

She answered instinctively, "Seven-thirty."

"Good, she'll find you soon enough, you in one bedroom and him in the other. Too late to do us any harm."

There was nothing Belov could do except submit, and within a few minutes he was tightly

bound, hands behind his back, his ankles tied
to his wrists. Brosnan gagged him and laid him
on his side.

"Not too comfortable, I hope?"

Belov's eyes flickered, and Brosnan gave him
an ironic salute, went out and closed and locked
the door, just as Devlin emerged from the other
room.

"All right," Devlin said. "Let's move it,"
and they went out quickly.

The fog was considerably worse, and it was
raining heavily by the time they reached Brie-
Comte-Robert. They found the airfield with
no difficulty, two miles on the other side.

The gates in the surrounding fence stood
open. The place was mainly in darkness, and in
the light from the Citroën's headlamps Brosnan
saw cracked concrete, grass growing high on
either side of the runway. There were four hangars. They loomed out of the fog, and a couple
of lamps high on the wall had been turned
on. In their light, the rain fell relentlessly.

A small door opened in one of the hangars
and a man was silhouetted there. "Mr. Devlin?"
he called in English, as Brosnan switched off
the engine.

Devlin got out first. "That's me."

"Come on in."

The hangar was dimly lit by only a couple of
bulbs. There were three planes. An old Dakota,
a Beaver, and a Navajo Chieftain.

"Barney Graham." He held out his hand, a small, wiry-looking man with faded blue eyes. He wore a World War Two flying jacket and sheepskin boots.

"You've heard from Savary?"

"Sure, you want to go to the Lake District. Come in the office." They followed him and saw that several charts and maps had been laid out across the desk. "A dirty night for dirty work."

"You mean you're not prepared to do it?" Brosnan said.

Graham laughed. "You don't say no to the *Union Corse*. They own this place. They're my bread and butter plus a considerable amount of jam. Now where exactly do you want to land?"

"An old RAF station from the war days, south of a place called Ravenglass. Tanningley Field."

"That's bad flying country," Graham said. "Friend of mind hit the top of a mountain near there back in '43 in a Lancaster bomber. Only the rear gunner survived, and he had both legs broken." He was going over the map as he spoke. "There it is. No longer in use."

"Apparently the runway is perfectly usable," Devlin said. "The man we're after is familiar with the place. He's flying up there now. Left around two."

"What in?"

"A Cessna 310."

"There's a head wind tonight," Graham said.

"I've checked the weather. That cuts him down to about a hundred and forty in one of those things. I'd say he'll get there about seven or seven-thirty. Maybe five hours, which would be about right. Dawn coming up, you see, and on a field like that with no facilities he can only make a visual approach, so he needs light," He folded the maps. "Just like us."

Devlin checked his watch and saw that it was four o'clock. "So, he's got a two-hour head start on us."

Graham shook his head. "My Navajo can better his speed by a hundred miles an hour, and we won't be as bothered by that head wind. I reckon we can make it in three hours."

"Arriving at around dawn." Brosnan turned to Devlin. "Right up his backside, so let's get moving."

"Just let me explain one thing before we leave," Graham said. "I'll need a destination to keep the air traffic people happy. I've already told Orly I'm making an emergency flight to Glasgow to pick up a supply of blood needed for an operation in Paris this afternoon."

"Blood?" Brosnan said.

"Yes, a rare group. You know the sort of thing. A trick we use occasionally when we need to make a flight that's a little out of the ordinary. Jean-Paul's already arranged it by telephone with a contact in Glasgow since he spoke to you, so that gives me a legal reason for the flight."

"And where do we come in?"

"The Lake District is directly en route, and it isn't controlled air space. At the right moment, I go down fast, you jump out, and I take off again and keep my fingers crossed it isn't noticed on anyone's radar screen. A fair chance at that time in the morning."

"And if it is?"

"I'll think of something." Graham smiled. "I took my wings in the RAF in nineteen thirty-nine, Mr. Devlin. I've been at it a long time. Not much they can teach me. If I say I had instrument problems, they've got no proof otherwise. Anyway, let's get going."

They got the hangar doors open, and Devlin and Brosnan climbed into the Navajo. It was roomy enough inside, with seating for ten people. Graham climbed in after them and pulled up the door.

"I've only got my wing lights to go by," he said. "With this fog the take-off's going to seem worse than it is. If you don't like heights, just close your eyes."

The engines roared into life, and Devlin and Brosnan strapped themselves in as he taxied outside, moved to the end of the runway, and turned into the wind.

"You know what they say in the theater, Martin?" Devlin said. "It's bad luck to wish somebody good luck."

"Thanks very much," Brosnan said. "Just what I needed."

And then they were plowing into the fog, Graham easing back the stick at precisely the correct moment for lift-off, refusing to sacrifice power for height, pulling the stick back into his stomach when instinct told him it was right to do so.

At eight hundred feet they burst out of the fog; he gently applied foot pressure on the right rudder and started to turn to starboard.

Anne-Marie had slept for some time and awoke to find the first gray light of dawn seeping across the sky. In the far distance to port, the Isle of Man was a shadow on the horizon. She could see from the altimeter that they were flying at two thousand feet. When she looked down, the sea was a desolate waste below.

She was aware of Barry's voice over the roaring of the twin engines as he spoke into his mike. "Ronaldsway. This is Golphe Alpha Yankee Yankee Foxtrot. I am diverting to Blackpool."

He switched to autopilot and turned to her, the handcuffs in one hand. "Not that I think you'd be silly enough to start a fuss that would kill the both of us, but I'd feel happier if you put these back on."

She didn't struggle, there was little point. She simply held out her wrists to receive the handcuffs.

"Good girl." He grinned. "Now just sit tight and enjoy yourself. This is the exciting bit."

He took over the controls again and went down fast.

FOURTEEN

Henry Salter had the forethought to take a pair of twelve-inch wire cutters with him when he drove out to Tanningley Field. They sliced through the rusting chain that was padlocked to the main gate easily enough, and he got back in the Land Rover and drove inside.

There were signs of neglect everywhere. Grass was growing through cracks in the old runway, and the roofs of two of the hangars had fallen in.

The third looked in reasonable enough condition. It still bore the legend in faded white paint *Tanningley Flying Club*. With a bit of an effort, he managed to roll back the doors and venture inside. Rain dripped through the holes in the roof. It was cold and depressing, and he shivered, turning up the collar of his coat. And then, in the distance, he heard the plane and ran outside.

The Cessna came in from the sea very low, banked to starboard, and dropped straight in at the far end of the runway. Salter ran out waving his arms, and the Cessna turned toward him and taxied inside the hangar, the roaring of the twin engines filling the place with their clamor. Barry switched off, opened the door, and climbed out on the wing.

"Mr. Sinclair," Salter said weakly.

Barry reached inside the plane and pulled Anne-Marie out and helped her to the ground. Salter looked her over, noting the handcuffs with dismay.

"All right, let's get moving." Barry ran Anne-Marie to the Land Rover and pushed her into the rear, taking the driver's seat himself, starting up as Salter scrambled into the passenger seat.

"But where are we going?"

"The marsh. Your boat, the *Kathleen*, is still moored down there on the creek, I hope?"

"Of course she is." Salter was bewildered. "I don't understand."

"You will," Barry said, and turned out of the main gates.

"Hang on," Salter told him. "I'd better close them or someone might notice and wonder what's been going on."

Barry halted, and Salter went back to the gates. He paused beside the Land Rover as he came back, head turned, listening. Barry said impatiently, "What is it?"

"I thought I heard another plane. I must have been mistaken."

"Get in, man, for God's sake. I haven't got

all day," Barry said, exasperated, and he drove away quickly without giving Salter time to get the door closed.

The sound Salter had heard was the Navajo making its first approach, but the weather had already deteriorated so much that the ceiling was down to eight hundred feet, and Barney Graham turned out to sea again.

"It's too bloody dicey to go in blind. We'll be into the side of that mountain before you know what's happened."

"You've got to get us down one way or another. It's absolutely essential," Brosnan said.

"Maybe you'd like to jump out?" Graham swore softly. "Okay, I'll try a sea approach."

He turned out to sea, banked, went down low and burst out of the fog at five hundred feet, the mountain rushing to meet them.

It was Devlin who saw the runway and hangars a few hundred yards to starboard through driving rain. Graham went in fast and so low that when he banked at the last moment, just before putting her down, the starboard wingtip was only six feet off the ground. They bounced heavily and ran toward the hangars.

"Out!" Graham shouted. "Now!"

He was out of the cockpit and dropping the Airstair in seconds. Brosnan descended, and Devlin went after him so fast that he stumbled and fell. The Airstair was hauled up behind them, and as they ran to get out of the way the Navajo taxied toward the far end of the runway, paused briefly, then roared forward and took off.

Within a matter of moments it had climbed into the mist and was only a fast disappearing sound in the distance.

Devlin said, "Let's hope this is it. No mistakes."

But Brosnan was already at the partly open hangar door, pulling it back on its rollers, disclosing the Cessna. "This is it, all right. So where's Barry?"

"I should think this fellow Salter will be able to tell us that, but just in case Barry intends to use this thing again let's make sure he can't."

Devlin produced a Browning from his pocket, took deliberate aim and fired at each wheel in turn. The Cessna lurched slightly as the tires deflated.

"That's it," Brosnan said. "Now let's move, Liam. According to that map, it's about five miles to Marsh End."

But luck was with them, for as they were walking along the main road five minutes later a farm truck with milk cans in the back passed them and stopped up ahead.

The man who leaned out of the window looked cheerful enough, in spite of the early hour. He badly needed a shave, and his pajama jacket showed under his old raincoat.

"In trouble?"

"We were last night," Devlin said smoothly. "Coming over the pass from the next valley when the car broke down."

"Wastwater?"

"That's right. We must have walked five or six miles."

"More like eight. Where are you making for?"

"You know Mr. Salter's place?"

"Pass it every day. If that's where you're going, hop on the back, and I'll drop you off."

"Thanks," Devlin said. "We can phone the local garage from there."

They climbed on board and squatted among the milk cans. Brosnan said, "You're never at a loss, are you?"

Devlin grinned. "All you have to do is live right."

Barry drove along the track beside the creek and braked to a halt at the end of the jetty. The *Kathleen* waited, silent in the rain, and fog draped the marsh in a gray blanket. He helped Anne-Marie out and walked her along the jetty, a hand on her elbow.

Salter hurried along behind. "But what are you going to do, Mr. Sinclair?"

Barry helped Anne-Marie over the rail. "I'm going to retrieve something that belongs to me, Mr. Salter, and for that, I need your boat. Afterward, you collect your five thousand, take us back to Tanningley Field, and I fly away into the gray morning like a departing spirit. I'm sure you'll be most relieved."

Salter stayed on the jetty, staring at him stupidly. "But we can't."

"Why not?" Barry frowned. "You told me when I was last here that you always keep the *Kathleen* ready for sea."

"The ignition key," Salter said. "I can't start the engines without that, and it's up at the house."

Barry swore. "Then go and get it, you bloody idiot, and be quick about it."

Salter turned, hurried along the jetty, and got into the Land Rover while Barry pushed Anne-Marie across the deck and into the wheelhouse.

"How are you liking it so far?" His smile was fixed, his eyes were alive with excitement, and when he lit a cigarette his hands trembled.

"Careful," Anne-Marie said. "You're coming apart."

"Who, me?" he laughed excitedly. "Not till hell freezes over."

He pulled down the inspection flap beneath the instrument panel. The Sterling and the Smith and Wesson were still in place. As he pushed it up again, she said, "So much for poor Mr. Salter."

"I know," he said. "But then I hate leaving loose ends. He shouldn't have joined, should he?"

He pulled her out of the way, lifted the lid of the bench seat, and rummaged around until he found the briefcase. He opened it, checked that the money was still there, and closed it again.

"The war chest?" she said.

"Something like that." He moved to the wheelhouse entrance and stood listening. "Come on," he said softly.

"Maybe he isn't coming back."

"Don't be stupid."

"Oh, I don't know. He looked frightened to death to me."

He turned and glanced at her, the smile wiped from his face, then grabbed her arm, pulled her out of the wheelhouse, and ran her along the deck and down the companionway to the cabin. He pushed her inside, locking the door on her, went back on deck, jumped over the rail, and ran along the jetty.

The milk truck drove away into the fog, and Devlin and Brosnan turned to the gold-painted sign beside the gate.

"Henry Salter, Undertaker. House of Rest and Crematorium," Devlin said. "Very tasteful. Let's see if he's at home."

The house was still, as if waiting for them, quiet in the morning rain as they moved toward the rear, keeping to the shelter of the rhododendron bushes. They paused, the courtyard before them, the barn door open. There was the sound of a vehicle approaching. The Land Rover turned into the yard and rolled to a halt. Salter got out and went in the back door.

Devlin whispered, "He has a look of a corpse about him, wouldn't you agree? I'd say that's our man."

Salter wasn't happy—wasn't happy at all. The whole thing had a bad smell to it, and Sinclair frightened him. On the other hand, he didn't really have much choice. He reached for the ignition key hanging on the key board above the refrigerator just as the door burst open behind him. Before he knew what was happening, he was lying on his back across the table, Brosnan's hand on his throat, the muzzle of the Mauser rammed against his temple.

Salter had never been so terrified. "Please, no!" he gabbled.

Devlin said, "You are Henry Salter, I presume?"

"That's right," Salter said, as Brosnan relaxed his grip.

"Where's Frank Barry?"

Salter said, "Frank Barry? But I don't know anyone of that name."

Brosnan's grip tightened. "You picked him up at Tanningley field no more than half an hour ago."

"That was a man named Sinclair, Maurice Sinclair."

"I see," Devlin said. "And he had the young woman with him?"

"That's right. When he took her off the plane she was in handcuffs."

"Where are they now?"

"Down in the marsh on my boat, the *Kathleen*. He sent me up for the ignition key—look."

He held up the key in his right hand, and Brosnan said, "I'll take that."

Devlin said, "He was here before?"

"That's right. A few days ago."

"To get that rocket pod?"

Salter looked bewildered. "I don't know what he was here for. I was paid to hire men for him. They were here for two days. They left. That's all I know."

He was obviously telling the truth. "How do we get to this boat of yours?" Devlin asked.

"Turn left on to the main road. There's a signpost to the right saying Marsh End Creek. The *Kathleen*'s tied up at the jetty there. You can't miss her. She's the only boat there."

Devlin reached up and ripped down the clothesline that stretched across the sink. He threw it to Brosnan. "All right, Martin, tie him up."

He went outside, got into the Land Rover's passenger seat and took out his Browning. He removed the clip, pushed the bullets out one by one with his thumbnail and reloaded very carefully. As he finished, Brosnan came out of the kitchen door and got behind the wheel.

He turned to Devlin, his face very pale. "He's mine, Liam, remember that."

Devlin said, "The Japanese believe revenge is a purification, but personally I doubt it."

He leaned back, eyes closed, holding the Browning in his lap as Brosnan drove away.

Frank Barry, taking the short-cut through the garden, saw the Land Rover through the trees, still in the courtyard and paused. What the hell was Salter playing at? Perhaps the girl had been right after all. He started forward and stopped, blinking, for coming out of the house and crossing the yard was his dead enemy, Liam Devlin.

Barry's instinct was to yell at the ghost, to frighten it away, but in fact it was he who was suddenly and strangely frightened. He cursed at himself. He wasn't a superstitious idiot. And then he saw Martin Brosnan come out of the kitchen door and go round to the other side of the Land Rover, then disappear from view. A second ghost? Feeling himself trembling, he tried to take courage from the weight of the Ceska in his pocket. How many times do you have to kill a man?

By the time Barry reached the jetty, panting from his exertion, he was in control again. That Devlin and Brosnan were still alive was a fact. Any explanation of the situation was of secondary importance at the moment.

He ran along the jetty and paused, listening. Already the Land Rover was close behind in the fog, and without that damned ignition key he couldn't move the boat, not under power anyway.

He cast off the lines at prow and stern, pushed as hard as he could against the rail and scrambled over, as the gap suddenly widened between the *Kathleen* and the jetty. In a moment the gap was ten or twelve feet, and then, suddenly the boat started to drift broadside on back toward the jetty. When he looked over the rail, the reason was plain, for the tide was moving in through the marsh strongly.

Anne-Marie heard him thunder down the companionway. The door to the cabin was flung open, he grabbed her and pulled her out and back up the companionway. She went cold, certain that he was about to kill her. Instead, he pushed her along the deck into the wheelhouse.

"What is it?" she demanded.

"The second coming," he said savagely.

And then, the Land Rover moved out of the fog, stopped at the end of the jetty, and her heart nearly stopped beating.

Two things happened very quickly. Barry smashed the side window of the wheelhouse with his elbow and Anne-Marie yelled at the top of her voice, "Martin, look out!"

Barry shoved her down and loosed off a couple of shots through the broken window as Devlin and Brosnan ran, heads down, along the jetty. The gap between the *Kathleen* and the jetty was only about three feet now, as Brosnan jumped for the stern and dived behind the deck housing. Devlin had chosen the prow and was down out of sight on the blind side of the wheelhouse.

"Now then, Frank," he called, "and how are you this fine morning?"

"Miracles is it now, Liam?" Barry called back.

"That's right. The Devil's sent us straight from hell to fetch you!"

"He'll have to wait a while yet." Barry got hold of Anne-Marie's hair in one hand. "I'm going to stand up with your girlfriend, Martin," he called. "If I go, she goes. Remember that. Try and pick me off, and my last act will be to squeeze this trigger."

He pulled Anne-Marie up with him and stood holding her as close as if they were lovers, her head dragged back painfully, the muzzle of the Ceska under her chin.

"Two choices," Barry said. "She dies now, even if I have to die with her, or you come out here and lay down your guns."

"No, Martin," Anne-Marie called, and Barry twisted his fingers in her hair.

"Don't muck about. Yes or no."

There was a pause, then Brosnan stood up holding the Mauser. "Throw it in the water!" Barry said.

Brosnan did so with an almost casual gesture, his eyes never leaving Barry's face. Devlin had

moved out from the other side of the wheelhouse and stood only five or six feet away. He
tossed his Browning into the creek without
being told.

"Right," Barry said. "Come closer." His voice
cracked, the first real signs of stress beginning
to show. "I said closer."

They stood together, just outside the wheelhouse. "Let the girl go, Frank," Devlin said.

"Sure, why not?" Barry shoved her out of
the wheelhouse into their arms. In the same
moment he reached for the button on the instrument panel, the flap fell down and he tore
the Sterling submachine gun from its brackets
with his free hand.

"My ace in the hole, Liam." He grinned. "I
learned the importance of that one from you,
remember?"

Devlin said, "What happens now? Another
execution?"

"Not yet," Barry said. "First, I'm going to
put you to work. A few hundred yards down
that creek there's a pool in the reeds with a
boat on the bottom. There's something in the
cabin I very much want. You can go swimming
for me, Martin."

"The rocket pod?" Devlin said. "Very in-
genious."

"You're remarkably well informed," Barry
said. "But enough conversation. Martin, you
and the girl move along to the top of the
companionway. Nice and slow. We'll have you

two below in the cabin while we get this thing moving." He swung the barrel at Devlin. "You walk ahead of them, right along to the stern."

Devlin moved first, and Brosnan pushed the girl in front of him and turned, backing away, protecting her with his body, his burning eyes never leaving Barry's face. Barry stayed where he was in the wheelhouse entrance, the Sterling ready.

Brosnan said, "You should have stayed behind at the farm, Frank. You made a bad mistake using rubbish like those three hoods from Nice. They wouldn't have lasted one bad Saturday night in Belfast."

"Yes, this time I'll see to it myself," Barry told him.

Brosnan turned, put a hand in Anne-Marie's back, sending her tumbling down the steps, dived over the rail into the creek, and went down deep into the brown stinking water, turning to pull himself under the hull, his feet kicking desperately in the thick ooze of the bottom.

The burst Barry fired from the Sterling chipped the rail, already too late, and he ran forward and fired again into the water. Of Brosnan there was no sign. Anne-Marie reappeared, crouching in the companionway. Barry ran to the other rail and loosed off another burst into the water.

Devlin said, "No good, Frank, you've lost him."

"You shut your mouth," Barry said.

Devlin took his time lighting a cigarette, and Brosnan, clinging to the prow, heard him say, "You always were a small man when it came down to it, weren't you, Frank?"

Barry stepped toward him. "Big enough to bury you."

"You tried once and made one hell of a mess of it." Devlin walked forward slowly. "I don't think you can do any better now."

Barry fired a single burst of four or five rounds that shredded Devlin's raincoat on the left side of his chest, spinning him around. He cried out and bounced off the side of the deckhouse.

Anne-Marie crawled toward him, pulling herself along on handcuffed hands, and Brosnan slipped under the port rail and reached inside the wheelhouse for the Smith and Wesson.

Barry, aware of the movement, started to turn and Brosnan shot him in the right arm, the force of the blow knocking him back. Barry tried desperately to hold onto the Sterling, but it slipped from his grip and slid over the rail, disappearing under the surface of the water.

Barry stood there clutching his bloody arm. Brosnan said, "The keys for the handcuffs, Frank. Let's have them."

Barry felt in his pocket with bloodstained fingers, found the keys and dropped them on the deck where Anne-Marie retrieved them and set about unfastening herself.

"By God, but you're the tricky one, Martin,

you always were, but I never thought to see you end up working for the opposition."

"This isn't for them," Brosnan said. "This is for Norah. For what you did to her. She died screaming, Frank, strapped to a bed in a mental hospital, and that's down to you."

"Whoever told you that is a liar." Barry looked genuinely horrified. "It was the French who did that to Norah, those SDECE Service Five bastards. You know what the *barbouzes* are like. They tried electricity to break her. When that didn't work, they moved onto drugs and went too far."

Liam Devlin, leaning against Anne-Marie, blood on his shoulder said weakly, "You're lying."

"It's the God's truth." Barry turned wildly to Brosnan. "Kill Norah, is it? Martin, she was the only woman I ever loved. The only person I ever put before myself."

"Liar!" Brosnan cried and fired three times very fast, his first shot catching Barry in the shoulder, turning him, his next two in the back, driving him headfirst across the rail into the water.

Birds called wildly to each other, rising from the reeds in clouds. Brosnan clumped down on the deck housing.

"Liar," he whispered and looked at Devlin. "Wasn't he?"

But Devlin's eyes were closed in pain and there was no answer there, only the pity in

Anne-Marie's face that he turned away from. He had to steel himself. The hired guns like Barry would always be replaced by other hired guns. Even the French torturers would be replaced by others. The blame went with the responsibility, whoever gave the orders. Ferguson? The Prime Minister?

He wished she wasn't a woman. It would be easier to kill a man.

Devlin's waistcoat had proved its worth again, taking the brunt of the burst Barry had fired at him, but one round had caught him across the right shoulder and another had gone through his upper arm.

Brosnan finished bandaging it expertly, the boat's first-aid box open on the bunk beside him. When he was finished, he took out one of the emergency morphine ampoules.

"That should take care of the pain for a while."

Devlin, his face gray, managed to smile. "You'd have made a fine doctor, Martin."

Anne-Marie said, "He needs a hospital now."

"Yes, but not here, not in England. The surest way to a prison cell. Do you still have that launch in Nice, like the old days?"

"Yes. Why do you ask?"

"So you could handle this?"

"Of course, no problem. This is a superb craft."

"Good. I reckon you'll make Ireland in eight hours. Liam will tell you where to go in."

"Liam?" She frowned. "You mean you're not coming? But I don't understand?"

He ignored her, picked up Barry's briefcase, which he had found in the wheelhouse and opened it, showing the money it contained to Devlin.

"At least thirty thousand quid there, Liam, probably more. Give me one name, one man in London who will do anything for that kind of money. No politics, just an honest crook."

Devlin said wearily, "Leave it, Martin. There's no profit in it now."

"Ferguson lied to us about Norah, Liam."

"All right," Devlin said. "So he lied. He thought the end justified the means. He wanted Frank Barry dead."

"They all wanted Barry dead," Brosnan said in a low voice. "Ferguson, D15, the Cabinet, the Prime Minister. Where does it stop? Somebody has to pay, Liam. I'm tired of being used for other people's purposes, dragged through the fire like some corn king for the sake of the rest of you."

Devlin shook his head. "No, Martin."

Brosnan said deliberately, "You owe me this one, Liam. You got me into it in the first place."

"I helped you get free, damn you!" Devlin flared.

"Free?" Brosnan laughed harshly. "Who's free?"

It was Anne-Marie who astonished them both by saying, "Tell him, Liam. Give him what he asks, and let's get out of here. Let him go to hell his own way."

She turned and went up the companionway. Brosnan said, "Well?"

Devlin reached for a cigarette, and Brosnan lit it for him. "I can't give you the name of a man, but there's a woman I knew some years back. Nothing to do with politics. Not even Irish. A German Jew originally. Lily Winter. She used to have a place on Great India Wharf in Wapping. I think she might be what you're looking for."

Brosnan closed the briefcase and stood up. "And Ferguson's telephone number."

Devlin told him, and Brosnan nodded. "Thanks. Good-bye, Liam," and he turned and went up the companionway.

Anne-Marie was searching the wheelhouse, and he took the ignition key from his pocket. "Is that what you're looking for?"

She took it from him and switched on. The engines rumbled into life. "That's all right then," Brosnan said.

"What do you want me to say?" she demanded angrily. "May you die in Ireland?"

It was the most ancient of Irish toasts. Brosnan said, "An excellent sentiment, but hardly likely."

He stepped over the rail and watched as the *Kathleen* pulled away from the jetty and turned downstream, disappearing into the fog. Only then did he walk to the Land Rover.

Jack Higgins

* * *

The selection of clothing in Salter's bedroom was so extensive that Brosnan could only assume that over the years the undertaker had made a practice of robbing the dead. He showered, washed the stink of the creek from him, and chose a gray tweed suit, woolen shirt, and a tie to go with it. He selected a raincoat and went downstairs to the living room where he'd left Salter tied to a chair.

He glanced at the clock. It was still only nine A.M., and he said to Salter, "What time does your staff come in?"

"After Sinclair phoned me, I told them to take the morning off."

"So they'll be in around noon?"

"That's right." Salter moistened dry lips.

"I'll do you a favor and leave them to find you tied up. That way it gives you a chance of claiming to be an unwilling part to whatever took place here, when it comes out."

Salter said, "I'm very grateful. May I ask you something? Is Mr. Sinclair dead?"

"Yes," Brosnan said, and he went out, closing the door.

A few moments later Salter heard the sound of the Land Rover starting up. It moved away down the drive and faded into the distance. He eased his hands as much as he could and sat there trying to work out what he was going to say to the police.

FIFTEEN

At one time, the Pool of London and the lower reaches of the Thames had been the center for world shipping. Those days were long gone, and as Brosnan walked down toward the docks through Wapping that Tuesday evening he found only decay, rusting cranes pointing at the sky, empty warehouses, their windows boarded.

Somewhere a ship, easing down the river, sounded its fog horn. Except for that somber sound, he might have been the only living creature left in the world.

He turned onto Great India Wharf, walked on past docks empty of shipping, and came to a warehouse at the end facing out across the river. The sign said *Winter & Co—Importers*. Brosnan opened the little judas gate in the main entrance and stepped in.

The place was crammed with old furniture of every description. It was very dark, as it had been on his last visit, but this time music drifted down from the small office high above, at the top of a flight of steep stairs.

"Mrs. Winter?" he called.

The office door opened, the music flooding out. "Is that you, Mr. Brosnan?"

"Yes."

She switched on another light to see him and peered over the railing. She was at least seventy, her hair drawn back from a yellowing parchment face in an old-fashioned bun. She wore a tweed suit with a skirt that almost reached her ankles. Her right hand had a secure grip on the collar of one of the most superb dogs Brosnan had ever seen in his life—a black and tan Doberman.

Her English was excellent, but with a German accent. "You know, you interest me, Mr. Brosnan. Karl didn't make a sound the first time you visited me, and he hasn't now. I've never known him to do that before."

"You know what they say?" Brosnan said. "Children and dogs, they can always tell."

He went up the stairs and gently caressed the dog's head as he followed her into the office. A cassette recorder on the desk was the source of the music. The song was *A Foggy Day in London Town,* but Brosnan didn't recognize the singer.

"Al Bowlly," she said. "The best there ever was. He was killed in the London Blitz. I used to hear him sing at the Monseigneur restaurant in Piccadilly with Roy Fox and his band. That was back in nineteen thirty-two before I was foolish enough to return to Germany after my father died."

Brosnan lit a cigarette and sat down on a chair on the other side of the desk, listening to that haunting voice singing a song from another world that for some reason touched something deep inside him.

"You like it?" she said.

"Oh, yes. I always loved cities by night or very early in the morning. Fog, wet streets, that total certainty that somewhere up ahead, just around the next corner, something marvelous and astonishing is waiting. That's when you're young, of course, and still believe."

The song came to an end, and she switched off the cassette player. "I stopped believing in Dachau, Mr. Brosnan."

She pushed up her sleeve and showed him the number tattooed on her arm. Brosnan took off his jacket and unbuttoned the cuff of his shirt. She pulled his arm across the desk and examined his prison number incredulously. "But you couldn't have been in the camps, you're too young, I don't understand."

"Somewhere similar," he said. "We didn't have the ovens, but the usual way out was feet first."

"Except for you?"

He pulled on his jacket. "You might say I was an exception."

She fitted a black gold-tipped cigarette into an ivory holder and looked at him searchingly as he gave her a light.

"You've brought the money?"

"Yes." He put Barry's briefcase on the desk and opened it.

She looked at the packets of twenty-pound notes inside and picked one up. "How much is there?"

"Thirty-five thousand pounds."

She sat staring down at the case, then closed it. "That's a great deal of money. After Dachau, when I came back to England in nineteen forty-five, money was the only thing that mattered to me, Mr. Brosnan. I'd stopped believing in people, you see." She got up, went to a side table, and poured coffee from an electric pot into two cups. "I became, by chance really, a receiver of stolen goods, the most successful in London before I was finished. I dealt with all of them. All the princes of the underworld. The Kray brothers, the Richardson gang. . . ."

"And Liam Devlin?"

"Liam, dear Liam." She smiled. "He was different. Him, I liked."

"And the business he was involved in?"

"Didn't interest me in the slightest. When he needed passports, I got them for him. Arms dealers in Europe or the name of a reliable doctor. Things like that, but all that was a long time ago. Now, as you can see, I deal only in furniture." She paused, then opened the briefcase again. "It really is a great deal of money."

"All yours, if you can help me."

"To do what, Mr. Brosnan, that's the thing? What do you intend?"

"That's my business."

She shook her head. "You have an angry aura, Mr. Brosnan, and that is not good. Give me your hands."

"My hands?" he said.

"Yes. I'm clairvoyant. Psychic. Surely you are aware of that? I'll show you."

Her hands were cool and flaccid, making him remember, for no accountable reason, his maternal grandmother in Dublin when he was a child, clean linen sheets, rosemary and lavender, and then she tightened her grip and he was aware of a sudden tingle as from a minor electric shock. She had her eyes shut and opened them and reached out and touched his face and she was smiling.

"Yes," she said. "Now I see it all."

Brosnan said, "I don't understand?"

Her voice had changed, and she was brisk and businesslike now. "The woman you seek may be found at home tomorrow evening."

"At home?" Brosnan's voice was hoarse. "But that's Ten Downing Street. No way known to man of getting in there."

"On the face of it, an impossibility. No one gets in without a personal invitation or official pass checked very thoroughly by the police on the doors and by officials inside. However, it is an interesting fact that all reception and official dinners are organized by outside caterers."

"So?"

"Tomorrow evening at six-thirty the Prime Minister is giving a Christmas party for at least a hundred people. Mainly staff, past and present. Office workers, typists, the cleaners—they'll all be there. The function will take place in what's called the Pillared Room. I've already put arrangements in hand for you to join the staff the caterers are using as an extra waiter."

Brosnan was stunned by the enormity of it. "Can we get away with it? I mean, I don't even know my way about."

She opened a drawer and took out a folded sheet of paper. "There's a plan of the ground and first floors. It's quite simple."

He opened it up to examine it. "But where did you get this?"

"Information freely available in numerous magazines and newspaper articles over the years," she said. "You'll need an official pass with your photo. That kind of forgery presents no problem at all to the particular man I use. However, the question of your personal appearance is of prime importance. It will be necessary to alter it considerably before the photo is taken."

"And how do I do that?"

"I have an old friend who specializes in such matters. I suggest you return here later on. Say, at ten o'clock, and check out of that hotel room. Better if you stay here now."

"All right."

He got up and went to the door. She said, "Oh, I almost forgot. I have made suitable inquiries in Dublin. Devlin is at present a patient in the Mountjoy Nursing Home. He is apparently doing well."

"There was a young woman with him?"

"That's right. She moved yesterday to Devlin's cottage in Mayo."

Brosnan nodded. "Well, that's all right then."

He went down the steel stairs, and the Doberman went to the railing silently and watched him go. Only when the outer door banged did he return to his mistress.

It was dark in the Prime Minister's study, the only light the single reading lamp on the desk. She was writing busily when Ferguson was shown in.

"Brigadier Ferguson, Prime Minister," the secretary announced, and left.

She didn't bother looking up, simply kept on writing, and Ferguson, forbidden by protocol from sitting without an invitation, was forced to stand before the desk like a schoolboy. Finally she stopped writing and sat back in her chair and looked up at him. The face was calm, but the eyes were cold.

"I've read your report on the Brosnan affair, Brigadier. May I take it that nothing has been left out?"

"Nothing within my knowledge, ma'am, I give you my word," Ferguson assured her.

"Right, then to take the most important item first. You stated in your report your intention to seek for this rocket pod, according to instructions given you by the man Brosnan. Have you had any success?"

"I'm happy to report that we recovered the item in question this very afternoon, Prime Minister. I was present myself." A fact that he would long remember and he shuddered, remembering the bodies brought up by the divers, one by one.

"Which at least gives us some hope of restoring confidence between ourselves and the West German government." She opened the file and tapped it with a finger. "In the copy of your original report, found in the possession of the Baxter woman, there is no mention of the girl, Norah Cassidy. Details of that disgraceful business are only made plain in the report you have just submitted. Why, Brigadier? Were you perhaps ashamed?"

Ferguson could think of nothing to say.

She carried on. "So, you lied about the Cassidy girl to Professor Devlin and, through him, to Brosnan."

"I thought it necessary, ma'am, I needed Brosnan's anger, you see, and then, as so often happens with these things, it all got out of hand."

"I don't believe that the end justifies the means, Brigadier. I believe in moral imperatives." She was angry now. "I don't hold the slightest brief for Martin Brosnan or anything he stands for. Or, if it comes to it, for Devlin, however devastatingly charming the rest of you seem to find him. A terrorist is a terrorist in my book, and that is exactly what these men are."

"Yes, ma'am," Ferguson said.

"Having said that, you lied to Brosnan, conned him, and for that he not only blames you but me through you. Would you say that that is roughly the situation he outlined to you when he telephoned you the day before yesterday?"

"Yes, Prime Minister. To be explicit, his actual words were, 'Somebody's got to pay. In the circumstances, I'll deal with the lady herself direct.' Then he hung up."

She nodded, very calm, not in the slightest bit ruffled. "Do you think he intends to assassinate me, Brigadier?"

"God knows, ma'am. He has a rather complex mind, this one."

"I should say so." She leafed through the file. "Roses. What a conceit." She closed it abruptly and sat up. "I usually make my mind up about a man in ten seconds, and I don't like to be proved wrong. In the circumstances, I'm going to put my personal safety in your hands, Brigadier. Now, how does that strike you?"

"As a very grave responsibility, Prime Minister."

"Good, it's nice to be taken seriously. I haven't the slightest intention of changing my schedule,

I'm far too busy. Another thing, I don't wish to
see Brosnan's face next to mine on the front
page of the *Daily Express*, with melodramatic
headlines such as mad IRA gunman stalks
Prime Minister. Whatever you do must be handled discreetly."

"As you say, ma'am."

She handed a typed sheet to him. "There's
my schedule for tomorrow. You will also find
waiting below special passes for you and your
aide, which will enable you to move in and out
of Downing Street or the House of Commons
at will." She picked up her pen. "Catch him,
Brigadier; I should have thought it a simple
enough task. Now you must go. I've got work
to do."

She pressed a buzzer, and, by the time he
reached the door, it was already being opened
for him by the young secretary who had brought
him up.

Ferguson told his driver to stop on the Em-
bankment and said to Fox, "Let's take a walk,
Harry."

They walked along the sidewalk, the driver
trailing them, and finally Ferguson stopped
and leaned on the wall, looking across the river.

"Bad, sir?" Fox inquired.

"She was not pleased, Harry. The last time I
got a working over like that was by my house-
master at school. I was twelve at the time." He

took out his wallet, produced a card, and gave it to Fox.

"What's this, sir?"

"Special pass, Harry, to get you into Downing Street or the Commons whenever you want. She's put me in charge of her personal security until this thing is sorted."

"I see." Fox put the card away carefully. "I shouldn't think her personal detectives will be pleased about that."

Ferguson produced the schedule she had given him and unfolded it. "This is what she's doing tomorrow. Read it to me."

He took a cheroot from a leather case and lit it carefully. Fox studied the sheet. "Good God, sir, she starts at six-thirty in the morning and doesn't stop until one A.M. the following day."

"I know. Just give me the important features as they strike you."

"Cabinet meeting in the morning for a couple of hours. That's at Downing Street." Fox frowned. "I say, there's a possibility, sir."

"What's that?"

"Memorial service for Earl Mountbatten. You think he might chance his aim there?"

"I don't know," Ferguson said. "What else is there?"

"Back to Downing Street. House of Commons at three o'clock. Then back to Downing Street for a meeting with Ministers. Let's see, then she gives a radio interview and receives the West German ambassador who's apparently retiring."

"Anything else?"

"There's a staff Christmas party in the Pillared Room at six-thirty. She's due back to the Commons for dinner just before nine. After that, back home to work on papers." He handed the sheet back to Ferguson. "I wonder if they pay her overtime, sir?"

Ferguson said, "So, the only soft spot seems to be the Mountbatten memorial service at St. Paul's Cathedral. Who else will be there? Prince Charles, Princess Margaret." He grimaced. "The last place we want a bomb."

Fox said, "But Brosnan's never gone in for bombing, sir."

"There's always a first time."

"Do you really believe that, sir?"

"No," Ferguson sighed. "Not his style. He's the last of the samurai, our lad, riding into the guns, sword in hand."

They went back to the Bentley and got in. "Still, the only soft spot is that service at St. Paul's," Fox said. "Everything else is either at Downing Street or the Commons, and he certainly hasn't a hope in hell of ever getting into Number Ten."

"The Commons is a tricky one," Ferguson said. "Lots of people come and go. Constituents up to see their MPs and so on."

Fox said, "So what's our next move, sir?"

"Convene a meeting of all interested parties."

Ferguson glanced at his watch. "We'll meet at my office at headquarters at eleven. No refusals accepted. Utmost priority. I want to see all heads of relevant departments at D15. I also want Special Branch there. You know who to talk to?"

"Yes, sir," Fox said. "We'll get him, sir. Bound to."

"Wish I could be so sanguine," Charles Ferguson said, and he leaned back and closed his eyes.

Brosnan sat in front of the dressing table, a towel around his shoulders, and watched as the old man ran a steel comb through the long hair which was now a pale straw color.

"Good," he said. "I'm really very pleased with that. Now, of course, most of it must go."

He picked up a pair of scissors and went to work, humming to himself. He was easily as old as Lily Winter and so similar in features that they might have been brother and sister.

Sitting on a stool watching, she lit a cigarette and passed it to Brosnan. "Shlomo is so clever. He started in Yiddish cabaret in Amsterdam. Got out just ahead of the Germans."

"I was at Elstree for years." The old man had exchanged the scissors for a cutthroat razor now. "Margaret Lockwood, James Mason. I've worked with all the greats. Mr. Noel Coward gave me a cigarette case once. It was engraved: *To Shlomo the Magician from the Master.*"

Brosnan's hair was now considerably more conventional in length, and the old man quickly blow-dried it and parted it neatly. Amazing the difference it made, especially the bleached eyebrows.

"Fantastic," Brosnan said.

"Not yet. Now you just look different. When I'm finished, I make you look like someone else. Stretch your upper lip and keep it stretched till I tell you to stop."

Brosnan did as he was told. The old man carefully fitted a blond moustache into place. He reached for the scissors and trimmed it. "I do this for famous people sometimes. You know, pop stars who want to go shopping at Harrods without being chased by the fans."

"And me?" Brosnan said. "Who do you think I don't want to be chased by?"

"I don't wish to know. I'm not interested. You seem like a nice boy to me." Shlomo shrugged. "If Lily's satisfied, that's good enough. Open your mouth." Brosnan did as he was told and the old man inserted cheek pads gently. He looked at the face over Brosnan's shoulder. "I don't think we need nose rings, eh, Lily?"

She shook her head. "Just the glasses."

They were gold-framed, tinted blue, and looked vaguely continental. The effect was quite astonishing. The man who stared back at Brosnan from the mirror was a total stranger.

"We'll not make you a foreigner," Lily said. "I mean, if we say you're Danish, you can be certain you'll run into a real Danish waiter, so plain George Jackson from Manchester will have to do." She looked over his shoulder again and nodded. "That really is very good. Now come and have your photo taken."

Ferguson stood to one side of the steps at the main entrance of St. Paul's Cathedral and watched the Royal party get into their cars below. The memorial service for Mountbatten was over. It had passed off without any kind of incident whatsoever. The Prime Minister, in a black suit, descended the steps, got into her car and was driven away.

Fox said, "Well, that went off all right, thank God," and they went down the steps as the Bentley drew up. "The thing is, sir," he added as they got in, "as that really was the only time today when she was a soft target, what do we do now?"

"Stick to her like glue, Harry," Ferguson told him. "That's all we can do." He rapped on the glass panel, and his driver moved away at once, following the Prime Minister's car.

Below stairs at Number 10 Downing Street was a hive of activity as six-thirty approached. The first guests were already arriving, for many retired staff members had been invited. The back entrance, a uniformed police sergeant on duty inside, stood open as half a dozen waiters ran back and forth, carrying crates of wine and other essentials for the function from a parked van.

Brosnan was one of them, and as he staggered in carrying two cartons of bottled beer the police sergeant said, "You can drop one of those off here any time you like."

Brosnan grinned and kept on going to the kitchen, where he was immediately ordered to help with the glasses. Some of the other waiters were already at work, he'd seen them go. It suddenly occurred to him that this might be it. That the sum total of all his efforts was going to be that he got as far as the kitchen, and then the headwaiter came in and tapped him on the shoulder.

"You—what's your name?"

"Jackson, sir."

"Right, put your gear on and get in there. You're needed."

Brosnan took off his dark alpaca working jacket and hung it up. Then he put on his white waiter's coat and took white gloves from the pocket. He pulled them on carefully and slipped a hand under his jacket, touching the Smith and Wesson flat against his back in his waistband, under the shirt. Then he picked up a silver tray, took a deep breath, and went along the corridor.

*   *   *

The Prime Minister, wearing a green evening dress, moved among the guests with her husband and daughter, thoroughly enjoying herself. From the other side of the room Brosnan watched, as he worked his way through the crowd with glasses of white wine on his tray.

When it was empty, he went back to the serving table, and the headwaiter told him to collect empty glasses and take them to the kitchen. Brosnan did as he was told, journeying back and forth to the kitchen three times.

Now that he was here, the truth was he had no idea what came next, and then, as he returned from the kitchen for a third time, he noticed the Prime Minister part from a group of people, a smile on her face, and go out through the open double doors and start up the main staircase.

He remembered the plans he had studied so carefully. Her private study, the White Drawing Room, and the Blue Drawing Room were all up there.

They were just opening champagne bottles at the serving table. He waited his turn with the other waiters and took one. Everything was busy confusion. He took a couple of glasses from the end of the table, placed them carefully on the tray with the champagne, then walked through the noisy crowd into the hall. It was, for the moment, empty. Without hesitation, he mounted the stairway to the first floor.

*   *   *

The Prime Minister was sitting at her desk, reading a memo and making notes, when there was a knock at the door. It opened, and Brosnan entered. He closed the door carefully behind him and stepped forward.

She glanced up in surprise. "What on earth have you got there?"

Brosnan's throat was dry, his heart pounded. He was acutely aware of the Smith and Wesson digging into his back. His voice was low and rather hoarse when he said, "Champagne, ma'am."

"I didn't order any champagne."

"Well the headwaiter told me to bring it up, ma'am, with two glasses. He was very specific about that."

"Two glasses." She smiled suddenly. "Oh, I see. Well, just leave it there on the table."

She was writing again, and there was sweat on Brosnan's forehead as he put the tray down on a small coffee table. He straightened and looked toward her, and his right hand slid under his jacket feeling for the butt of the Smith and Wesson. In three seconds it would be over.

For her, not for him.

Would it ever be over for him?

"You can go now," she said without looking up.

I don't exist for her, he thought, and yet I

am her death. Oh Norah, will this or anything else avenge you?

He saw the roses in the crystal vase on the table to one side. White Christmas roses with long stems.

"Will that be all, ma'am?"

"Yes, thank you," a touch of impatience in her voice.

She still didn't look up, even as, his heart beating rapidly, he slipped a rose from the vase and laid it on the silver tray between the bottle of champagne and the two glasses.

He opened the door, went out on the landing, and closed it again quietly.

The hall was still deserted as he went down the stairs past the portraits of all those prime ministers who had gone before her. He moved straight into the crowd, picked up a tray, and started to collect empty glasses. When his tray was full, he went back to the kitchen.

The passage was a frenzy of activity as the party drew to a close, and the back door stood open, waiters carrying crates of empty bottles out to the van.

Brosnan went into the kitchen, took off his white waiter's coat and hung it up. Then he pulled on the dark alpaca working jacket, picked up a crate, and went out into the passage, past the sergeant standing at the open door. He joined the queue at the back of the van, passed up his crate, then walked around to the other side and cut across a small courtyard with a little lawn in the center.

Downing Street was crowded with departing guests, many of them on foot, moving on to look for taxis elsewhere. Brosnan joined the cheerful crowd, turned the corner into Whitehall, and walked briskly away.

It was perhaps five minutes later that the Prime Minister finished her memo. She got up, went around the desk and started for the door, intending to go downstairs again. She glanced casually at the champagne and glasses on the tray as she went by, and stopped abruptly. Then she turned and hurried back to her desk and flicked the intercom.

Ferguson said, "He's gone, ma'am, not a sign of him.

"There wouldn't be, would there? Not now."

The rose lay on the desk between them. Ferguson said, almost plaintively, "I don't understand. What on earth was he playing at?"

"But it's so simple, Brigadier, don't you see?" She picked up the rose. "No one is safe, that's what your Mr. Brosnan is saying to us. The kind of world we've created."

Ferguson went cold, and she laid the rose down very carefully. "And now, Brigadier, I'd better get back to whatever guests I have left."

He opened the door for her and she passed through.

* * *

Music was playing again as Brosnan stepped through the judas into the warehouse, and the light was on in the office high above him. He went up the steel steps slowly and opened the door. Lily Winter was sitting at the desk examining an antique necklace with an eyeglass. The Doberman got up and pushed himself against Brosnan.

She took out the eyeglass and looked up at him for a long moment. "So, you went to make war and made peace instead."

"How did you know?"

"Fool." She took a bottle of brandy from a drawer and a glass and filled it. "Here. Do you think I would have helped you in the first place if I had not sensed it in you?"

"I stood as close to her as I am to you," Brosnan said, and the glass shook in his hand. "There were some winter roses in a vase. I put one on the tray and left."

"A fine romantic gesture, and what does it prove?"

"I've made a separate peace," Brosnan said. "A separate peace." He lay down on the bunk against the wall and stared up at the ceiling. "Suddenly I feel old—really old. You know what I mean?"

"I know," she said.

Her voice seemed to come from a long distance. He closed his eyes, and after a while the glass slipped from his hand, and he slept.

SIXTEEN

In a private room on the third floor of the Mountjoy Nursing Home in Dublin, Liam Devlin tried to possess himself in patience as the staff nurse removed the dressing from his shoulder and arm. The matron, a formidable lady as stiff as her starched headdress, stood behind the surgeon, watching as he inspected his handiwork.

"Very nice," he said. "Very nice indeed." He nodded to the staff nurse. "Fresh dressing, please."

Devlin said plaintively, "For God's sake, Patrick, when can I go home? A terrible place, this. Not a drink in sight, and they even try to stop you smoking."

"A week, Liam," the surgeon, himself a distinguished professor of Trinity College, said. "Another week and I'll think about it." He turned to the matron. "Terrible injuries these car crashes cause. Terrible. He's a lucky man."

"And tobacco and whisky won't help," she said. "I'm sure you agree, professor?"

"Yes, of course. You're quite right." She opened the door for him, and he turned to

Devlin and shrugged helplessly. "I'll look in again tomorrow, Liam."

When the door closed, Devlin said, "God, she's a hard one, and that's the truth."

The staff nurse smiled as she finished replacing the dressing and bandages. "Now you don't really expect me to comment on that, do you, Professor Devlin? I'll bring your tea in half an hour."

She went out, and he lay back against the pillow. There was a timid knock at the door, and a young probationer looked in. She carried a long thin parcel wrapped in gold paper with a bow on it.

"And what in the blazes is that?" Devlin demanded.

"Interflora. It's just been delivered. Shall I open it for you?"

"That would seem to be a sound idea."

He lay there watching as she stood at the table removing the wrapping. "That's interesting." She turned, holding a plastic tube containing a single rose. "Somebody loves you, professor."

Devlin lay there looking at it for a long moment. "Is there a card?"

"Not that I can see."

"No, there wouldn't be."

"You know who it's from?"

"Oh, yes," Devlin said softly. "I know who it's from. Just leave it on the bed."

She went out, and he lay there looking at the

rose and then he smiled. "Now then, Martin," he said softly, "a small celebration would appear to be in order, surely."

He reached over, wincing with pain, got the cupboard open at the side of his bed, and took out a bottle of Bushmills and a pack of cigarettes.

It was one of the most beautiful evenings Anne-Marie Audin had ever known. She sat at an easel on the edge of the cliffs below Devlin's cottage, painting very fast, trying to catch the last of the evening light. Killala Bay was below her, and across the water in the far distance, the mountains of Donegal were a purple shadow.

There was a step behind her. She didn't look around, some sixth sense telling her who it must be, and Brosnan said, "You get better all the time. That background wash is fantastic."

She looked up and frowned. "What happened to your hair?"

"It's a long story." He lit a cigarette and crouched beside her.

"A change of heart?" she asked.

"Something like that. I'd forgotten how peaceful it is here."

She stopped painting and turned to look at him, her face somber in the evening light. "But for how long, Martin?"

He had no answer for her—no answer at all. The sea was calm, and the sky the color of brass. A storm petrel cried harshly as it dipped above their heads and fled across the water.

About the Author

Jack Higgins is the most famous pseudonym of Harry Patterson, a former don and now one of the world's most successful thriller writers. Every one of his books since *The Eagle Has Landed*, including *Solo* and *Luciano's Luck*, has been an international bestseller.